TWO IDIOTS

WAHEED MUGHAL

Bright Pen

A Bright Pen Book

British Library Cataloguing Publication Data.
A catalogue record for this book is available
from the British Library

Urdu poem in this book is of Haider Geelani and translated into English by the author.

ISBN 978-0-7552-1386-3

Authors OnLine Ltd
19 The Cinques
Gamlingay, Sandy
Bedfordshire SG19 3NU
England

This book is also available in e-book format, details of which are available at www.authorsonline.co.uk

By The Same Author

Beyond London

Chapter 1

On the 16th September 2008, Kamal was finally on the plane; he had been waiting for this moment for a long time. He was flying high, not only physically, but also in his imagination, taking in all the possible pleasures during the journey. He was curious to use all passengers' facilities on the plane, but at the same time he was very nervous. It was his first time travelling by air and he was very careful not to be looked at as a fool. Every time his fellow passengers made any move, he followed them. He took the English newspaper, so he could pretend to be well educated and started reading, despite knowing he had never read this kind of paper before. He would only read the advertisements about the student visa services "No ILETS, 100 % visa guaranteed, bank statement facility until you get visa, no visa----no fee, etc". The Sunday editions were full of such advertisements.

He soon got bored, because of his poor reading skills and lack of vocabulary. He warped it back up and looked at the mini TV ahead of him. He could not find any channel that interested him. He took the headphones and started trying to plug them into the different holes along his seat, so he could listen to the music.

The fellow passenger noticed his nervousness and asked him, "Can I help you?" "NO, no I am OK", he replied with self-belief. He adjusted the headphones around his ears in alacrity, smiled at his fellow and said, "Thank you". Yet, there was no sound.

He took a brief look outside the window, but he could not see anything except tiny plots of green fields. He closed his eyes, pushed his head back into the seat and was soon lost in dreams. He recalled the happiest day of his life when he got student visa for the UK. The whole family was so very pleased. Friends and relatives came to his house to offer their congratulations. Every one of them wanted to be the first to host his farewell dinner. Since that day his life had completely changed. He had become more important for his friends and family members. This visa was an assurance that his dreams could come true, a hope of a new life full of riches, the likes of which his family had only dreamed of. His optimism was very high. It was even higher than the plan flying high above the earth.

Kamal was 23 years old; was of 5-8" tall with dark brown coloured skin, big eyes, long curly oily hair and a small arrowed moustache. His face had big cheeks, and a long nose which curved straight at the end. He had a particular village look, with strong body and big shoulders.

After his graduation, he started working at a telecommunications company but he was not satisfied with his salary. He wanted to earn more, to have an affluent life. He desired to compete in society, especially with his rich relatives. His uncle, Raheem Chaudhry, had moved to the UK a long time ago and had become a rather wealthy person. Kamal wanted to be wealthy like his uncle, but not to be a stingy; he wanted to support his family back in Pakistan.

He was organising his priorities; first he was to pay the loan his father had borrowed (from different sources) for his tuition fees and travelling expenses; second, to complete his MBA degree; third to find a good job; fourth to support his one younger brother and two sisters so they could also get a good education; fifth to send his parents to Makkah to perform the Hajj; and finally getting married his cousin, Tanzeela, daughter of his uncle Raheem Chaudhry.

He was lost in his dreams when the air-hostess came with a dinner trolley and asked him for his preferred lunch and drinks.

"Are you vegetarian or non-vegetarian, sir," she asked him.

He could not understand exactly what she was asking. He looked at the trolley and said, "Yes please two *Nans* with vegetables."

She just smiled as she had to deal with hundreds of such people every day and passed him a vegetarian meal. It was tasteless to eat, but he pretended to his fellow passengers that he was in a mood to have such a dish.

****

Rehmat Chaudhry, Kamal's father, was a small landlord in the village. He was once a famous *Kabaddi* player. He was sitting amongst a small group of people in his *Havailee*—a big sitting place in villages separate from main house. He was over sixty, a tall man with a fatty figure and long thick moustache curved upward at both ends. He wore a white long turban all the time. He had never been very rich, but he led a comfortable life within his limited sources. Seasonal agricultural crops were the main source of his income.

He was talking about his son, Kamal Chaudhry, who had left for the UK that day.

"He has been very good in his studies since his childhood," Rehmat praised his son.

"I know, I never seen him without books, there is no doubt he is very clever," an old man said in confirmation.

"His consultant told me that Kamal had gotten the UK visa because of his ability", Rehmat boasted about his son.

"Rehmat Chaudhry is right; the British do not give visas to every one." Allah Ditta, an old friend of Rehmat, told them before asking further, "Chaudhry, I think you have spent a lot of money to send your son *Walliat* (foreign)."

3

"Yes, more than five hundred thousand rupees," he replied, like a king.

"Rehmat Chaudhry is a rich person; money is not a problem for him." Another old man sitting there said in admiration of him.

"Wealth is for children; we are not going to take it to our graves." Rehmat said purposefully.

"Rehmat Chaudhry, your fate has changed now, your son has gone abroad," another man of his age said enviously.

"You are right, these days only those people who are prosperous and those who have some family members in foreign lands." Gama *mochi*—cobbler, said.

"I have already asked Chaudhry Noor who wants to sell some of his agricultural land, in the village, not to sell it yet. For Rehmat Chaudhry's son is going overseas, he will buy it soon," Gama further said and looked at Rehmat for his approval.

"Yes, tell him wait for some time and I'll buy his land," he said proudly.

Chaudhry Noor is also a small landlord in the village and rather a rich man. He is a rival of Rehmat Chaudhry. One of his sons entered into Italy illegally through an agent long time ago and settled down there after seeking immigration. He is earning good money in Italy. Noor wants to sell a small piece of agricultural land in the village to buy a bigger one outside the village.

I have heard the Prime Minister's children are also studying in England," Gama asked.

"Yes, not only the Prime Minister's but the children of the President of Pakistan are also studying over there", Rehmat said by nodding his head cheerfully.

"I know only rich people send their children abroad, we poor cannot even send ours to another city." Gama said with a deep sigh.

"Will Kamal only study there or get a job?" Baba (an old man) Nazar asked.

"He will do them both", Rehmat told him.

"Chaudhry, do not mind if I say that your brother has not done very well. He has been in *Walliat* for a long time and become a very rich man yet, he has never helped you." Baba Nazar said in criticism.

"It is not a problem; brothers are not meant to leave in life. God grant him a long life!" Rehmat replied satisfactorily.

"Will Kamal stay with his uncle?" Baba Nazar further asked.

"Yes," he gave a short answer.

Gama continued, "It would be a matter of shame if Kamal stays somewhere else while his uncle is living there."

"Your brother has only three daughters; you should ask him to marry one of them to Kamal." Baba Nazar advised him.

"His uncle himself wants such a marriage to happen. That is why he asked me to send Kamal to England", he explained to him.

"You should have asked him to bring his daughter here for marriage and then return with Kamal. Why have you spent so much money to send him over there?" Allah Ditta said sagely.

"You do not understand Allah Ditta; his daughters are well educated. They no longer speak our language, rather they only speak English. Once Kamal completes his education there; he will be able to speak English fluently and then they can get married." Rehmat told him.

"Rehmat Chaudhry is right," Baba Nazar agreed.

"Kamal is a clever boy, he'll learn English in few days," Gama flattered him.

"He can already speak very good English, he just needs to polish it," Rehmat told them.

"I know. Once he helped Ramazan *fogi* (soldier) to read a letter in English. *Allah khair kery* (God give him a favour) our Chaudhry's ability is not less than his cousins in the UK," Gama complimented, before started to laugh in an awkward way.

****

Kamal finished his dinner and began to think about his cousins in the UK. Nabeela is the eldest, aged 25; Tanzeela 22 and Shakeela is the youngest aged 19.

He has some good memories of childhood with Tanzeela. She used to come to Pakistan in her summer holidays with her father. They played together and had lot of fun. She tried to learn Punjabi and Kamal wanted to speak English with her. They both were language teachers to each other. He recalled the days when they played hide and seek in the fields. She fearlessly stood behind him on the running bicycle and asked him to ride fast. She spread her arms around him from the back and made loud noises, "Ride fast, faster", and enjoyed herself. She was always scared to swim under the running tube well. When Kamal dived deep into the water and held him long under it she became worried and shouted, "Kamal are you there?"

He took her to the fields and they played together. She was very happy playing in the orange gardens. He was not able to understand her language but still she was very friendly to him. He also remembered when she insisted she could climb an orange tree and he wanted to explain her she would fall down. He did not know how to tell her in English. He climbed up himself and fell down intentionally to show her the danger. She laughed madly.

She stopped visiting Pakistan at the age of twelve. He recalled the day when she was going back to the UK during her final visit she cried bitterly at the airport and he also started to cry. She waved him warmly and with tears before she entered the airport lounge. He started missing her and when he grew young he found himself in her love. He was fond of writing daily diary since his college life. He recollected all of his memories with her and recorded them in the diary. He was going to complete his love story by going to the UK. He was going to see her after ten years.

How the things had changed in ten years he wondered. She had become a pretty young lady. Would I recognise her at the first instance? He sketched her personality in his imagination.

Would she remember everything about me as I did for her? Would she return my love for her? He took out his diary from the hand luggage and started reading his past memories.

Nabeela visited Pakistan only once in life. Being the eldest daughter she helped her mother at home when the father was out of the country. They were Tanzeela and Shakeela who visited their native country frequently in their childhood.

Kamal was absorbed in the diary when the airhostess came with a trolley of drinks. "Sir would you like tea or coffee?" she inquired. He noticed his fellow was having coffee. He asked for coffee as well.

"How many sugars you would like to take, sir?" she asked him, while pouring coffee in a cup. He could not understand and said in confusion, "No I am OK."

"Would you like anything else, Sir," she further asked.

He was looking at the tray and wanted to have muffin but did not know what muffin called in English.

"The rounded fruit cake please," he asked and pointed towards the muffin.

"Oh, you mean muffin." She gave him the muffin with a large smile and tried to stop laughing.

He had never had black coffee in life. He took the first sip, felt its bitterness and showed it through his face expressions. His fellow noticed his misery and offered him his extra packet of sugar. He hardly drank the coffee but enjoyed the muffin.

****

Raheem Chaudhry, is the younger brother of Kamal's father. He is in his sixties and is very similar to his elder brother, Rehmat, in figure but not in physique. He is not physically strong, like his brother. He has a small trimmed beard mixture of black and white hair. He is bald on top, but has thick hair all around his head. He always wears a white thread netted round cap on his head, to hide his baldness. He moved to the UK forty years ago and worked in different businesses. Finally, he started a property business and had grown very wealthy in the past ten years. Yet, He is a very stingy person. Since he started his own business he had no time to take his daughters to Pakistan for holidays as he used to do in the past.

He was busy organizing the room for Kamal. He had a large four bedroom house. All the rooms are occupied, except a small one on the top floor which, used as a store room. He was cleaning and arranging it, for his nephew, by disposing of unwanted stuff.

"These girls are so open-handed; they buy the things they don't need actually", he muttered.

"Can you please come to help me Sadiqa?" he called for his wife.

"I am busy," she shouted from down-stairs.

"What are you doing?" he shouted back and walked downstairs.

"Oh, you are busy watching TV," he said ironically, moving his head up and down.

Sadiqa is a short woman, in her late fifties. She is somewhat fair with a round face, wide forehead and big eyes. She clearly looks like a village woman from her appearance, and the way she dresses.

She just jolted her head in annoyance, without looking at him.

"I know madam, why you are in a bad mood," he said angrily.

"Listen to me, he is coming here for studies at his own expense. I have not sponsored him. Did you get me?" he made it clear to her.

"I know the reality. You sent him money, but you did not help my brother's son when he wanted to come to the UK," she spoke harshly.

8

"You are the most stupid woman I have ever seen in my life. Your nephew is not a capable person. He wanted to come here on visit visa, how could I help him? Kamal is a clever boy. He got his student visa through his own abilities," he said praising his nephew.

"You always say that my family is dull, while yours is intelligent. If this is the case, why did you marry me then?" she said in high tone.

"O' my God, I have told you hundreds of times that it was an arranged marriage. I could not disobey my elder brother," he replied in the same way.

"I spent my whole life with you like burning in fire, but I don't want my daughters have the same distressing life because of arranged marriages. I want you to make it clear right now." She said tearfully.

"What do you want me to say?" he asked her.

"I know your intentions; don't think that any of my daughters will marry your nephew," she said this and left. He kept staring at her, until she disappeared in the drawing room. He went back upstairs to organise the room for Kamal.

****

There is an announcement that the plane is going to land at Heathrow Airport in half an hour. Kamal's heart beats hard with the thought of London. He thinks that all of his cousins, aunt and uncle will anxiously be waiting for him at the airport.

"I will say *Assalama Allikum* to my cousins. No. I will say 'hello' to them. No, I will say 'hi, I am Kamal Chaudhry'," he thought to himself.

"Will they recognise me? We last saw each other in our childhoods. But I think I can identify them easily. How will Tanzeela be looking? I guess that she has got long silky hair, fair colour, and slim body. What colours will she be wearing? I think pink or light green. How will she greet me? She will say '*Assalama Allikum*, I am Tanzeela'. I will say 'hello I am Kamal Chaudhry'. She will bow her head with shyness. I will ask her, 'How are you Tanzee?' She will say, 'I am fine.' Then she will ask me, 'How are you Kamal?' I will say 'I am good.' She will ask me, 'How was your journey?' I will say, 'It was really rather perfect.' He practised the questions and answers with himself.

The plane has landed. He is coming to the lounge for immigration checks. He is totally astonished by the environment all around him. He does not know exactly where to go. He is just following the other passengers, looking here and there in amazement. He is holding his luggage tightly standing on the running ramp. He could not balance himself on the ramp and kept falling down till the end. He did not look at the other people around him because of his embarrassment and puzzlement.

He stands in a long queue to wait for his turn to go to the Immigration Officer. He organises his admission papers and travel documents, to show him and repeats all the questions answers his consultant told him for immigration clearance.

"What is your name?" the Immigration Officer asks him.

"My name is Kamal Chaudhry and I am come from Pakistan for education in the UK," he gives a long answer in his broken English. The Officer looks at him with interest.

He becomes nervous and starts reciting some prayers in his heart, for the success of his entry clearance.

"Can I see your admission letters?" he asks him.

He gives him the letters. The Officer starts looking at them one by one. Kamal's legs are trembling with tenseness. He has forgotten all the answers he learnt for this occasion.

"Can you please tell me the name of your proposed course in the UK," The Officer asks him.

Kamal can not understand the question, he pauses for a while and says, *"My name is Kamal Chaudhry and I am come from Pakistan for education in the UK."*

"I can see from your passport and admission letters that your name is Kamal Chaudhry and you have come to the UK for studies, but my question is what is the name of your course of study?" the Officer asks him politely, realising Kamal's anxiety.

He thinks for some time and again says, *"My name is Kamal Chaudhry and I am come from Pakistan for education in the UK."*

"Do you have any family or friends already in the UK?" the Officer asks him the next question. The politeness of the Immigration Officer gave him some confidence and he started to understand the questions.

"I have no friend in the UK," he answers, rather confidently this time.

"Any relatives?" the Officer asks him.

"No," he tells him, as his consultant advised him not to mention about relatives already in the UK.

"Where will you stay then?" he further asks him.

"In the college hostel," Kamal replies.

"Have you already paid for your accommodation?" the Officer asks him.

"Yes," he replied and the Officer took out his letter of accommodation from his papers.

"Oh, you have paid one year advance rent for your room," he says, surprised.

"Yes sir," he answers with self-belief, whilst knowing that it was a fake letter.

"What is the name of your course?" The Officer once again questioned him.

"Level 6 diploma in business management and IT." This time, he answers correctly.

"What will you intend to do after you complete your studies in the UK?" asked the Officer.

"I will go back to my country," he repeats the same words his consultants taught him for this question.

"OK, thank you very much Mr. Kamal Chaudhry, I allow you to enter in the UK as a student." The Officer stamped his passport and let him go.

The next challenge for him is to locate the luggage collection point. He starts asking people and finally reaches the exact place with great effort.

He drags his luggage and starts walking towards the exit. The thought of his uncle's family, especially Tanzeela, makes him nervous again. "I'll say sorry to them for have to wait so long," he thinks.

He looks here and there to find his cousins or his aunty, but they have not come to greet him at the airport.

Only his uncle was waiting for him outside. This was the first shock Kamal had as he arrived in London.

****

Chapter 2

Kamal's family are very happy that he has successfully arrived in the UK. His parents, two younger sisters and one brother are embracing one another cheerily.

"Once I complete my college education I too will go to London for higher studies," his younger brother tells his parents.

"O' my son, don't worry, Kamal will soon send you a visa; he is very clever," his father taps his shoulders.

"Father, when will you buy me a motorcycle? You promised me one a long time ago," the son reminds him.

"O' son, now we will buy a car. When I'd pass through the village in my car people say, 'O' see Rehmat Chaudhry is going," he extends his chest and spreads his arms open. "I will go to the college in a car then. I will drop my sisters at their school first. When people will see us in a big car, they say, 'look, Rehmat Chaudhry's children are going!" Kamal's younger brother imagined out-loud.

"O', yes my son, I want to my competitors in the village jealous. Chaudhry Noor thinks that only he can drive a car, but I will tell him that Rehmat Chaudhry can also drive. I have already asked Gama *mochi* to inform him that I'll buy his land soon. My son has gone to England. Now we have no problem," he boasted.

"I will buy a new mobile phone, with a camera," one of his daughters spoke this time.

"Why not honey, I will buy new mobile phones for both of you," Nusrat, their mother, assured them. Nusrat is a tall lady with brown colour. She has put some weight on her. She has a long face and big eyes. Her hair gone white but she always colours them with henna. She is a pure village woman with no formal education.

"The coloured ones, with cameras," the other daughter said.

"O' yes, the coloured one my darling," she guaranteed her too.

"You know mother, Chaudhry Noor's daughter makes us jealous in the school by showing us her mobile phone every day," she further added.

"Do not worry, I will buy you a better one than she possesses," the mother replied.

"I will go to perform the Hajj first," she told her husband.

"Sure, we will go together my pious wife," Rehmat confirmed with her.

The whole family talks about its rich future and dreams of a luxurious life.

The children have gone to sleep. Rehmat and his wife are now in their room. "Chaudhry, we have borrowed five hundred thousands rupees to send our son to *Walliat* and we promised to give it back in six months. Will we be able to pay it all back in six months time?" Nusrat shared concerns with her husband.

He gave her surety, "I think we will be able to pay earlier. Kamal's consultant told me that he could easily earn one thousand pounds per month."

"How much is one thousand pounds?" she asked.

"One hundred and thirty five thousands rupees, the consultant told me", he said.

"Then there will be no problem for us. We will be very rich soon," she dreamed.

"Your brother never helped us in life. Yet, when his daughters needed to get married he remembered we were his relatives," she complained.

"No matter, after all, he is my younger brother. I love him so much. When my father was dying he asked me to look after him. I got him married first. I am happy he is a rich person and having a good life," he sang the praises of his brother.

"I want Kamal to marry my niece. She is very pretty and has good manners, but Kamal was very keen to go to *Walliat*. We did not have enough money to give him. When your brother asked you to send him to the UK, so that he could marry his daughter we borrowed the money. I thought of my two daughters. They are becoming young women soon. We have to think about their marriages. We'll need a big amount of money to arrange their weddings. You know we are not big landlords. Kamal remained worried about our financial position. That's why he wanted to go abroad, but I miss him and I feel very sad," she started weeping.

"I miss him too. You know, we average people have our compulsions. The people of the village think that we are rich. If we sell our lands so our daughters can marry, it will be matter of shame for us. I also wanted to send Kamal abroad so that we could manage our future expenses."

'We have to sacrifice all the time in life. In this materialistic world your social position depends upon money. People judge you by your wealth, not by your character. We've never been able to give a rich life to our children. We are forced, by our limited resources, to send our Kamal abroad. You know how difficult it is for a father to send his young son to another country. Now I have gone through this experience, only my God knows my feelings," he spoke and also started sobbing. They both cried until they went sleep.

****

Kamal was arranging the stuff in his room. A single bed, a

cupboard, a small folded metallic chair and a table, there is no space for anything else.

"O my God, this room is too small for me," he whispered.

"I don't know where to put my big briefcase and two heavy bags," he said while trying to adjust them on top of the cupboard.

"Here is tea for you," his uncle entered the room with a cup of tea. "You must be tired, it is better if you take some rest. Your aunty has gone to market for shopping. Nabeela always comes late from the bank, her job is like that. Tanzeela and Shakeela have gone to attend a birthday party. I have to go to collect the rent of one of my properties. No one is at home to give you company," he tells him.

"No problem uncle," he says satisfactorily.

"Tanzeela could not come to the airport because she was busy," Kamal thinks, lying on the bed.

"When she will see me she says, 'sorry Kamal I could not come to receive you. I will say 'no problem Tanzeela, I know life is very busy in the UK," he once again lost in thoughts.

In the evening his uncle comes to him and asks him to get ready, they all are waiting for him, for dinner. He takes a shower and goes down stairs into the dining hall.

"*Assalam Allikum*," he greets them warmly. They also greet him with smiles, nodding their heads, but without showing any of the warmness he was expecting.

"This is Kamal Chaudhry, the eldest son of my brother Rehmat Chaudhry," Raheem introduced him happily as they did not know about him.

"This is Nabeela. She works in a bank, Tanzeela goes to university and Shakeela goes to college," he pointed towards them, one by one.

"This is your own house Kamal; feel free here," he encouraged him.

The three sisters were just looking at him with smiley faces, but without saying anything. His aunt is completely silent and cold. They start eating. He does not know how to use knife and fork, laid out on the dining table. He is making a lot of noise by striking them on the plate. The sisters are trying to stop laughing at his awkwardness. Raheem feels that Kamal is having difficulty trying to use them. He asks him to eat by hands. He does not look around him in nervousness and keeps eating, bowing his head down.

As the dinner finishes, the sisters go to their rooms and their mother gets busy in washing dishes. Raheem takes him to his room, where he asks him about the relatives and the village people one by one, in detail. He also makes tea for him, and they talk till late in the night on different topics.

Kamal was in his room. Thinking about why his cousins did not talk to him. He realised the cold behaviour of his aunt in first instance, but the silence of his cousins really worried him. He was expecting a long dialogue with them, but they did not even greet him properly.

"Perhaps, they did not like me?" he asked himself.

"Tanzeela had turned out to be a very pretty young girl. She was very friendly with me when she came to Pakistan, but today she did not even talk to me," he felt sorry for himself.

"She was just a child when she visited Pakistan, I thought she had forgotten all about her childhood but I remembered everything. I will remind her," he said to himself.

"My classes are going to start next week. I must find a job this week," he started planning his life in the UK.

"We have to pay our loan in six months time. I know my uncle is a tight-fisted; he will not give me any financial help. I have to manage my educational expenses by myself and also save some money to pay off my debt. My fees are paid for one year, if I earn one thousand pound per month, I will keep one hundred pounds for my monthly expenses and send nine hundreds pounds to my father. Nine hundreds pounds will be one hundred twenty five thousands rupees. It will take me four months to clear my debts. But if I work hard, I can earn more than one thousand pounds in a month. I have to work hard anyway because I need to pay my college fees after one year. I will save five hundred pounds for six months for my next year college fees, and send rest of money to my family. If I send them at least five hundreds pounds every month it will become seventy thousands rupees. They can easily pay off loan in six months," he kept thinking until he fell asleep.

****

This is the weekend. Everybody is at home and having extra sleep. Kamal gets up early in the morning, as usual. His uncle makes breakfast for him and teaches him how to use knife and fork at the dining table. After they finish breakfast, he takes him outside.

Sadiqa is sitting among her daughters on the lawn. They are having morning tea.

Nabeela is very pretty. She has fair complexion and short silky hair. She is a slim and smart lady with five feet and four inches height. She has got dark brown eyes and a round face with long narrow red lips. There is a small cut under her chin. She fell from the bed when she was a child and injured her chin. She looks like a pure professional lady from her style.

Shakeela got average height and she is very similar to her mother in her appearance. Being the youngest she enjoys all kind of favours and loves at home. She is rather a quiet lady and spent most of her time in reading magazines or browsing internet.

"Your father brought his nephew here to marry one of you. I already told him none of my daughters will marry him," she told them.

"Who will marry this idiot who even does not know table manners?" Tanzeela spoke first.

"I am a professional banker; I socialize with a high class

18

people all the time. How can I marry this stupid villager who has no education, no job and no manners? How can I introduce him to my friends? I will marry a person who is equal in education and status to me," Nabeela said.

"I need to complete my education first. I have not even thought about getting married. I don't believe in arranged marriages anyway," Shakeela joined in.

"Yes, you are right Shakeela, my marriage was an arranged one and you see I never have had a peace in life. I don't want you to go through the same experience I have," the mother supported them.

"I tell you, just keep away from him," she advised her daughters.

"I am all with you, if your father forces any of you we shall inform the police," she further encouraged them.

"He does not suit us, by any means, how can we marry him? It is so strange, isn't?" Tanzeela said.

"Marriage is someone's personal decision, no one can impose it on us," Shakeela added.

"He can not speak English even, how will we communicate with him?" Nabeela continued.

"You must hire a translator first if you want to marry him," Tanzeela joked with her sister.

"My foot," she answered in hatred.

"One of my friends got married to her cousin in Pakistan and they separated after six months," Shakeela informed them.

"It is so unnatural, how you can lead your life with a person who is not known to you very well? I used to visit Pakistan with my father in childhood. I remembered we shared some part of our childhood together but it did not mean that when we would grow young we marry. That was my childhood which had passed then", Tanzeela said in brief.

"Now you have a chance to understand him, so go ahead," Nabeela teased her.

"I will never marry this *lamboo*, (tall man) with a moustache," she said and they all started laughing. The sisters continued making light jokes at each other's expense and their mother kept them encouraging not developing any friendship with him.

****

In the evening, Kamal returned with his uncle. Again, they all gathered at the dining table. He avoided using a knife and fork this time.

"Kamal is going to do his MBA," Raheem praised.

"How long it will take you to complete your MBA Kamal?" he asked him.

He tried to speak English to impress his cousins.

They giggled at his poor and broken English but he continued to speak. Raheem helped him wherever he stopped or spoke incorrectly.

"Two and half years," he replied.

"Two and half years!" Nabeela looked at him in surprise.

"It is one year degree course; I completed it in one year," she told him.

Tanzeela and Shakeela smile sardonically. He felt uneasy.

"Actually, in the first two years I will complete my level 6 and level 7 diplomas and then top up to an MBA in six months," he explained.

"What are these level 6 and level 7 diplomas? I don't understand," she said, again   surprise.

"My visa consultant, in Pakistan, designed this course for me," he said perplexed.

"Okay, so you did not select this course by yourself," she did not change her startled tone.

"My consultant told me that I could not get admission directly into an MBA because I had no prior management experience," he continued explaining.

"MBA is a very expensive degree, isn't?" Tanzeela spoke for first time in his presence.

"Of course it is expensive, it cost me more than twenty thousand pounds," Nabeela told her.

"That means he is going to spend twenty thousands pounds to get this degree. It is lot of money," Tanzeela said and frowned.

"No, it will cost me eleven thousands pounds. First year fee is three thousand and then four thousands for the second year. Once I complete my level 7 diploma, I can do top up MBA in six months by paying extra four thousand," he explained in more detail.

"I've never heard of this course before," Tanzeela continued.

"Where is your college?" Nabeela asked him.

"In Whitechapel," and he told the long name of it.

"I'm hearing this name first time, to my surprise," Nabeela said and it further increased his uneasiness.

He knew that he was being ridiculed by his cousins. He went to his room immediately after he finished his dinner.

He was lying on the bed, both hands under his head, fixing his eyes on the ceiling, and thinking about his discussion with them.

"They are rich people. They can go to the good colleges and universities. We are poor people and can only afford diplomas education here. Our first priority is to end poverty, not getting education. They don't know how it is difficult for us to arrange the money to come here. They can spend twenty thousands on their education in one year. We are not able to do that."

"One day I will be successful like them. When I complete my MBA I will also get a good banking job in the UK. I am more hard working than them. I will compete with them in life. I will be equal in status with them and they say proudly to their friends, 'this is Kamal Chaudhry, our cousin'. Once my college starts I will have a chance to socialise with my English classmates. I will learn English and talk to my cousins freely. They were laughing at my poor English today, but very soon I will prove to them that I can speak good English."

"I know that I cannot eat with knife and fork. But to eat with knife and fork is not a status symbol. Anyway, one day I will be able to use them properly. This is not a big thing to learn".

"Will Tanzeela marry me? She can marry me, but I need to prove to her first that I am a successful person. When she will come to know how much love I have for her she pays me back all my loves. I need to develop a friendship with her, so that we can understand each other in a better way. I'll remind her the glorious moments of our childhood once we shared together".

"What about my job? I will ask my uncle tomorrow to arrange job for me. He has got good contacts. If he does not help me, I will search myself. I can find a good job. There is no problem for me. My consultant told me that finding a good job in London was not a big deal. I must not waste my time; I should find a job this week as next week my classes are going to commence. If I go to college three days a week, then I can easily work for remaining four days. Can I make one thousand pounds by working four days a week? I will try to make it. I am hard working," he continued to think such things, to himself, for a long time.

****

Rehmat Chaudhry is boasting about his son everywhere in the village. He tells peoples that his son has reached England before they even ask him. He is sitting at Gama *mochi's* shop with three other men this time.

"I heard the British officer at the airport had a long interview with Kamal," Gama asked him.

"O' yes, Kamal told me on phone that the officer asked him many questions but he answered skilfully," he told him.

"No doubt, Chaudhry's son is very clever," another man sitting there said.

"It is not easy to speak English with the British but Kamal spoke it very easily at the airport," he said in admiration of his son.

"Has he started a job?" Gama asked him.

"A Job is not problem for him, he can speak their language, and I asked him to get some rest," he replied.

"His uncle is there, finding work is no problem for him," Gama added.

"Chaudhry, you must definitely be missing your son," the old man continued.

"Yes, we are all missing him, it is the first time he's gone so far from us," he replied sadly.

"Chaudhry *Sahib,* keep patience, he's gone there for your betterment," Gama comforted him.

Babu *Mussali*---a person, who works in kiln, pops into the shop. A *Mussali* is from a caste in rural Pakistan who makes bricks form wet soil. The owners of big kilns hire them on an annual basis. They also do other kind of labour, like watering crops or working with masons. The dark black colour is their unique identity. They are famous for flattering the landlords in villages. They keep moving their permanent residence because of the nature of their work. Usually, they are victims of the forced labour in Pakistan.

When Babu sees Rehmat, he puts his hand on his forehead in a salute and says, "Millions of congratulations Chaudhry *Sahib, chotay* (small) Chaudhry *Sahib* (Kamal) has gone to *Walliat.*"

He is doing this in order to get some money from him. Rehmat Chaudhry gives him one hundred rupees. He refuses to take it and tells him that when Chaudhry Noor's son went abroad he gave him five hundreds rupees. He demands him one thousand. He hesitates to give him this amount, but he remains firm by consistently putting his hand on his forehead. The people, who are passing by, stop there to enjoy this style of greetings and congratulations. Babu starts singing songs in praise of Rehmat Chaudhry's family.

Rehmat has no choice but to give him one thousand rupees, to save face in the village.

The story spreads all over the village and by evening nearly everyone knows that he has given such a big amount to Babu. Some more people like Babu, start coming his house to congratulate him on his son's arrival in the UK. He has to give them more or less the same amount for sake of his honour.

****

It is a lovely Sunday morning in the late September. The sky is clear of clouds; sunlight is smashing through the windows, making the room even brighter. Kamal is taking tea with his uncle.

"I think I should find a job before my classes start," he told his uncle.

"Don't worry, I have already spoken to some of my friends about it. They are trying to find a suitable job for you."

"I need to find a job as early as possible," he answered eagerly.

"How much money you have spent on your visa?" he questioned.

"I paid fifty thousand rupees to my visa consultant, three thousand pounds to my college and fifty thousand rupees on my air ticket and on some shopping", he gave the details of his expenses so far.

"Oh, that means you have spent five hundred thousand rupees!" Raheem says in exclamation. "Your father has become a rich person," he continued joyously.

Kamal does not tell him that they borrowed it from different people and promised to repay it in six months.

"OK, Kamal. I am very busy today. I'll see you in the evening," he walked downstairs, carrying the empty cups.

Kamal takes out his diary and starts writing his daily routines as usual.

"Now I am in the UK, I must write in English," as he thinks this, he writes 'Kamal Chaudhry in London' on the very first page. His understanding of spoken English is very poor. But his writing skills are reasonable. This is because of educational system in Pakistan, in government schools and colleges. The teachers give lot of attention to grammar but there is no proper source of improving speaking and listening skills.

He starts writing about his journey from Pakistan to London. The rays of sunlight coming through the window are spreading across the room. He pulls the curtains open and lets the sunshine in. He looks down through the small window of his room, which opens down on to the garden. The sun has evaporated the dew. A big round plastic table, with four white chairs, lying in the green lawn is fascinating to him. Three are two apple trees in one corner and a palm tree in the other; they are giving a beautiful look. There is a row of roses, in full bloom, between the two corners, along the wall.

He sees Tanzeela coming to the garden, carrying a cup of coffee in one hand and a book in the other. She is wearing loose jeans, a short black *kameez* with white embroidery on the chest. Her long, shiny, silky hair reaches her knees. She has brown colouring, black eyes and wide chest. She has a round forehead and there is black mole on the left side of her nose, which can be seen from a distance. She is a perfectly attractive young lady, more than five feet tall.

She pulls up a chair, turns it towards the sun, leaves the book on the table and starts sipping her coffee.

Kamal is watching her constantly from the window. He briefly looks at himself, standing before the long mirror along his cupboard. He oils his hair and moustaches, combs them properly, and looks at himself in the mirror again and again till he is satisfied that he will give the impression of being a handsome man.

He also takes a book and goes to the garden.

"Hello Tanzeela," he says warmly.

"O hey, you all right," she takes a quick glance at him and turns her face to the sun again.

"I am fine, I am fine, you OK?" he asks in a friendly tone.

"Not too bad," she replies without looking at him.

There is a pause. He wanted to ask her whether she was taking sunshine but he did not know how to say this in English. He remained silent for some time and sat on one chair. He opened his book and pretended to read. He repeated so many sentences in his heart to speak correctly.

"You are putting sunshine on you?" he asked lovingly, after thinking for long time.

She could not stop laughing while replying, 'yes'.

He realised that he had spoken incorrectly. He felt embarrassed and remained silent for other ten minutes. He wanted to tell her that his family was paying compliments to her. He again repeated several sentences in his minds to speak correctly this time.

Finally he says, "My father, mother, sisters and brother sent you *Assalama Allikum,*"

"That sounds good, how were they, were they all right?" she turns her face towards him and asks.

"They all are fine. They were all remembering you," he says happily.

"It is strange, I'm not friend with any of them, why do they remember me?" she puts him in shame.

"Actually you visited us in your childhood, so they remember you," he says in lingering tongue.

"I do not remember anything about them," she said, took her book and went back to her room, leaving him in panic.

He sat there for long time, fixing his eyes on the book but without reading it. He recalled his past again and remembered everything he had in his recollections about his childhood friendship with her.

He went back to his room and continued writing his diary with broken heart.

****

Kamal was very excited, the next day he was going to the college. He was organising his school bag with notebooks and some stationery. He was undecided as to what to wear for his first day at college in London. "A two piece suit would be the best idea," he thought. He was looking at the title page of the college prospectus. Three white boys, two white girls and one black girl carrying school bags were smiling at each other, standing at main gate. "They could be my classmates," he said to himself.

He turned the pages one by one and took a brief look wherever he saw any picture. He imagined himself within that picture, and soon got fascinated. A huge library hall, a big computer lab with dozens of computers lined up on beautiful desks with colourful chairs, a vast yard with lavished plants and trees, comments from some students about the high quality education at this institution and the list of high profiled teachers were stunning him.

He thought about his very first day at college in Pakistan, how he was mocked by some of his seniors. A group of scoffers stopped him in the corridor and asked his name. He told them Kamal Chaudhry.

"What is the meaning of Kamal?" they asked him.

"Perfection," he said hesitantly.

They asked him to stand on one leg when he did that then they asked to lift the other one up too.

"I can't do that," he said and they started laughing.

"You are not perfect though," they ridiculed him by calling him 'Chaudhry Perfection'.

Then he was known as 'Chaudhry Perfection' in the college. His classmates teased him by calling him by this name in later years.

"Will my seniors make fun of me tomorrow?" he asked himself. "No, this is the UK, a civilised country, they would not do that," he sighed long with satisfaction.

"How will I greet my fellows at college?" he wondered.

"Hello, good morning, my name is Kamal Chaudhry, I am from Pakistan" he thought about the greeting. *"No, I would say, Hi, how are you? My name is Kamal Chaudhry. I come from Pakistan."* he looked at himself in the long mirror of his cupboard and stood poised as if greeting his fellows with a smiley face.

He practiced greeting his future classmates before the mirror many times, with different styles and words. He tried to memorise the route to the college, mapped out by his uncle earlier. This would be the first time he going out all alone. Previously he would go out with him. He set the alarm to get up in good time the next day. Raheem told him that he would prepare his breakfast as usual. He had been making his breakfast since Kamal had arrived at his house. For the first three days he ate dinner with the whole family, but after that Raheem began to bring his dinner for him to eat in his room. In the very first week he realised the cold behaviour of his aunty and cousins. They were not taking any interest in him. It was the uncle who was looking after him.

He dreamt about his college, his classmates and bright London life as he lied down in his bed. He could not get to sleep till late that night for he was so excited.

****

Raheem was having an argument with his wife in his bedroom, over her cold manners toward his nephew.

"He is a child, you should not treat him that way," he said angrily.

"What did I do to him? 'I never even spoke to him." She retorted

"Do you think that is fair not to speak with a guest?" he questioned

"Guest------guests are for some days, they are not permanent," she murmured.

"You don't like him staying in this house?" he raised his voice.

"Did I say something like that?" she replied

"Then what do you mean by permanent?" he asked.

"Nothing, this is your house, you can make it a guest house," she nodded and turned her face away.

"What is your real problem? Tell me please," he asked harshly.

"You know we have three young daughters at home, this is not right to allow a young man to stay with us," she said without looking at him.

"Good madam, finally you have thought about your young daughters," he said dryly.

"Yes, I remain worried about them. They are equally young and are of marriageable age. I am a mother and always think about them." She told him.

"You have already turned down three proposals for Nabeela, where will you find suitors for your daughters?" he responded disrespectfully.

"They are not cows or buffaloes to tie at any *khurley*---- animal eating container; after all they are human beings. They have their own likes and dislikes. How can I accept an unsuitable proposal for them?" she retorted.

"But you cannot bring grooms from the heaven anyway," he said sneeringly.

"When there it is my God's will, He will send suitors for them," she said satisfactorily.

"Look, Kamal is my nephew--- our blood relative, he is handsome and a gentle person. He will be the best suitor for Nabeela," finally he showed his intent to her.

"He is your blood relative, not mine, I knew your intentions from the very first day, he can never be a suitor for Nabeela, don't even think about it," she raised her voice this time.

"Listen, I worked hard to give you a wealthy life style. We have no son; all property will go to our daughters. I don't want someone who comes from outside and becomes the owner for nothing," he spoke softly this time.

"You are worried about your properties but not your daughters' lives. Is this fair?" she said irritably.

"You are a silly woman, you will never understand," he criticised her.

"He is not suitable for Nabeela by any mean; there is total difference in age, education and status," she negated him.

"I have given *zaban*--- verbal promise, to my brother. I can not take it back. This is my final decision being a father, I am telling you," he said decidedly.

"This is nonsense, absolutely nonsense, how can you give *zaban* to someone without asking your daughter," she said harshly.

"We don't ask daughters' decisions for marriages. We just tell them who to marry. Do you get me?" he insisted.

"My daughters were not born in a village and they were not brought up under your funny traditions, did you get me?" she insisted too.

"It is you who are spoiling them, by making them modern and liberal. I don't want them to adopt English culture," he said.

"You have always been very harsh to them, stricter than needed for young children. You always follow them and keep an eye on their activities. That is not fair. When they have reached marriageable age and you want to impose on them your own decision. You never allowed them to live a free life, not even in childhood. This is not fair," she ranted.

"Do you think I have not loved them? They are very dear to me. What I am thinking is in their best interest. You are a stupid woman. You can never understand it," he whinged.

She nodded impatiently, turned her face away and pulled the blanket over her to fall asleep.

****

Chapter 3

Kamal excitedly got ready for his first day at college in London. He was standing on the footpath, waiting to cross the road with a map in his hand, carrying a college bag on his shoulders, one hand in his trousers pockets. He was continuously looking at the other side of the road to find out his bus number. Suddenly he noticed a stationary long queue of vehicles on the both directions and drivers looking at him expectantly. He got confused. An old white lady, first in the row, smiled at him. He smiled too in return but did not move. A young black guy from the other direction pressed his horn noisily and murmured something in anger, which he was unable to hear. Kamal looked at him and gave him a smile in puzzlement. He said something loudly and pulled away at full speed. The old lady yelled at him, "Young man, you are standing at pedestrians crossing, aren't you?" Then he realised that his foot was on the lines and he hastily crossed the road.

He followed the route mapped by his uncle by using buses, trains and asking people in his broken English and poor accent and finally, he came out of the Whitechapel tube station after a long struggle.

The next challenge was to find the way to his college. He took a sigh of relief as he saw many Asian faces around him. There was a long queue of stalls on the both sides of the footpath, mostly run by people look like him. This scene reminded him of

Old Anar Kali bazaar in Lahore, where people sold clothes, shoes and other things along the same lines, it was always crowded with customers, especially women.

He thought that everyone here knew about his college, because it was always a famous place in any locality. He started asking the stall men but no one knew about it.

"They are all uneducated, how can they know about the college," he muttered.

He stopped a gentleman seemed to be well educated and asked him about it.

"I have never heard about this college, I am afraid," he replied.

Kamal showed him the address and he just directed him towards the road mentioned on it. He walked along the road, and looked carefully on both sides to find the college, the road finished but he could not succeed in locating it. He was looking for a big building, huge gate, vast lawns, big trees and large number of students coming in and out of the main gate. At the end of the road, he looked at the sign board and matched the spelling of the road name with his college given address over and over.

"Oh my God, this is the same road but where is the college?" he questioned himself in irritation.

By this time, he was tired and hungry. He found a fried chicken shop, with a big, 'Halal' logo, on the other side of the road. His uncle had advised him to eat only at *Halal* shops. He went there and felt satisfaction by reading different verses from the Holy Quran, written on the walls. A smart man with a short black beard serviced him and talked to him in Urdu. He ordered two pieces of chicken and chips and a cold drink.

"Are you a student?" the man asked him while he was having his meal sitting on a long seat near his counter.

"Yes, I am a student," he replied.

"Are you from Pakistan?"

"Yes."

"When did you come to the UK?"

"Just a week ago."

"Oh, I see."

"Was everything OK in Pakistan?"

"Yes, all was OK."

"There is a terrible situation there, a bomb blast every day. I really feel sorry for the people when I see all this," the man said in grief.

"What kind of Islam are the *Taliban* promoting over there? This is not Islam, to kill innocent people in the mosques and in the markets through suicide attacks or to cut throats in front of children," the man continued and became emotional.

"You are right, we do not like them," he said while struggling with the chicken.

Another man popped in. He was wearing white *shalwar qameez* and had long beard mixture of grey and white hair. The shopkeeper greeted him warmly.

"Mian *sahib* have you heard there was another bomb blast in Lahore yesterday," the man asked him.

"O *bhai*, (Brother), this is all conspiracy against Islam," Mian *sahib* said intensely.

"Some external forces are playing this obnoxious game by using the local people," he said further.

"I tell you one thing today, the day America leaves Afghanistan; there will be no bomb blast in Pakistan. It was a big mistake to send troops into tribal areas. The Pakistani army is fighting its own people. Only the Muslims are being killed from both sides. I told you it was a big conspiracy against Islam. Tell me one thing if innocent people are killed in Drone Attacks, would their relatives not fight back to take revenge. The regular Drone Attacks are increasing militancy in the region. The external forces are making Muslims to fight with Muslims," Main *sahib* started a lecture. They both engaged in warm discussion over *Taliban* and criticised US politics in Afghanistan.

Mian *Sahib* comparing Afghanistan with Iraq and proving by his arguments that America went to Afghanistan to get control of the natural resources of Central Asian states same like it invaded Iraq for oil only. The war on terrorism is just an excuse to get sympathies and support to reach its real targets. Once USA blamed Iraq that it had mass destruction weapons but no single weapon of this kind was found over there.

"I tell you one thing, the US cannot win this war by killing innocent civilians in Drone Attacks. This war will finish USA by paralysing its economy. The world will see soon the ever worse defeat of any super power in this modern age. There is no supreme power but Allah. Whenever any human or state claimed to be the super power it distinguished from the face of the earth sooner or later. Allah has mentioned those people in the Holy Quran in the following words:

"And when it is said to them, 'Do not cause corruption (destruction, transgression etc) on the earth', they say, 'We are but reformers'. Unquestionably, it is they who are the corrupters, but they perceive (it) not". (2:11-12).

They think that they can do whatever they like because they are super power and no one can challenge them. But they forget that there is a supreme power watching over them and giving them respite only. The Holy Quran says about them:

"And if Allah were to impose blame on the people for what they have earned, He would not leave upon it (i.e., the earth) any creature. But He defers them for a specified tern. When their time comes, then indeed Allah has ever been, of His servants, Seeing". (35:45). Mian *sahib* said final words before he left.

Kamal finished his meal and asked the shopkeeper about the location of his college. He did not know about it, but directed him to the road number.

He was standing by the exact door number. This was a small sized building, three storeys high. The names of the offices were written in small fonts with a door bell. He found his college's name on the second floor and headed towards it. The picture of the college on the front page of its prospectus was still fixed in his mind, and he thought that it could be an administration office and the campus would be somewhere else. He knocked at the door and entered the room, after waiting a long time for an answer.

At the reception there was a small rounded desk, with a computer on it and a young Asian lady was sitting there on a revolving office chair absorbed in typing some thing. There were three wooden chairs in front of the desk. Two Asian boys were already sitting there gossiping with each other. On the right hand side, there was a small room and written on its door was, 'Principals Office'. On the left hand side there was another small room, labelled as a class room. Its door was open and there were only six chairs in a row on two sides, one computer on a table in one corner and white teaching board standing on the opposite side.

"Hello, my name is Kamal Chaudhry and I am come from Pakistan," he tried to get attention of the receptionist, a fair coloured and beautiful teenaged girl.

"Hang on," she replied without looking at him. The two boys sitting there looked at him and gave him a big meaningful smile. One of them pointed him to sit on the chair. He started whispering him in Urdu.

"Have you come to the UK recently?" he asked him.

"Yes, a week ago."

"What is your course?"

"Diploma in business management....."

"Advanced diploma or just diploma?"

"No, level 6 diploma."

"What have you done in Pakistan?"

"I completed university degree".

"You should have been admitted into the level 7 advanced diploma then."

"My educational consultant designed this course for me."

"How much did you pay to the college?"

"Three thousands pounds."

"Three thousands pounds fee just for level 6 diploma!" the boy raised his eye brows in astonishment.

"I think you are a rich person. You should have gone to a good university. What are you doing here? "Anyway, my name is Ajay and I am from India, nice to see you," he shook his hand.

"My name is Kamal Chaudhry and I am come from Pakistan," he also shook his hand more warmly. Ajay smiled at his poor English.

The receptionist called Ajay's name, handed over two papers with some instructions. He took the papers, said goodbye to Kamal and left. A boy came out from the principal office and passed her a paper. She talked to the principal on phone, but in some code words and asked the boy to sit there until she typed the letter for him. She sent the next person to the principal's office.

"Hi, you OK," the new one greeted Kamal.

"Yes, I am fine"

"Are you a newcomer?"

"Yes."

"Where are you come from?"

"Pakistan"

"Which part of Pakistan?"

"Punjab", Kamal replied.

"I am from Pakistan too," he shook his hand warmly.

"Have you found a job?"

"No."

"Where are you staying?"

"With my uncle."

"Lucky you!"

"How did you find a job?" Kamal asked him.

"It is very hard these days my brother. I've been struggling for the last three months but could not find one yet," he told him desperately.

"What should I do to find a job?" Kamal asked.

"Just keep trying," he replied shortly.

The receptionist typed the letter for him. He took it and also left.

It was Kamal's turn to go into the principal's office. The principal was a good looking young man with long curly hair, a smooth forehead and of a fair colour. He dressed himself in a decent way. There was a big table taking half of the room space, a big luxury revolving chair and two small leather chairs at the front. There was a flat screen desktop computer, with beautiful keyboard and some necessary stationery on the table. On the right hand side there was a golden name plate, embedded in dark brown wood was written 'A. Karim Principal'. He greeted Kamal speaking to him in Urdu.

"How are you Mr. Kamal Chaudhry?"

"I am fine."

"Good."

"You are lucky that you have come to our college. Don't worry we will look after you," he said with a big smile.

"I think this must be your administration office. I was wondering, where is your campus?" Kamal asked him, hesitantly.

"This is our college, we have no other campus, don't worry we will look after you. Tell me have you found a job, or not yet?" he said with a large smile.

"Not yet, I was wondering, how many days a week I have to come to the college? The offer letter said only 15 hours a week. I want to get a part time job on my free days."

"Don't worry! You do not need to come to the college at all. We'll keep your attendance record updated. After one year, we would issue you with a diploma. If you want the next level diploma you would have to pay four thousands pounds extra. You can pay it in two instalments. We will also help you in extending your visa next year. You know that you cannot get extension without our confirming your attendances and enrolment. But don't worry we will take care of you, if you pay your fees on time," he warned him, he will give him favour only if he pays the money, and on time.

"OK, please go to the receptionist she will give you some letters and your college identity card. If you have any problem come to see me in my office anytime," he asked for his secretary, over the intercom, to send the next person in and gave Kamal a farewell smile.

The girl at the reception desk, asks him to wait until she finishes typing the letters for him.

A cold wave of disappointment and sadness was running through his body. He sat on the chair, putting his bag in the lap and appearing to be deep in thought. "Was that the college I had dreamed about for so long?" he was wondering.

All his dreams, about his English classmates, a huge college building with lavish green lawns, a big computer lab and a vast library, have shattered.

The receptionist gave him three letters; one for the bank, to allow him to open an account; one for GP, to let him register with a doctor; the final one was his enrolment letter. She also issued him a college identity card.

Kamal was standing outside the building in dissatisfaction. He saw Ajay who was coming back to the college. He told Kamal that there was some spelling mistake in one of his letters and he came back to get it corrected.

Kamal told him about his meeting with the principal, with deep disappointment.

"Don't worry, this is what happens here," Ajay said.

"I have no friend here, and I don't know what to do next, I do not want to tell my uncle's family about it." Kamal told him with sorrow.

"I'm your friend. You can call me any time, to ask me any thing."

They exchanged telephone numbers with each other. Ajay assured him that he would help.

****

Tandoor is a centre point for women in the village, where they gather twice a day—lunch time and in the evening, to bake their breads. It is planted into the ground, by digging it deeply.

This particular *Tandoor* is owned by Bhagee *machin*. *Machi* is a tribe in rural areas, who bake bread for weddings, funerals or any other special occasion. People also hire their services to cut the trees. They are also used as messengers to invite people to a wedding or to inform of any death from outside the village. The person who receives the good or bad news, from a *machi* is bound to give him some money. If there is a wedding invitation it is called *bhaji* or *bulawa*. *Bulawa* is a Punjabi word meaning invitation, but *bhaji* is taken as return. If someone has already attended your wedding ceremony, and given you some money, it is called *bhaji*. There is a proper register, in every house, where people keep a record of the *bhaji*. Whenever they go to any wedding ceremony, they check this register first to find out how much money the bride or groom's family has already gifted to them on their weddings in the past. If they go for the first time to attend a wedding ceremony and give some money to bride or groom it is called *nai bhaji* --- new *bhaji*. If they have already received some money, then they give little bit extra in return and this continues on for generations. *bhaji* at weddings are also called *naindra*. When a *machi* is used as a messenger to pronounce, a death to the friends and relatives living outside the village, they all give him money but no record is kept of it, however, he is bound to tell, verbally, details of the money he receives from each individual, to the family who used

40

him as a messenger. This is a tradition in rural society in Pakistan.

There is a special reason why people call upon a *machi* to cut or trim their trees, he does not demand money as a wage but takes some part of the tree as reward. They need this wood to kindle the *Tandoor* twice a day. Usually, *machis* serve a landlord through out the year, free of charge and get wheat and wood in return on an annual basis.

The village women are gathered at *Tandoor* and they are served on a first come first served basis. They knead the dough and give it to the Bhagee. She kneels down, into the *Tandoor* and slaps the flattened dough onto its inner walls. The women give her big piece of dough as a wage for her services. She has a vast container beside her, where she keeps all the dough given to her. At the end, she bakes bread for her family and for the customers who buy them for cash. If there are no customers, then she leaves the breads to dry and sells them to farmers, who use them as food for their animals.

It is evening time and the *Tandoor* is crowded with women. They are sharing their news with one another and discussing the different affairs going on in the village. Kamal Chaudhry becomes a topic of discussion when his mother arrives. They all praise Rehmat, for his generosity to Babu *Mussali* and the other *Kammies* in the village. Kamal's mother started boasting about her family and especially about Kamal, so felt the need to fabricate some stories about his life in London, she would have something to say to impress the village women.

"How is my son? Have you talked to him on the phone?" Bhagee asked her.

"I talk to him every day. He phones us daily," she told Bhagee.

"It is very expensive to call from *Walliat*, isn't?" she asked kneeling down into the *Tandoor*.

"I told him 'son, don't waste money by phoning us every day', but he does not listen to me", Nusrat said.

"Money is not a problem for you, after all you are Chaudhries," Bhagee flattered her.

"Babu *Mussali* is our special servant, if he demanded of us even two thousand rupees we would give it to him," she proudly told them pretending to be the richest family in the village.

"Have you found a girl for him?" another woman asked her.

"His uncle Raheem wants him to marry his daughter."

"Now he is an *Angreez babu* ---an English man, he needs *Walliati* girl," the woman said and started laughing, as did the others.

"Since he's gone to London, I have been receiving lot of proposals for him, both directly and indirectly. I asked him to send us his new pictures, to show the people," she further boasted about her son.

"Has he started to work?" Bhagee asked her.

"No, I asked him, take some rest, concentrate on your studies, we don't need his money. Allah has given us a lot already."

"I asked him the day before he was going to *Walliat*, what he would get for me from there, he said, *Amman*---mother, whatever you ask me I will buy for you." Bhagee sang in his praises.

"Don't worry Bhagee, I know he would buy you whatever you asked."

"It is getting cold now, please ask him to send me a woollen jacket," she demanded.

"I will ask him," she assured her.

The wife of Gama *mochi* is also there. She says, "Kamal is my son too, he played in my lap, he also promised to send me a tea thermos. Next time, when he phones you, please remind him his promise."

"Don't worry, I will." She reassured her too.

"Please also ask him to have his marriage ceremony here. I will take his *bhaji* to every door in the village," she further says.

"No, my husband will do it," Bhagee interrupted her.

42

They both start arguing; each of them claiming that she deserves more and is closer to Kamal.

"Don't worry, I'll equally distribute all of his wedding invitations among you to give out", she placated them.

"I have already told Rehmat to ask his brother to bring his daughter here; we want marriage ceremony in the village," she explained further.

"I fear they will snatch your son from you," Bhagee showed her concerns.

"I want to see Kamal happy and to be prosperous in life, if he comes to see me once a year, it will be fine with me," she said as tears appear in her eyes.

"You will definitely miss your son," Bhagee stated.

"Since he went to London, I have not eaten properly. I can not sleep well. I miss him all the time. I wait for the postman, standing on the doorstep every day with hope of his letter and fresh pictures. I go to his room daily, touch his things and remember him", a stream of tears floating out her eyes. She hides her face in her hands and places her head on her knees.

Some other women were also shedding tears, in remembrance of their sons who are also away from them. The others comfort them.

****

Kamal was sitting on a chair, his arms folded across his chest, bending his head onto the table in his room.

"My dreams of studying in London have been crushed to dust. I do not have any money to transfer to another college. I did not know about the cheating and blackmailing by colleges in the UK. My consultant even kept me in the dark. I believed in what I saw in the prospectus or what the consultant told me. They don't know how hard my family worked to arrange this money for my

43

foreign education. I will not be able to compete with my cousins here. Tanzeela is going to a good university, how can she marry a person like me? I have no future prospects here. When she sees me at home every day, what will she think about me? How can I tell them why I am not going to the college?" he was lost in his thoughts when his uncle entered the room, with a tray carrying his dinner for him.

"How did your first day at college go Kamal?" he asked while putting his tray on the table.

"It was good, really good," he said hesitantly.

"How were your new classmates and teachers?"

"They were good," he replied shyly.

"Have you had any lectures today?"

"No, today I just completed registration things."

"I see--- the very first day at college is always like that. Did you feel any difficulty getting to your college?" he asked.

"No, I found it very easily," he said unconvincingly.

"OK, you enjoy your dinner. I am very tired today and want to go to sleep early," he said before leaving.

Kamal took the dinner half-heartedly and was soon again lost in his thoughts. He phoned Ajay to seek his advice.

"Hello Ajay *bhai*---brother, Kamal speaking."

"Hi Kamal! How are you?"

"Very confused *bhai*, I don't know what to do? You know I stay with my uncle and I do not want to tell them about my college things."

"Forget about the college Kamal. We will see it again after one year. I have been with this college for the last four years, just pay them some money and keep getting the extension for visa. It is better that you look for a job" Ajay told him.

"But what I tell to my uncle family?"

"They are not chasing you all the time. You don't need to tell them any thing."

"I don't know how to find a job" Kamal said.

"OK, I tell you the steps, first of all; go to the local job centre and apply for a national insurance number as early as possible. They will guide you how and where to apply for it. Then go to any bank, with your passport and college letter and open your account. Also, go to your local surgery and get registered with a doctor. You can also go to the local library to use the internet and computer facilities for free. Compose a good CV at the library, make plenty of photo copies of it and go to each and every shop and supermarket in your area and ask all around for the job opportunities."

"Thank you Ajay *bhai*, I will start doing that tomorrow" Kamal said in thanks.

"Any time you need my help, don't hesitate to ask me" Ajay reminded him.

"Thank you Ajay *bhai*, you are really very helpful" Kamal said as they ended the call.

Kamal forgets about his college and starts following Ajay's instructions. He leaves early in the morning and comes back late in the evening pretending to his uncle that he goes in search of a job after he finishes college. No one in the house interacts with him but his uncle. He has some discussions with him, about his studies and job hunting activities and the things going on back home in the village. He also keeps him informed about his struggle in finding him a job.

Kamal does not forget to write his diary every day, before he goes to sleep.

****

It is the weekend. Nabeela is sitting with her mother in the TV lounge. They are watching some Indian movie. Nabeela was anxiously waiting all weekend, because her mother told her that she wanted to discuss with her, something important. She had no time during the week, as she came late from the work and was busy with her own things. Her father is always at home during the week and her mother does not want to talk to her, about this serious issue in his presence at home.

"Mum, you wanted to talk to me?," she asked, lowering the TV volume using remote control, which she had been holding in her hands for a long time.

"Your father wants you to marry Kamal," she said, revealing her secret.

"What?" she replied in surprise and switched the TV off.

"Yes, he told me and he had given *zaban* to his brother already." Her mother revealed more.

"I can't believe it. How it is possible someone takes decision of my life without asking me?" she said agitatedly.

"I know, but your father does not understand it. You know when he came to know about your friendship with a black man at university he became ferocious. You remembered he broke everything in his room in anger and threatened to put the whole house on fire if you did not stop seeing him. He wanted you to marry Kamal from the beginning", she made known to her.

Muhammad Ibrahim was ex-boyfriend of Nabeela. He was a Nigerian classmate of her at university. She fell in his love but when her father protested violently against it she had to break this friendship. Her mother was also not happy with her on this affair. She wanted her to marry a Pakistani Muslim that suited her in education and social position but she was totally against the arranged marriages within family. Nabeela had to stop seeing him under the family pressure.

"But I can't believe it. Just tell dad that I do not agree with him," she said, stomping her foot on ground. She pushed the table away with her leg angrily, threw the remote control onto the sofa with all her strength and went to her room.

She was furiously pacing in her room, from one corner to other. After some time her mother came in.

"Don't worry my baby, as long as I am alive, it won't happen," she told her affectionately.

"This is not fair. We have always obeyed him in life. We did whatever he asked us to do. He remained with us like a shadow wherever we went. We wore whatever he asked us to wear. We have been forced to choose our friends on his likes and dislikes. Now he wants to impose on us husbands, of his own choice too. This is totally unfair," she sat on bed, took her face in hands and started wailing.

The other two sisters heard her wailing and rushed to her room.

"What happened? *Appi*--- elder sister," Tanzeela held her in her arms.

"Your father has given *zaban* to his brother, for Nabeela," the mother said wiping tears from her face, with one corner of her scarf.

"Don't worry *Appi*, it will not happen," she comforted her.

"Everyday, we face new challenges in life. Our success tomorrow depends on how we deal with them today," Shakeela came forward and sat on her knees on the ground by raising her head to Nabeela's chest. Nabeela tapped her head lovingly.

"Look *Appi*, you are not going to marry this idiot; we are all with you, aren't we?" she said, sympathetically.

Their mother sat on the bed amongst daughters and told them the story of her marriage to their father.

"I had never seen him before. My family was happy that he lived in the UK. I wanted to go to college after I completed my school education in the village. We lived in a village that was near to your father's village. I had a passion to become a doctor. My family did not want me to go to college in the city. They thought that the colleges spoiled the girls. My friends were envious of me, because I would go to London after my marriage. I was not as happy as my family was, to receive this proposal. But girls had no voice there. I had no other option than to accept their decision, for the sake of my family's honour."

"You know your father was against your college education, but I did not want same thing to happen to my daughters. I wanted to see you highly qualified, so that you could have an independent life."

"Nabeela you have become an independent girl. You are doing a good job. I want my other two daughters to have the same as you. Most of the men keep women financially dependent, so that they can rule over them."

"I have already told your father, none of my daughters will marry his nephew but he is not listening to me. He has given *zaban* to his brother, without asking me or you. Shakeela is right this is a challenge for us. This marriage will never happen." She ended her story.

A cold war had started in the house. The sisters and their mother are supporting Nabeela, and Raheem is in favour of Kamal. Every night he has an argument with his wife, on this issue. He gives lectures to his daughters, on the benefits of getting married within the family.

At the same time, he pushes Kamal to complete his MBA as early as possible so that he may be able to find a good job, becoming equal to Nabeela in education and status.

On the other hand, Kamal is struggling to find a job, forgetting about his education completely. Sometimes he asks his uncle to help him finding a job, who gives him some references but they don't work.

His status in the house is just like that of a stranger. His only friend in the house is his uncle. Sometimes, he feels lonely and wants to talk to his cousins and aunty, but they do not come near him and avoid his company. If he goes to TV lounge, or into the garden, in their presence, then they leave him alone or do not join him there, if he is sitting there already.

He does not tell these things to his parents back home, because he wants not to disrupt family relations. He knows that his father loves his brother very much. After a long time, they have come together. He does not want to create any hatred between the brothers, because of him.

He spends most of his time outside, hunting for a job and comes back home late in the evening, when his uncle is at home and leaves early in the morning.

Ajay is his only friend, who guides him in every thing and talks to him on phone daily.

He belongs to Gujarat in India. He is twenty five years old with an average height and dark wheat colour. He has big cheeks, small button styled eyes and long smooth hair. He is a man with a big heart and mind who makes friends easily. He has a retail security job, in a store in central London.

They both have some common characteristics, like writing daily in a diary, making friends easily and shy of girls.

****

Chapter 4

After three weeks in London. An owner of a chicken shop offers Kamal a volunteer job. He is a Pakistani, and is known as Malik *Sahib*. He works there for two weeks without any salary. When he demands him a paid job, Malik *Sahib* releases him and gives the same job to another student who wants some training and references. This is a trick of Malik *Sahib*; he exploits the students on the name of training, experience and references for two to three weeks without giving them a penny. The only benefit students get from him, is the improvement in their CVs; they can add work experience and have a future reference for hunting another job. Kamal also gets this benefit and starts hunting a new job, after adding this UK work experience to his CV. He walks miles, all over in different parts of London in search of job. Every day he finds several students like him, in the same situation wandering on the roads and the supermarkets looking for work. Some of them have been doing this for three to six months, but still they have not succeeded in finding a job. When Kamal listens to their stories he becomes disappointed, but his family's loan, which he took to come to the UK, and dreams of becoming equal to his cousins make him to continue in his struggle.

The reality of London life, for the international students who come to study with hope to find a good part time job, has been revealed to him. He has no choice, though, except to work hard to earn the money back, that he has already spent and to fulfil his dreams of becoming a rich and educated person.

After a long tedious struggle lasting three months, he finally succeeds in securing a job at a big grocery store owned by a Sri-Lankan, on thirty pounds per day from 7:00 am to 7:00 pm seven days a week.

Kamal Chaudhry, who has come to the UK with high dreams, is now working in a grocery shop for 2.50 pounds per hour. Loading and unloading the heavy stuff from delivery trucks, arranging shelves with commodities, helping customers to put their heavy shopping in cars and mopping the shop floor twice a day, is all his job.

He receives his first wage of 210 pounds. He was very happy that day and decided to send it to his mother.

****

Raheem was sitting in Kamal's room one night.

"Kamal, you get very busy these days. You leave early in the morning and come in late in the evening", he said.

"Yes uncle, I go to college first and then to my part time job."

"You are really working very hard. I am proud of you." he told Kamal.

"Kamal, I know your cousins and aunty are not friendly with you, but don't worry everything will be fine."

"I don't mind it uncle," Kamal replied, disheartened.

"This is your aunt's fault; it is she who feeds the daughters' minds against us because she is not from our family." Raheem informed him.

"I know it."

"That's the reason I want to marry my daughters within the family."

"This is a good thinking uncle." Kamal agreed

"Kamal, I have asked your father to get ready for your wedding." Raheem revealed.

"But uncle first I need to complete my studies." Kamal objected.

"The marriage will not affect your studies. Nabeela is doing a good job. You can live in this house. You do not need to do part time job after wedding, just concentrate on your studies."

"Nabeela!" he said surprisingly.

He loved Tanzeela and wanted to marry her but the sudden announcement of his uncle left him in panic. He could not tell his uncle on his face that he loved his younger daughter.

"Will Nabeela accept it?" Kamal asked him.

"I am her father and I know what is best for her," he said with a firm voice and left the room.

Kamal got worried but could not raise voice before his elders according to the family traditions.

He pondered over Ajay advice, who asked him to marry his cousin as early as possible, to secure his immigration status in the UK. But he did not want to get married just for his immigration status. He wanted to get admission into any good English language school, to improve his skills so that he could communicate with Nabeela confidently. He also wanted to go to a good college to complete his studies, after the marriage. He wished to become equal to her.

He phoned Ajay and explained the situation to him. He also asked him to find him a good English language school. Ajay told him to take the day off from work the next day and they would visit, together, some institutions for this purpose.

****

Raheem wanted his wife, Sadiqa, to talk to Nabeela about the plans for her wedding to Kamal.

"Did you talk to Nabeela about Kamal?" he asked her one night.

"I did, but she was not agreeing with you. None of my daughters was happy with this decision," she told him.

"She does not know what I know, so tell her that is my final decision." He told her.

"But you can not force her, can you?" she said angrily.

"You are her mother; it is your duty to make her agree. She is a child yet. She cannot understand the fruits of getting married within family." He explained.

"She is not a child anymore. She can decide things for herself. She is a matured woman. If we force her she could go to the police, women agencies or the human rights organizations. You know the government has passed tough laws against forced marriages," she warned him.

"You are threatening me, aren't you?" he said lividly.

"I am not threatening you, but telling you the reality," she said softly.

"Do you think that my daughters can dare to go to the police or somewhere else to register a complaint against me?"

"If you oppress them they can do that."

"You stupid woman, I am not oppressing them. I am doing the best things for them being a father."

"Raheem, I am telling you this marriage will not happen."

"And I am telling you *Begum*—wife, this will happen. My name is Raheem Chaudhry and I am leader of the house, here only my orders will work."

"What kind of father you are? You are going to compete with your own daughter!" she declared in annoyance.

"I am not competing with anyone. I am going to do what I think is better for this house."

"I am not agreeing with you and I am telling you this will not happen," she roared.

He slapped her with his full force. She fell down on the bed and started to cry loudly.

"OK, here I am, beat me more," she stood up close to him.

When the daughters heard this noise they rushed to the scene.

"Here you go, beat me up. Why have you stopped?" she was howling bitterly.

The daughters held their mother. Their eyes were full of tears too, but they kept quiet in respect of their father. This was not the first time this had happened. They had seen it many times in their lives. This was a common habit of Raheem, when he had been defeated in an argument, he beat his wife.

"Tell him Nabeela; you will not marry his nephew," she yelled.

When Kamal heard this noise, he also came downstairs, stood behind the door, and listened to their conversation by hiding himself from them.

Raheem was sitting on a sofa, sighing long with anger, his wife and daughters were on the bed. The girls are still holding their mum who is shivering and sobbing in grief.

"Since your nephew has come to this house our peace has finished" She told him.

"What is he doing to you? He leaves early in the morning and comes back late at night. No one among you speaks to him. Is this the way to treat your relatives?" he fluttered.

"We know better about how to treat our relatives, but you are forcing him on us as a proposed husband for Nabeela. Is this the way to arrange marriages for girls?" her eyes were filled with tears of rage and temper.

"He is not unknown to us. He is my nephew--- the son of my real brother," he stressed the last sentence.

"*Ma'shallah*---what is God's will, today you remembered your brother, when your daughters have grown up," she said jokingly.

"Nabeela, tell him to his face today that you will not marry this unwanted guest in our home, his nephew, Kamal Chaudhry, who does not even know how to use the toilet or the bathroom," she murmured the last words under her breath.

Nabeela is looking down to her lap, holding one of her mother's hands gently. Everyone is looking at her, waiting for her answer.

"He is not my suitor, I am sorry to say," she said softly, without lifting her head up.

"What do you mean by suitor? He is your real cousin. You both belong to the same blood. He is young and handsome. He will be equal in education with you in two years time. What is this 'suitor'? You know when your mother came to the UK, she could not speak one word of English, and even then I accommodated her. It took her two years to speak little bit English. She had a complex. When she brought you up, she did not speak to you in her native language. She spoke to you in English only. That is why today you are not able to speak your parents' language properly. This is her fault not mine," he gave his lengthy logic.

"You are forgetting one thing Raheem Chaudhry; you accommodated me because we had the same native language but Nabeela's native language is English now," Sadiqa gave her counter argument.

"He will learn English, as you learnt and he does it quickly because he is going to college."

"This is not the question, whether he speaks poor English or good English. The question is, we were both brought up in two different cultures. We have a difference in age, education, career and sociology. How we will accommodate each other?" Nabeela spoke this time, but still bowing her head down. A stream of tears was pouring from her eye.

"Look darling, two or three years age difference is not a big deal in weddings, and what 'culture' is this? He is a Muslim like you, he does not drink, gamble nor is he involved in any immoral activities. He knows how to respect elders, how to look after family and people all around. He knows how to speak with the people. He is hard working. Once he has lived in this society for some time, he will learn the sociology as well. I am unable to understand, why are you are all so negative about him?" he said more positively this time.

He gave a brief look to all of them and then continued to speak, "I worked hard throughout my life just for you. I always tried to be a good father. I know sometimes I treated you bit harshly, but it was for your betterment. Once you have children you will come to know why sometimes parents have to be strict with them."

"I love all of you and what I am thinking, this time, for Nabeela is the best for her," he tries to convince them.

"But marriage is a life time decision. How you can lead your life with a person you don't like?" his wife, again, negated him.

"OK, fair enough, that is the reason I have kept him in this house, so you can get to know him better. But you avoid him, don't talk to him, don't socialise with him. How can you develop an understanding with him? What is the reason for your hatred of him? Is he burden to you? Are you giving him money for his studies? Are you cooking and doing washings for him? He is limited to his room. I make his breakfast and dinner not you. He never comes out of his room. If he sometimes does, you leave him alone and he goes back in embarrassment. You are not only hurting him, but me as well. I am just observing your attitudes towards him. This is enough now. This is my final decision, Nabeela will marry him," he declared, like a judge.

"OK, you will also listen our final decision, Nabeela will never marry him," Sadiqa told him, spreading her chest wide open in a challenging way.

"I had been kept quiet before you for the whole life, just because my daughters were very young. I tolerated your abusive behaviour, faced your beatings and obeyed your fair and unfair demands. Now my daughters had grown up. They are able to look after me. Listen carefully, Raheem Chaudhry, if you try to slap me again or force my daughters to marry your nephew I will call the police straight away and put you behind bars for rest of your life," she spoke to him, just like a man would have.

Raheem was shocked at the bravery of his wife, sitting amongst her daughters.

Kamal heard all this and went back to his room. Shakeela took the mother to her room, leaving the father all alone.

A storm of thoughts was coming across Kamal's head. He kept changing his position in bed and sleep was miles away from him. He spent the whole night in restlessness. The next day, early in the morning, he phoned Ajay and asked him to arrange accommodation for him. He told him that they would look a room after visiting some languages schools, which they had already planned for the day.

****

"Why are you leaving your uncle's house Kamal?" Ajay asked him, on the way to an English language school in central London.

"I am an unwanted guest in that house," he said sadly.

"You were going to marry your cousin. Weren't you?" Ajay asked.

"None of my cousins likes me, they think I am an idiot who can not speak good English; doesn't know table manners, doesn't know the rules of using a toilet and bathroom, doesn't have good qualifications, brought up in different culture and doesn't know English sociology. So, I am useless to them," he said and Ajay saw water floating at the corners of his eyes.

They visit three colleges and select one of them, a rather cheaper one, which has good learning facilities.

It was a sunny day, in mid December. The markets and high streets were colourfully decorated. Christmas shopping time was at its peak. There was an extra rush of people everywhere. They were walking down Oxford Street, famous for its shopping malls all over the world. Sometimes, they stopped in front of the big shopping stores and enjoy their decorations and did some window shopping.

Everything seemed to be colourless to Kamal. Ajay realised that he was not taking interest in anything. He wanted to make him happy. He took him to the Merlin Entertainments London Eye for some fun.

"Kamal do you know that the London Eye is the tallest Ferris wheel in Europe? It is 135 metres (443 feet) tall, situated on the bank of the Rive Thames. It carries 3.5 million customers every year", Ajay told him.

"I never have been to this place before. It is really amazing," he replied, looking at its height.

They walked along the bank of the river and sat on a big stone bench, a rather lonely place, facing towards the sun. Ajay kept quiet for some time, looking deep into the flowing water.

"OK, you love Tanzeela, your uncle wants you to marry Nabeela, her elder sister, but none of your cousins likes you. So, you have decided to leave the house, because you do not want to be a bone of contention in your uncle's family, right?" he asked him.

"Yes Ajay, I don't want to cause any problems in the house. I will live separately and make my life without my uncle's support. I want to prove to my cousins that I am not as much worthless as they think I am," he showed his determination.

"What will you do to prove that?" Ajay asked.

"I will take English classes for six months, to overcome my language deficiency. Then I will try to complete my MBA and get a good job to make my life. I will become equal to my cousins, in education and career-wise and one day I will go before them as a successful person."

"Fair enough, I appreciate your good thinking." Ajay said.

"Did you find an accommodation for me, Ajay?" Kamal asked.

"Yes, I talked to one of my friends; there is a vacant box-room in his house. He is demanding 250 pound per month inclusive. The four Pakistani students are already sharing this house. You can also share cooking with them." Ajay told him

"OK, thank you very much Ajay *bhai*." Kamal replied.

"Kamal, can I ask you something personal?" Ajay asked

"Go ahead."

"How much do you love Tanzeela?" Ajay questioned

"I fell in love with her, unconsciously, before I came to the UK. I have some memories of our childhood from when she visited Pakistan." Kamal revealed.

"Did you ever express your love to her?" Ajay asked

"No, she does not like to talk to me." Kamal replied

"For how long you have been staying in her house?" Ajay continued his questions.

"About four months."

"In four months you could not express your love to her!"

"No, I couldn't." Kamal replied

"Some people can't express their love in four months, some in four years and some other ever," Ajay took a long sigh.

"Ajay *bhai*, are you in love with someone?" Kamal asked

"Yes *bhai*, no human being is without love."

"Who is she?" Kamal asked

"This is a long story *bhai*." Ajay replied

"Would you not share with me?" Kamal asked

Ajay fixed his eyes on the dancing waves in the river, as these waves had some meaning for him in life. He held his chin and cheeks with his palms, putting his elbows on his knees bending his body down.

"She used to work with me in a supermarket in London," he kept quiet and was lost in thought.

"What happened then?" Kamal asked him anxiously.

"Nothing happened; it was a love story written on the waves

and it fled away into the deep silent waters," he said, and stood up, walked to the boundary at the bank of the river, put his arms onto the cemented wall and started looking down into the water. Kamal also followed him.

"I want to listen to this story Ajay *bhai*." Kamal told him

Ajay looked up to the sky, took a long sigh, kneeled down onto his arms and sank his face into them.

"It was her first day at work. I was impressed by her at very first sight. She had long silky hair, brown colour, slim and smart body, narrow long eyes and was of more than average height at the age of twenty. Her name was as unique as she was. She belonged to same part of India where I come from, but she was born in this country. We had the same religion and the same native language. When she spoke Guajarati, no one would believe that she was a British. She was very friendly with everyone at work but totally reserved outside of the workplace. I did not believe in love at first sight before I saw her. I fell in her love the very first day. I did not miss any opportunity to be near to her and talk to her. She disappeared soon because she was a seasonal worker and would come to work only in her holidays. She was studying at a university in London. I waited for her restlessly. Every time I went to work, I used to check the rota, to try and find her name," he lifted his head up onto his arms and started to walk along the bank putting his hands in his trousers. Kamal also followed him. He took a long pause to start again.

"Kamal, you know one sided love makes you mad. It hurts you a lot," he stopped, gave him a deep look and continued.

"A true love is just like an island---completely surrounded by water, if you lose your boat, it drowns you into the deep waters. I lost my way back when I saw her for the first time. I kept drowning in her personality day by day."

Kamal looked into Ajay's drenched eyes and felt sympathy in his heart for him.

"Ajay *bhai*, you never told me before that you were so broken-hearted in life," Kamal said in a grieved voice.

"This river, this bank and this place are very dear to me. Whenever I have some free time I come here, sit for hours and remember her," he looked at a ferry coming from the west side of the river and enjoyed the ups and downs of the waves running with it.

"What a beautiful scene!" he got the attention of Kamal towards it.

"One day, I asked her if she was really very pretty or if my eye sight was weak. And you know what she said?" he asked him

"What?"

"She said innocently that she was little bit pretty," he said this and started to laugh.

"One day, I was doing the shopping and she was serving me. I joked with her that I had a big family to feed, just five children. She surprisingly said 'just five'. I said, 'yes', I did not believe in a large family and she laughed madly."

Kamal saw brightness on his face, when Ajay was talking about her laughing.

"And you know one day, we were working together, all the male customers came to her to get served. I told her that it was because she was very pretty and they did not want to miss a chance to talk to such a lovely girl. She shrunk with shyness and said, *Na*—no. She was looking so innocent at that time, I was feeling like time had paused to appreciate her."

"But you know Kamal when we finished work and walked together to car park, she used to tell me that our journey finished there. From that point, our destinations were separated," his face had gone weepy as he said that.

"My love story is from the store to the employee car park," he held his head from its back with his hands, pressed it hard between his arms, took a long sigh and said hysterically 'Oh my god'-----'Oh my god'; this love kills you."

Kamal was still wondering what the link was, of that place with his love story. He asked him about it, "Ajay, why is this river, its bank and its uncontrolled waves so important to you?"

"I am getting late to work. Today I have to do a night shift. I will tell you next time," he looked at his wrist watch and rushed to the bus stop.

"You did not even tell me your complete love story," Kamal said to him, walking behind him at the same pace.

"I'll tell you next time," he said.

Love is a feeling, which is not dependent on words to express it. It has no voice but it speaks louder in human hearts. It has no shape but reflects in minds. It gives happiness, sadness, restlessness and calmness all at the same time. It hurts and gets hurt. It develops unconsciously inside us.

It is above race, colour and faith. It has one name, love, and only love. Once you feel it for someone it remains there for ever. Wherever you go, whatever you do, it is with you. When you are quiet it speaks. It is companion of your loneliness but makes you alone when you are among the people.

Ajay's love was 'love at first sight". It is natural and beyond someone's control. It happens all of a sudden, comes like a storm and takes you far-off where you cannot find a way to come back. It leaves you helpless. It does not wait for the response of the other person. It behaves one sided. You do not want to miss any opportunity to talk to your beloved or to be near to them. You are always looking for them amongst thousands of people. When you see them you feel like all the colours of life have come to you. You forget everything when your love is with you and you too forget all when they are not with you.

You start loving all the things associated with your honey. Love at first sight is madness in a real sense and is a sweet poison that melts inside you all of sudden, kills you slowly but silently.

He told that his love story was limited from the store to the employee car park but when he said, 'it was a love story written on the waves and it fled away into the deep silent waters', it meant that the River Thames had some link to it.

****

When Nusrat, Kamal's mother, received her son's first week wage in Pakistani currency, twenty-five thousands rupees, she was very happy.

"First of all, I will get cook two *daigs*---a big rounded cooking pot used to cook food for a large number of people, of sweet rice and distribute them on Miran Shah's shrine. It was my *mannat*-- a holy commitment," she tells her husband.

"It has happened with Miran Shah's blessing," she said in devotion.

The Shrine of Miran Shah has a significant place in the village. No one knows the exact history or biography of the sacred man buried there. There are many different stories about him. The most common belief is that, once there was a severe flood in the village some three hundreds years ago. The whole village was under water. Miran Shah ordered the water to leave the village and within a short time, all water went away and the village was saved. This shrine is famous for that *Karamat*—miracle. This is the reason that whenever anyone in the village falls into trouble, they come to this shrine for prayers and blessings. It is situated on a high pitch, on the west side of the village. The grave is covered with a dark green velvet cloth embroidered with verses from the Holy Quran. There is a small green minaret, which is oval shaped, high above the grave. The shrine is surrounded by a boundary of bricks.

There are a lot of small, horse shaped, toys made from the soil scattered around the grave. They are called 'Shah dey Ghorady'—horses of Shah. When people come to visit the shrine they lift them up, kiss them sacredly and rub them on their faces and chests. There is a superstition that at night time, they become real horses and race with each other. In the morning, they come back to shrine, turn into soil again but human eyes are not able to see them when they become real horses. If a head or leg is broken off any of the horses, it meant they fought with each other at night time and Miran Shah had punished them.

All the brides in the village first come to the shrine for blessings on their wedding day, before they leave for their husbands' houses.

When the visitors' prayers are granted, they come to the shrine and fulfil their *mannat* -whatever they have committed before. Usually, this is in the form of commodities to distribute among the people.

This shrine is very special place for the children. They play around it the whole day and whenever they see someone coming to fulfil his *mannat* they gather there and compete and fight with each other to get maximum quantity of the distributed things.

"It is a good idea. Kamal used to go to Miran Shah's shrine every morning to pray to get UK visa," Rehmat appreciated his wife decision.

"Kamal told me that this was just one week salary," she told him cheerfully.

"Our son is very clever," Rehmat boasted about Kamal.

"Mother, tomorrow we will go to city to buy new clothes for us," one of the daughters said.

"Why not my dear baby, I will buy you a new mobile phone too," she patted her cheeks.

"No, mobile phones are not good for girls," Rehmat opposed the idea.

She blinks her eyes in a way to show her approval to buy it, but hiding it from her husband.

She told every woman of the village that Kamal had sent her a lot of money, and she was going to distribute two *daigs* of sweet rice at Miran Shah's shrine the next day. She invited all of them to come and get their share. Some of them were praising him but most of them were feeling jealousy. They wished their sons to be like him. Nusrat also told them false stories about her son's rich life in London as usual.

****

When Kamal got home, in the evening, he saw Tanzeela sitting on the stairs like she was waiting for someone. He greeted her; she nodded without giving any welcome expression. He went to his room and found a letter for him on the door step.

Mr. Kamal Chaudhry Sahib,

Since you come to our house our life has been disturbed. Every day my parents have had a row because of you. My mother is a heart patient and I am afraid that if this continues she could lose her life.

Last night my father slapped her because he wanted my Appi to marry you and she did not like this proposal. You know it better; you are not a suitor for her from any aspect. You are not a suitor for any of us.

Would you like my mother in the hospital and father behind bars? I think you would not, would you?

Can I please ask you to leave our house and let us live peacefully? I hope you will not tell our father about this letter.

Thanks for your cooperation.
Tanzeela

He had already decided to leave the house; this letter made him to leave right away.

"I should have left it before," he cursed himself.

He packed his luggage and got ready to leave. He did not wait for his uncle, as this house was stinging him. He dragged his suitcase and two heavy bags down the stairs. Tanzeela was standing with her mother and her younger sister, Shakeela, in the corridor. In the mean time, Nabeela had entered the house. She told her mum that she had come home early that day as she was not feeling well.

Kamal carried the two bags on his shoulders and took the suitcase in his right hand. They were all watching him silently. When he passed by them, on his way to the main gate, he stopped and said, 'I am sorry'. He wanted to say something more, but his tongue did not support him. He gave a quick fleeting look to Tanzeela; she started looking down to her feet.

He paused before stepping out of the door to thank them for their hospitality, but the stream of tears running from his eyes stopped him from turning his face back to them.

****

Chapter 5

Today, Nusrat was very happy. She was going to distribute two *daigs* of *zarda*--sweet rice at the Miran Shah Shrine in the afternoon. The cook of the village—*Nai,* was cooking the *daigs* at the shrine. The children had gathered there much earlier with their pots. They were very impatient to get the rice and were competing with each other to stand first in the queue.

Rehmat Chaudhry was sitting beside a big oak tree on a *charpie*-a big bed with four legs made of straight threads of unravelling old linen cloth, with some other people of his age. There was a big *hookah*---a pipe with a long, flexible stem, arranged so that the smoke is cooled by being made to pass through water. They were all smoking it, turn by turn, and talking about the sugar cane crop that was ready to cultivate.

"I cannot understand, we produce sugar cane on a large scale but still our country is suffering from sugar shortage," one farmer said.

"This is the game of mill owners, they give a small amount of money to the farmers, hoard the crop and play with the government to earn extraordinary profits," Rehmat said.

"Most of the mill owners are the part of the government, no one can question them," another man said.

"We work hard in the fields, cultivating the sugar cane but when we go to the market to buy sugar, we have to queue for hours, this is not fair to us," the old farmer again said.

"Our political leaders are corrupt; they are involved in the smuggling of sugar. They do this intentionally to create shortages, so that they can import sugar and get a huge commission on it from foreign sellers," Rehmat said.

"We are an agricultural country but we have a shortage of wheat, even the vegetables become scarce sometimes. It is matter of shame for us," another old man said.

"I told you it was all because of poor governance and wide spread corruption in our country," Rehmat said.

"Rehmat Chaudhry, I ask you please contest the next elections. You have no money problem now because your son is in *Walliat*," the old man suggested him.

"Election is a game of millions of rupees, you know it," he said.

"Your son is earning good money in *Walliat,* so you can easily afford the elections. We all assure you our support," the old man said again.

They all convinced him to contest the next election at local level because they think that he has become rich after his son went to the UK.

When the *daigs* were ready, *Moulvi Sahib*---the head of the mosque, came to recite some verses from the Holy Quran, for blessings. First of all, the cook gave a big pot of rice to *Moulvi Sahib.* When the rice was ready, Kamal's mother came there to distribute it with her own hands. She argued with those asking for their relatives' shares, for those who were unable to come. She was discouraging the children, who turned up over and over. The people had specially gathered there, with pots and plates. When she put the rice in someone's pot, she asked them to pray for Kamal. If someone spoke nice words for her son, she gave them extra rice.

The whole village was envious of Kamal and his family. They took it as a sign of wealth if a family member was abroad, especially in Europe. Every young person desired to go to the UK, by fair or foul means. The fresh graduates in the village, who were unemployed, were asking for Kamal's contact details to get some information and guidelines from him in applying a student visa for the UK. Those who were clever were already in contact with some agents, in the big cities, for this purpose.

Nasir, a fresh graduate with A grades, son of the village school teacher, was zealous to go to the UK than anyone else in the village. He thought that he was more intelligent than Kamal and deserved to go abroad. His father wanted him to do a teaching course and start career as a teacher, but he insisted to go to England. His father did not have enough sources to afford his foreign education.

Nasir's mother also came to the shrine for rice. She was praying more for her son to go abroad, than praying for Kamal's success.

"I did a holy pledge, *mannat,* on shrine to distribute three *daigs* of *zarda* if Nasir succeeded in getting visa," she told her husband.

"But where will the money come from? He asked me for five hundreds thousands rupees! How could I arrange such a big amount?" he said irately.

"He told me that the agent would help him in maintaining the bank statement," she further asked him.

"Yes, he told me too. But you know he would charge eighty thousands rupees for keeping the required money, in Nasir's account, just for one month and he would also charge fifty thousands rupees for a visa consultancy fee," he explained to her.

"We have some jewellery at home. I went to the goldsmith yesterday, he told me its value was about three lakhs rupees (three hundreds thousands). I asked my brother to lend us one lakh too. Could you please arrange another lakh from somewhere?" she said.

"Look, we have got three young daughters; it took me ten years to make this jewellery for them, so that we could marry them honourably. We should not sell it. I am hardly feeding you with my salary, from where should I borrow one lakh rupees?" he said.

"Kamal's mother told me that he was earning twenty five thousands rupees per week. Our son is cleverer than him. He can do better than what Kamal is doing. We can make this jewellery again in just three months time. Anyway, we are not going to marry our daughters this year. I have told my brother that we would give him his money back after six months and he agreed," she convinced him.

"OK, one of my colleagues took out one lakh loan from the bank. I will get information from him tomorrow and if possible I will apply too," finally he was agreed with his wife to send his son to the UK.

****

Kamal's father was having an argument with his wife that night.

"I asked you not to buy a mobile phone for girls", he said

"No problem, they will not misuse it. You know Chaudhry Noor's daughter is making them jealous everyday, showing them her mobile phone. We are not less than them," she said proudly.

"But you will have to keep an eye on them, mobile phones are not good for young girls," he warned her again.

"Rehmat Chaudhry, times have changed. On TV, every second commercial is about a mobile phone, we can not keep our children away from this modern age," she said thoughtfully.

"We never talked to each other till our wedding day. Even after our engagement I stopped going to your village. It was a matter of shame to go to one's fiancée's village in our times. That age was better; boys and girls had some limitations. This media is spoiling the young children. Most of the mobile phone commercials on TV are showing boys and girls in friendship. This is not good," he said worriedly.

"Rehmat Chaudhry could my Kamal be happy in *Walliat* without us?" she said, with all her motherly love to change the topic.

"He is a young man; he should learn to live without parents by now." He said.

"He told me that he liked Tanzeela and wanted to marry her rather than Nabeela", she said.

"He is a stupid man how the younger sister can get married before the elder one", he said angrily.

"You know Nabeela is older than him", she said.

"Look, in blood relations these things are not considered. This is a matter of shame if the younger sister gets married first. The people will think that there is some fault with the elder one. This has never happened in our family before", he negated his son desires.

"I know but the time has changed now. We must respect our children likes and dislikes", she favoured her son.

"I want him to get engaged to Tanzeela but your brother insists on Nabeela", she further argued.

"He has already given me *zaban* for Nabeela", he explained her.

"If you have give zaban for Nabeela then it is fine. I know this is a disgrace for you to turn down your verbal promise. I'd explain to Kamal and I hope he understands this", she also agreed when she knew the verbal promise of her husband. In rural society this is dignity of a man to respect his verbal promises.

"You are ten years younger than me but your father did not show any objection on this big age difference between you and me", he said.

"I was just informed by my family that I was going to marry you, there was no other question", she said.

"The same thing is my brother doing. He has told Nabeela that she meant to marry Kamal. We are noble people and the daughters are our family honour. We know better how to defend and respect this honour. We are not so shameless people to ask our daughters about their wedding decisions. We select grooms for our girls by ourselves. They are not so *bi-gheyrat*---dishonourable, to find their husbands by themselves", he spoke his mind.

Nusrat was also not in favour to give freedom to girls to go out and find their husbands. She changed the topic and said, "You know Rehmat, a mother always thinks of her adults as children. Whenever I start to eat I think about him, if he has eaten or not. He is bad in the cold; I heard that there was always cold in London. I am worried about him".

"Don't worry he is staying in his uncle's house. All of his cousins will be looking after him. His uncle and aunty will be taking extra care of him, after all he is going to become their son-in-law," he said satisfactorily.

"OK, ask your brother that we want them to get engaged. I want to celebrate my son's engagement in the village," she agreed on Kamal marrying Nabeela, finally.

"I will phone him tomorrow and talk to him on this issue," he assured her.

"First, we should pay off our debt, otherwise our lenders will think negatively about us. Time is passing fast and our promised date is falling nearer," he showed his concerns.

"Don't worry Rehmat; Kamal has already started sending us money. If he sends us twenty five thousands every week, we will be able to pay back soon, if we are one or two months late it will not be a big problem," she made an estimate.

"You are right, our lenders are our close friends or relatives, if they are getting some money back every month they will not mind it," he said.

"I cannot wait to celebrate my son's engagement. All the women of the village ask me about it at the *Tandoor* every day," she showed her impatience.

"Tomorrow, I will talk to my brother and fix a date for engagement," he said affirmatively.

****

Kamal came out of the house, he did not know where to go. He phoned Ajay but it went to his voice mail box. He remembered, Ajay had told him that he was working that night. He left a message for him. He was planning on leaving the house in two to three days, but Tanzeela's letter forced him to leave all at once.

He stood at the bus stop for long time. He thought his uncle might come out in search of him and he did not want to go back to that house.

It was very cold out there. Whenever there was a sunny day in winter in the UK the evening would be much colder. He was shivering with cold.

His uncle was ringing him, over and over. He ignored his calls for some time, and kept thinking of what to tell him. Finally he attended his call.

"Hello, Kamal my son, where are you?" he asked him in broken voice.

"Sorry uncle, I forgot to tell you that I had a new night job in a hotel. They provided me with free accommodation and a night-time meal. The salary is also good. They wanted me to start from the same day, so I had to leave in a hurry. This hotel was near to my college and it was much easier for me to go to college by foot," he convinced him about his sudden depart from the house.

"OK, if there was a good opportunity then it was fine with me," he was satisfied.

He decided to spend night on the buses. He got on the first bus that arrived. He kept travelling from one destination to other for the whole night, with his heavy luggage. Most of time he slept on the buses, the drivers would alert him when the bus reached its final destination.

Ajay responded him at 7:00 am, when he finished his job. They decided to meet at a point in central London. Kamal explained to him the reasons for his rushed exit from his uncle's house. Ajay felt sorry for him.

He took him to East London, where he had already arranged a box-room for him. It was a two bedroom house. Each bedroom was shared by two people. Ajay helped him in arranging his luggage in his new room. This room was similar to his previous one, in his uncle's house, but there was no window there.

"Ajay *bhai*, I had only five hundreds pounds on me, which I paid to my language school yesterday. I have got nothing left to pay in advance here. I will be able to pay one months rent, in advance, in two weeks time," he told him his financial position.

"This house is owned by an Indian landlord; he is a nice person but does not give any relaxation in rent. I will pay your one month rent; you can give me back in two weeks time," he solved his problem.

"Thank you Ajay, you are always very helpful to me," he appreciated him.

"No worries, we all have some problems here", Ajay said.

Ajay introduced him to his two friends—Manzoor and Asif, who were already living in the house. They worked with Ajay at the same security company. They both were very nice and assured Kamal that they would all help each other. They had breakfast together.

Kamal was not feeling well. His eyes were red with sleeplessness. He was still shivering with cold. He phoned his employer and told him about his illness. He went to his room and fell into a deep sleep.

Asif came to his room in the late evening, to ask him to come down for dinner. Kamal was still in his bed. He had caught the flu and had a temperature. He hardly got up. He was feeling very weak. When Asif saw him, in such a poor condition, he brought food for him to the room, made tea for him and gave him some pills. Kamal again went to sleep, after having dinner and taking the medicines. He still had a high temperature, body pain with chills and a severe head ache, which almost made him faint.

He spent the whole night in that condition. The next morning, he felt some relief but was still not well enough to go to work. Asif prepared breakfast for him, gave him some more pills and asked him to take complete rest. The pills made him sleepy again. He took complete rest till noon. By the evening he felt so much better.

Ajay came to see him. He brought some fruit for him. They had a long gossip. He advised him not to go out, for at least two days, unless he again fell sick.

The first time he had more than a brief introduction to Manzoor and Asif when they were at home gathered at dining table.

Manzoor, was thirty years old, a single-body tall man with eye glasses, he had an Msc in Physics. He was working for a private company on a good salary in Pakistan before he came to the UK, three years ago, through the Highly Skilled Migrant Programme (HSMP) and was now doing a security job here.

Asif, aged 26, with strong athletic body, epic hair style, fair colour, and a smiley face, had done an MBA degree in London, and was also doing a security job.

"Kamal, what are your ambitions in the UK?" Asif asked him.

"I want to do an MBA degree," he replied.

"What will you do after doing MBA?" he further asked him.

"I would do a good job here."

"Do you have any previous management experience?" he kept asking.

"No." Kamal replied honestly.

"I had three years of work experience; I did an MBA through

a college, struggled hard in the market but could not find a job. I am not discouraging you, but telling you the reality," he said, his voice full of meaning.

"Two other people in this house have done master degrees, from good universities in London, one is working in McDonald's and other in a supermarket," he told him about the other people in the house.

"We had the same dreams, like you have, when we came to this country but we are doing low profile jobs. Our families boast about us, that we are living in the UK but they do not know what actually we doing here," Manzoor spoke this time.

"My past colleagues in Pakistan are working on better positions after getting experience in their fields, earning good money, enjoying recognition and respect in society, while I am worse than them, working as a security guard," Manzoor said desperately.

"I used to work in a bank in Pakistan before I came here, I did not greet the security guard over there. Today I am a security guard and people don't greet me. I can feel for him now but it is too late to realise. God has punished me for my arrogance. What is the difference between him and me? We both are *chowkidars*— door men. The difference is in places not in positions," Asif said philosophically.

"What should I do then?" Kamal asked both of them.

"Education is not bad thing. We are not against getting good education. We are just telling you the realities regarding job market in the UK these days," Asif said.

"OK, Kamal, we tell you the rules of this house. Four people share it. There is a time table hanging on the wall in the kitchen for cooking and cleaning. We will add your name today. We cook and clean on our fixed turns. On your turn you will have to cook the food for all of us and clean the whole house. There is no concept of lunch, just breakfast and dinner. However, if someone is at home during the day he can cook for himself. We do weekly shopping. One man is responsible for the shopping. There is a register on the kitchen shelf, whatever is bought is noted there. At the end of month we equally share the monthly expenditures. It is usually around one hundred pounds, or slightly above, per head." Asif explained.

"Our working schedules are different. You will hardly see all of us at one time, at home."

"We pay rent on monthly basis. Our landlord comes once a month to collect it. He is very strict in this matter. We don't blame him as he has to pay his mortgage for this house, every month on a fixed date," Manzoor briefed him.

Kamal went to his room and started to write about his ins and outs.

"I was earning 210 pounds per week by working seven days, now I have to go to the language school for three days and also spare one day at home for cooking and cleaning. I would be able to work just three days a week, which reduces my income to ninety pounds per week. It would become 360 pounds per month.

My rent is 250 per month, food expenses 100 and travelling around 80, phone bills 50, if I include 50 extra for other necessities it becomes 530 per month.

My English language course is for six months. It will cost me 1500 in total. I have paid 500 already, still need 1000 more. I need to save at least 170 per month to manage it. That means I need 700 per month. My family has five lakhs rupees loan, which I have to pay back in the next two months. How will I manage all this?" he put the paper and the pen aside, held his head in his hands and was lost in calculations.

"Should I pay my loan first or complete my language course?" he pondered.

"If I do this course, I will be able to speak good English and can compete for a better job, face people with confidence. If I don't pay my loan on time, my family will be in trouble. I can not see my parents bearing humiliation because of me. I do not want to damage my family's respect in the village. First of all, I should pay my loan back," he decided finally.

He dropped off the idea of doing a language course and planned to go to the college tomorrow to claim his fee back.

He was fidgeting on the bed with the thought of Tanzeela's letter. It hurt him deeply.

When he felt that he was unable to get to sleep, he started writing his diary:

"I can not understand why the people who are born in the UK think so negatively about their relatives back in their homelands. Why do they not want to mix with them? Why do they not want to get married to them? What is the reason behind it? I think it is because of the huge differences between the two cultures, a lack of understanding, communication and the financial gap.

Tanzeela, you did not need to write me this letter. You should have waited for me to leave on my own. I knew that I was an unwelcome guest in your home. I was fighting with my circumstances. You were not aware of the poor condition of my family and my problems. You did not even try to understand me. I have the burden of old parents and two young sisters on my shoulders. I have also a big burden of loan on me, as well. If you had given me some support, I could have easily unloaded all of these burdens. I came to this country with the hope of earning good money but I did not know that the things were totally different there for me. If I had known, I never would have come here until I had enough money. I still want to get good education to come equal to you."

He felt dizzy. He stopped writing and lay down on the bed to sleep.

****

78

The next day, he went to the school to claim his fee back. He told the administration that he had changed his mind, for some personal reasons. He got his deposited fee back. He called Ajay, to give him the money he borrowed to pay his rent. He told him that he was sitting at the same place by the London Eye, where they had met last time.

The weather wasn't very good that day. A typical winter day in London, the dark black clouds had fully covered the sky; it was looking like there would be rain soon.

"What is he doing there in this chilly weather?" Kamal thought about Ajay.

He found him sitting on the same stone bench, covering his head in a black hoodie and folding his arms across chest.

"What are you doing here in such a cold weather?" Kamal confronted him.

"I love this place," he replied serenely.

"What is so special here? Does it make sense to sit on a river bank, on such a cold day?" he asked.

"This place is very special to me Kamal," Ajay said totally.

"Oh ho, I remembered, you told me last time about your love story, but I could not understand what the link to this place was?" he asked him.

"The same link that breaths have with body, beat has with heart and scent has with flowers," he took a long breath and looked to be in a romantic mood.

"Kamal, you know every time we finished work we looked for each other to say goodbye. One day, she left without seeing me. The next day I complained to her about it and she said that she looked for me but could not find me. She was looking so innocent when she was telling me this. I took her hand and walked through the shop floor. I wanted time to stop and keep walking for my whole life, holding her hand, but time never stops," he said regrettably.

"She was the fairy of my dreams, queen of my heart and last desire in life. I would talk to her in my thoughts and worship her like a goddess. I slept under the blanket of her memories and got up with a new hope to find her love. She lived inside me all the time and I saw everything with her eyes," he squeezed his arms as if he was hugging someone in his imaginations.

Kamal was becoming more interested in this love story. Once, he thought all those things about Tanzeela. He had not even had a chance to talk to her properly. He was envious of Ajay, who could see and talk to his beloved every day.

"Once, she told me that her birthday was falling in a few days, I asked for her phone number so that I could wish her a happy birthday. She wrote it with black ink on a small piece of till roll paper and said that I was the first person at work who she had given her mobile number. This was the only thing she ever gave me. I saved it for ever. I looked at it every day. Do you want to see it?" Ajay asked him.

"Yes, of course," Kamal showed his eagerness.

Ajay took out his wallet, opened a small zipped pocket, and showed him that paper.

"When did she give it to you?" Kamal asked him.

"Three years, eight months, thirteen days---he paused, looked at his watch and said--- three hours, 47 minutes and 23 seconds," he told him exactly.

"But, it looks like someone has just given it to you", he was surprised how well Ajay was taking care of that small piece of paper, and how he remembered that moment.

"Ajay, you love her so much," he said tenderly.

"Yes, I do," he replied touchingly.

It started drizzling and suddenly it turned into heavy rain. They ran to find a shelter.

They stood under the shade of a coffee shop.

"You see Kamal, how the river absorbs the rain as it drops into it. When love showers on someone, it immerses them in human feelings, runs into the body like blood, becomes oxygen for life, and lasts evermore. Humans are separated, but it still remains there. It spreads in the air like scent. You feel it with your every breath. It keeps falling and becomes a river one day that flows everlastingly and irrigates the souls eternally, even after our bodies become ash or are mixed with soil," he was continuously looking at the river.

"See how the rain drops are emotionally falling on the running water. How they were missing it, how they are anxious to become a part of it. When love showers on humans' soul it makes them clean and pure just like a heavily rain does to the trees.

When snow falls on a full moon night, when the sky becomes clear, stars shine and the moon light brightens everything, the world looks so pure, she was so pure."

"Once I saw her, she was touching feet of an old lady. She sat on the ground and touched her feet to pay her respects. She did this in front of dozens of people on the shop floor. See, how humble she was, like those rain drops, which are drenching their existence into water," he was lost in his memories of her.

"Ajay, I have come to give your money back, thank you for your help. Let's come inside, we'll have some hot drinks, I am feeling cold," Kamal took him inside the coffee shop.

A woman with four children, who had probably come to see the London Eye, was sitting on the opposite table. She was helping her children to eat the sandwiches she had brought from home. The children were making her crazy, by their mischievous behaviour.

"One day, I told her that I wanted at least eleven children in life, to make my own cricket team. She laughed madly and said that she wanted only two, so that she could bring them up nicely," he said while looking at the children.

"Ajay, you told me that she disappeared soon from the work place. Did she come back?" Kamal asked.

"She worked during her summer holidays and went back to her university. She came back during the Christmas time."

"Did you keep touch with her on phone?"

"No, I avoided phoning or messaging her. I did not want to disturb her during her studies. I wanted her to study hard, for her better future but I missed her a lot." Ajay told him.

"I could not sleep the whole night, just to wish her birthday next day. I wanted to be the first to send her birthday wishes. That night was the longest one in my life. I waited for it to pass restlessly. I did not want to disturb her sleep, by sending her a message too early in the morning. I sent her a birthday message at 8:00 am. This was my very first message to her."

"Did she ever send her best wishes on your birthday in four years?" Kamal asked him.

"She wished me on my last birthday, just once in four years whereas I wished her each birthday except the last one. Once, I joked with her not to forget my birthday, she said that she would not but she never sent birthday wishes to me. I was so hurt when she overlooked my birthday." Ajay told him.

"Why you did not send her best wishes on her last birthday?" Kamal asked him.

"I wanted to forget her. I controlled myself, not sending her any text. I switched my phone off and left it at home for the whole day. But she wished me on my birthday, which fell after hers--- the first time in four years. I was over the moon and read it over and over," he said ecstatically.

"OK, tell me what happened when she came back to work," Kamal was keen to know.

Ajay looked at the wall clock, gulped his coffee in hurry and said, "Sorry Kamal, I promised to see one of my friends today. I am already getting late. I'll see you some other day," and he rushed to the bus stop.

Kamal was still wondering why he came to this place in his

free time. What was so special about this bank of river Thames? What happened next when she came back at Christmas time? He wanted to know the answers of those questions.

****

Kamal went to see his employer, to tell him that he was feeling better and would be back at work the next day.

He was not happy with him. Kamal told him about his sickness but he was not ready to accept his excuse.

"We don't give work to the students. I gave you a favour but you let me down," he shouted at him.

"I am sorry, there was a genuine reason of my absence."

"First you come and beg us for work, when we give it to you, you start disturbing us," he said angrily.

"This is not begging. I came to ask you if you had any job opportunity was not begging. I offered you my services. I got money from you, for my hard work not as a charity," Kamal became furious at the word 'begging'.

"You are a student. You are allowed to work only 20 hours per week. I gave you 84 hours. Don't you think it was a favour?" he said in the same annoyed tone.

"But you are giving me only 2.50 pounds per hour. Is this basic wage rate in the UK?" he said.

He opened his drawer and took out handful of CVs.

"Look, they are all students and willing to work on two pounds per hour even," he spread CVs before him on the counter.

"Yes, they can work even on two pounds per hour, but they have not asked you for any charity. They are willing to work but they are not beggars," Kamal temper went high.

"I don't like a worker who argues. I sack you, right now. You can go," he fired him.

"I don't like to work with a person like you, who pays minimum wage and thinks me a beggar. Don't use this word for students," Kamal was still very emotional on the word of begging.

"What will you do?" he asked him rudely.

"I'll cut you into pieces and throw them out to dogs," a villager inside Kamal took hold of him.

When he saw the seriousness in his eyes, he left the counter immediately and asked his assistant to deal with him. He made amends and gave him his remaining wages and took him outside the store with the utmost humbleness.

"Tell your owner that we come here to work, not for begging. Basically, you are thieves who rob money from our wages and also cheat the government by stealing taxes," his temper was still high.

"I apologise on his behalf," he said humbly.

Kamal left the store and was full of anger. He kept walking for long time, in fury, just to get control of himself.

****

It was a Sunday afternoon. Everyone was at home in Raheem's family.

Raheem told his wife that he had fixed a date for Kamal's to Nabeela engagement, next month.

"How could you fix a date without asking us? It is not a doll wedding. It is something about humans and you know humans have emotions, feelings, likes and dislikes. Why are you willing to destroy your daughter's life?" she said in one breath.

"Why you don't want me to fulfil the responsibilities of a father? This is always the parents' job, to find suitable husbands for their daughters. Do you want them to go out and seek life partners for themselves?" he said furiously.

"The Parents' job is to find suitable husbands for their daughters, with their consent, not to force them," she said irately.

"Kamal is not being forced upon her, he is known to her---- her first cousin," he stressed on 'her first cousin'.

"She does not like him and you can not force her into getting married to him."

"OK, go to the police station and report against me, that's you want, isn't it?" he said in a challenging way.

"If you oppress us, we will definitely do that." She rose to the challenge

"Bear in your mind that the day you go to report against me, will be the last day for you in this house," he threatened her.

"What will you do?" she asked him surprisingly.

"I will divorce you," he said calmly. On the name of divorce she started to cry. He left the room, leaving her alone and went into the TV lounge where his three daughters sitting quietly, as they had been listening to their conversation.

He sat on a chair in front of them. The girls were sitting on a long sofa seat, squeezed together. They knew that their father was full of rage, they were also scared.

"She will go to police against me----against Raheem Chaudhry," he murmured.

"You know her father was a chowkidar ...security guard, in an office, an employee of the lowest grade in a government office, a servant of 'category fourth'. You know only the uneducated and poor people do this kind of job in our society. They have no social status, no recognition and no respect", he addressed his daughters.

"A daughter of a *chowkidar*," he said disgustingly.

"You know my elder brother proposed her for me. He asked me to marry her and I did not disobey him. In our family we don't disobey our elders. I could have been married to a better women but it was the order of my brother, who was just like my father," for the first time in their life he was talking in such a way, before his daughters.

"My brother took pity on her poor father; she is obliged to him for her whole life. He made her *Chaudhryan*---female Chaudhry---- from a daughter of a *chowkidar.* Today she is rejecting the son of the same man," he continued.

"Kamal is a son of a Chaudhry not of any *chowkidar,* I know why he has left this house. I am not a child. I know he heard our dispute last week. Since he came to this house your mother's mood was off. She was poisoning your minds against him. She does not like him because she is not from our family. She wanted to bring her nephew here and ask you to marry him. She is jealous of Kamal. I do not want my daughters to marry a *chowkidar* family," he started delivering a lecture.

"I want my daughters to marry a Chaudhry not a *chowkidar*, but your mother wants the opposite. You see, this is the difference between *Chaudhries* and *chowkidars,"* he said his last sentence in full pride.

"You are my ever dear daughters. I love you. I want you to see happy in life. I am your father not your enemy. What I am going to do is in your best interests. It is always better to marry within family. If your mother belonged to my family, she would never have hated Kamal. Just think for a moment, Nabeela, if tomorrow one of your sisters' sons came to your house would you treat him like Kamal? Your mother has a poor mentality because she is a daughter of a *chowkidar,"* he showed his contempt for her family.

"We are in old age now. If you all get married outside family, who will look after us? We have no son. Who will take us to hospital? Who will put medicines in our mouths? Your mother is a stupid women she is not even trying to understand all these things."

"Just tell me who will take care of us after you? She needs to understand it, but she is of a crazy character. She has fixed her mind on one point, 'none of my daughters will marry your nephew', that's all she knows, nothing more. She does not think something else", a daughter of a *chowkidar*, he repeated over and over by shaking his head in hatred.

The girls, who have always remained under his pressure, listening to him, bending over their laps, and not daring to negate him at any point he made.

"I want to distribute all of my property amongst you on equal basis; on top of that I will give this house to Nabeela as a gift. She and Kamal will live with us. You see this was my planning. Kamal will look after us in our old age. You tell me; am I wrong?" he looked at his daughters for a response.

They kept quiet as usual. Sadiqa came out of the room.

"They will not answer you, but I will, Mr. Raheem Chaudhry *Sahib*," she said bravely.

"You want a servant for your old age, not a husband for your daughter," she said strenuously.

"You want us die in a caring house," he said.

"You want to sacrifice your daughter for your own comfort, what a selfish father you are! Marriages are not decided on personal interests but they are done on understanding, likes and dislikes. She told you already that he was not a suitor for her. She does not want to marry him. Do you think daughters have no feelings, nor emotions? How she can lead her life with a person she does not really like?" she gave a motherly look to Nabeela.

"Today, you remembered that I was a daughter of a *chowkidar* after I had spent my whole life with you, gave birth to your three daughters and brought them up for you. If you did not like me you should have refused the very first day," she said depressed.

"We do not disobey our elders------you stupid woman," he said snappily.

"I don't want my daughters listening to the same words from your nephew in the future," she said.

"He has no objection, he wants to marry her happily," he said.

"Your daughter will be saying the same words to him in her later life, I am telling you today. Why do you want to destroy two lives for your own ego and pride?" she said.

"I'm not destroying someone's life but making it happy and easy for everyone, here in this house", he said.

"I am fed up with all this, you do whatever you like to do," she said in annoyance and walked back to her room.

"Nabeela, I have fixed a date for engagement, third Sunday of the next month. I have told Kamal's father already. I am going to invite only some close friends. You know we do not have any relative here. You can invite your close friends too. There will be a simple function at home," he informed her.

Nabeela ran to her room, fell on the bed, on her belly, pressed her face deep into the pillows and started to cry.

****

Chapter 6

The four house mates were together at home for the first time in a long while. Kamal got to know Arsalan and Zaman aged 27 and 31 respectively. Arsalan had a short curled hair, a broad forehead, a bit fatty face figure but looked graceful. Zaman had short smooth hair, which had mostly gone white, some scars on his face, a short, narrowed moustache, dark wheat colour and wide chest. He was 5-8"--- a bit taller than Arsalan.

All of them belonged to the province of the Punjab in Pakistan. Arsalan had done a masters degree in law (LLM) at a university in London and was working as a sales assistant in a supermarket. He was practicing as a lawyer in Pakistan before he came to the UK, three years ago.

Zaman had also done a masters degree in Human Resource Management (HRM) at a university in London. He was working in McDonald's as a shift supervisor. He did his masters degree, in Economics, in Pakistan and was teaching in a government college, as a lecturer, before he came to the UK three and half years ago.

They both were on Post Study Work (PSW) visas and were planning to apply for the Highly Skilled Migrant Programme (HSMP).

"Kamal, can you cook?" Arsalan asked him.

"No, I have never cooked in my life," he replied.

"How will you cook for us on your turn then?" he asked.

"I'll try to learn cooking, but I clean the house on my turn," he replied.

"Don't worry we all learnt here, you will learn as well," he encouraged him.

"Are you doing a job?" Zaman asked him.

"I was but I lost it today," he said.

"How did you lose it? You know it is very hard to find a job these days," he asked him.

"Actually, I remained sick for three days, my employer did not accept my excuse and he sacked me," he said.

"Where were you working?" he further asked him.

"At a grocery shop," he said.

"Ajay told us that you were staying at your uncle's house before you moved here. Why did you leave?" Arsalan asked him.

"There was no particular reason, actually I wanted to live with people like me so that I could enjoy my life," he hid the reality.

"Does your uncle have family here?" Arsalan kept asking.

"Yes, he has three daughters," he replied.

"No son?" he asked

"No, he does not have any son," he said.

"Oh, I see, you were feeling uneasy amongst the girls," he joked with him.

"Are they all young?" Zaman asked this time.

"Yes, they are," he gave a short answer.

"You should get married to one of them," Zaman advised him.

"I could be in the future," he replied.

"Good man, your life will become much easier," he said.

Asif and Manzoor were busy in cooking. Asif shouted from the kitchen, "OK, guys dinner is ready, arrange the dining table please."

They had their dinner of chicken curry and rice.

"Can you please help me in finding a job," Kamal asked them, when they were taking tea after dinner.

Zaman asked him to apply online, for a crew job at McDonald's and he would help him as soon as there was a vacancy available at his store. Arsalan asked him to give him his CV; he would drop it in at his store and try to help him too.

"Why you don't send him to Haji *Sahib*? He is running a busy cab office and looking for people all the time," Asif asked Arsalan.

"He never refuses anyone; he employs people on trial basis, rejects them after three days and takes on another one. He runs his cab office like that. Most of his victims are students who are desperately looking for a job," he said in a funny way.

"This is a big problem these days. Since the job opportunities are few most of Asian businessmen have been exploiting the students," Asif said sadly.

"Kamal, I suggest you go to the pizza shops, in this area, and ask for a leaflet distribution. I did this too when I came to this country", Zaman asked him.

"This is a good idea; at least you can earn some money for your daily expenses," Asif encouraged him.

"How is your security job going? ---highly skilled worker *sahib!*" Arsalan made fun of Manzoor, who was on HSMP visa.

"It's going well, Barrister *sahib*, by the way what was the rate of potatoes and onions today?" he quipped about his sales assistant job in a supermarket.

"Zaman *Sahib* is in a better position to draw some light on market prices, because he is the professor of Economics," they all laughed at Arsalan's remarks, for Zaman, who was once a lecturer of Economics in Pakistan.

"This is a big tragedy for our brilliant minds to be doing menial works here," Asif said seriously.

"What can they do? They have no other option. Most of the students who come here do so for economic reasons. Their aim is to take their families out of poverty. They feel insecure in their countries. The majority live in rural areas but they have to work in big cities. The life is very expensive over there. They cannot afford the costly living and feed their families back in the villages at the same time. They want to increase their income levels, so they think to go abroad. But they don't know that things have completely changed in developed countries, especially after the recent recession," Arsalan argued.

"The actual problem is family dependency. A number of people are depending upon us. Usually, we have big families. There is no social security system. Our parents, even grand parents and other members of the family depend on us. We have to look after them. We can't manage it on our small incomes and so we move to foreign countries," Zaman said.

"Our wedding ceremonies, deaths events and other social functions are very costly. We have to spend at least one years saving just to arrange them. The whole of our lives we are trapped in them. We believe in simplicity, but don't practice it in real life. We spend four times more money, on our engagement ceremonies alone than the White people spend on their weddings. We take hundreds of people to the bride's house—*Barat,* and put financial pressure on her family, we invite hundreds to our *Valimas*---groom wedding dinner. All these things give great financial stress," Arsalan said.

"These are the social problems, I admit, but our real issue is financial difficulties, which compel us to go abroad. If our government offers us good salaries, we would love to stay there. We want to serve our country, but can't see our parents dying without getting medical treatment and our sisters sitting at home waiting for dowry to get married," Asif said.

"It's OK if someone comes here just for education, but the problem is we try to settle down here and do minor jobs, this is a waste of education," Manzoor said.

"Again the same issue, I do a security job and send one lakh rupees to my family every month, but if my government give me the same amount I would be happy to go back and work in my skill-set of business administration. I was earning twenty thousands rupees per month in Pakistan, but that was not enough for my family's needs so I had to come here. I did an MBA here to find a good job, but no one gives us good administrative jobs, I had to do a security job eventually," Asif said.

"There are jobs for MBAs, but only if you get your degree from Oxford, Cambridge, Imperial College of London or some other good institutions like them. You cannot expect a good job through doing your degree from one of the low profile affiliated colleges," Manzoor said.

"Who can afford the forty thousand pounds fee for an MBA from a good institution?" Asif said surprisingly.

"Here graduate opportunities are for fresh graduates from UK universities, not for masters degree holders like us," Zaman said.

"My experience is, if we work hard in our country we can reach a better future. All of my old colleagues are doing really well. They are enjoying a better life. I am so ashamed that I am doing a security job in London and they are progressing in their careers," Manzoor seemed depressed.

"We are all depressed in one way or another. We want to do something for our country, but our poverty is a big obstacle. We are all here for nothing else but money. Our high calibre people are wasting their abilities working in pizza shops, cabs offices, restaurants, supermarkets and securities jobs. I work with a team of twenty security officers---twelve of them are master degree holders," Asif said miserably.

Kamal was listening to them with deep interest. He also had high dreams about UK life, but now was coming to face the reality. His case was very different to his house mates. He wanted to compete with his cousins in education. He wanted to become equal to them in social status. He knew that his uncle was going to marry him to Nabeela. He did not want to let himself down before her in education and professional career.

He had strong belief in destiny. "It is not compulsory I would do a security job after my MBA degree like my friends. I may find a good job. Once you have a degree, you are in a better position to apply for a good post. My fortune is definitely different from my friends'. I can not apply their experiences on my life. I could be better than them," he was thinking while lying in bed.

"When Nabeela will introduce me to her friends, she could at least say that I have done an MBA degree," he imagined his future life with Nabeela.

"Where will I get the money from?" he thought worriedly.

"I will have to really work very hard to earn the money for my education."

He kept thinking about his family back home, about Nabeela and Tanzeela and his financial problems until he went to sleep.

****

It was mid-day. The sun was shining at its full brightness, a lovely winter day in Pakistan. Kamal's mother and father were sitting in the big yard of their house. Rehmat was sitting in a bamboo chair, with long back, smoking his *hookah*. Nusrat was sitting on a *charpie* busy in knitting a wool sweater.

"Raheem has given me a date for engagement, it's in the next month," he told his wife.

"Thank God, I've been waiting to celebrate the bliss of my son for ages," she showed her delight.

"We will arrange a huge function at home. I want to invite the whole village," she said with pleasure.

"Kamal and his fiancée are in *Walliat*, we do not need to hold a big function. You can just send sweets to each house in the village," he suggested to her.

"No, Kamal is our first son; I want to have a big party for his engagement," she insisted.

"It will cost us lot of money," he said.

"We are not going to serve food to our guests, just tea and sweets. It won't cost us a lot," she argued.

"If you want to invite the whole village, even on refreshments, it will be very expensive," he said.

"Kamal's wedding will happen only once in life; I want to enjoy it by all means. If we don't hold a large function, what the people of the village think about us, especially when our son is in *Walliat?*" she said.

"You know we're already in debt, where will we get the money from for such a big event?" he said, blowing his *hookah.*

"Our son is earning twenty five thousands rupees per week, if we spend his two weeks salary on his engagement, there won't be any big difference," she said satisfactorily.

"I am thinking of sending something to Nabeela, after all she is our daughter," he said.

"What will you send? Dresses, shoes, make-up kit or jewellery? We don't know what kind of stuff girls wear there in the UK. It is better if we ask Kamal to buy things from there," she said.

"He is still a child, he does not know what to buy for engagement," he said.

"Tell him to buy a ring, three pairs of shoes, five dresses, and one make-up kit for Nabeela; two dresses for each of her younger sisters and one for his uncle and one for his aunty. Also, 10 kg of sweets, some dried fruit and some fresh fruit," she gave a list for engagement shopping, according to the traditions in the village.

"I don't know if he has enough money for this," he showed his concern.

"*Mashallah*, he is earning good money, don't think like that," she said contentedly.

"I recommend for you to invite at least one person from each house in the village and close relatives living outside; we don't need to invite all of them," he said.

"OK, if this is what you suggest, I don't mind," she agreed with him.

"There are more than three hundreds houses in the village. We need tons of sweets. We will have to order in advance," he said.

"You can ask village *halwie*---confectioner, to come to our house three days prior to the function to make sweets for us," she said.

"I will ask him," he said.

****

Kamal had come to know about his engagement. He had to do the shopping as advised by his mother. He also had to send money back home, to pay for his engagement function in the village.

The dire need of money made him to leave early in the morning in search of a job. He walked from street to street, area to area and kept asking each and every shop; restaurant and office for a job opportunity to come his way. Some of them asked him to drop in a CV. He desperately walked for miles, but there was no positive response from anywhere. He came back home unsuccessful. The next day he decided to go some other area. He repeated the same practice, in different areas for one week but in vain.

He phoned Ajay, and explained him his situation. He promised to help him in finding a job.

But there was a big problem with Ajay, every time when Kamal wanted to see him he had to go the London Eye. He would spend his spare time sitting on the bank of River Thames, as if he had lost something there or was waiting for someone to come. Kamal could not understand this mystery about his friend.

He knew that he could help him, but he had to pursue him to London Eye.

"Ajay *bhai*, I can not understand why you are so addicted to this place," he said, while approaching him who was sitting at the same place as usual.

Ajay greeted him with a big smile.

"Bhai, tell me weather your beloved committed suicide in your love by jumping into this river or you are planning to do so," he asked him humorously.

Ajay laughed at his remarks and asked him, "What is your sad story today?"

"My engagement has been fixed with Nabeela. I already explained you my situation on phone," he said.

"What a story! You love the younger sister; your engagement has been fixed with elder one, you need money for a big shopping, you need to send money back home, you don't have a job, what a story!" he laughed madly on his own remarks.

"Ajay *bhai*, you are the only person here with whom I can talk openly," he said innocently.

"You are like my brother Kamal," he tapped his shoulder.

"Ajay, I am really worried," he said.

"Don't worry bhai, *mein hun na*-----I am here," he delivered an Indian movie dialogue in heroic style.

"I have a friend who is livingly illegally in the UK and does private building works. He is working in a house somewhere these days. I talked to him about your need for a job and he told me that he had three weeks work and was looking for someone as a helper. You can start tomorrow. He will give you forty pounds per day. You do this job until I find you a better one. I know this is hard for you but at the moment, this is the only job that is available," he told him

"Ajay, you know I am so desperate this time, I can do something even harder," he said poorly.

"*Kabutar ja ja, kubutar ja, phely payar ki pheli cheti sajan ko dey ay*--- pigeon go, please go and deliver my first love letter to my beloved," he sang an Indian movie song.

"Ajay, what's the matter? You seem to be very happy today," he asked him.

"You are going to get engaged so I am happy for you," he said merrily.

"I am going to invite you and my four house mates, will you come?"

"Why not *bhai*, I will be there for you," he showed his willingness.

"I also need your help in shopping", Kamal said.

"Don't worry we will go to Southall for your engagement shopping", Ajay replied.

"When is your engagement Ajay?" Kamal asked him.

"You know, once I asked her 'please find me a girl' and she said that she would do that. I further asked her to find one who was similar to her and she said, 'Na---she would be better than me'. I said, 'no----I did not want anyone better than you but same like you'. She smiled a lot but did not say anything. I was jealous when she talked to some other boys at work. I felt pleasure in her presence and became sad after she left," he was lost in his memories of her.

A white man passed by them and asked Ajay if he had a light for his cigarette. None of them smoked. He said sorry to him.

"You know Kamal, once we were working together at kiosk at night time. I had finished half an hour earlier than her. I came to her and asked her for a packet of cigarettes. She said, 'no, you don't smoke'. She said it in such a way, as if she never wanted me to smoke. Actually, I went to her just to see her again before I go home. She was painting some thing on her palm, with a pen. She was looking very pretty. I sat on one side hiding myself from her and kept looking at her until she finished work," he said lovingly.

"OK, Ajay tell me please what happened when she came back?" Kamal asked him.

He took a deep sigh, folded his arms around his chest and said,

"One night, in the last week of December, I saw her again in the store. After a long time, I went to her to greet her. It was my routine, if she was there I used to see her first before I started work. I got busy in my work. After a short while, she had her tea break but she did not go to the canteen, she came straight to me and said, 'I missed you so much Ajay, I was praying that you were still there working in the store'. For the first time, we hugged each other. It was an unintentional emotional hug, very natural and full of feelings. I felt her heart beat and quivering on my chest. I hugged her again. I wanted to tell her how much I loved her but I could not say that. I simply said, 'I missed you too'. I joked with her that the emotional fire is burning equally from both sides. She said, 'no, we are just friends'.

"This is the problem with me. I don't know how to express my love to someone in words, especially to girls. The only thing I could say to her, 'If I had the chance, in life, to select a girl for me, from the whole world I would select you'. She just smiled with shyness on my claim and said, 'Oh, do you?' She kept walking with me on the shop floor during her break time. I was feeling love for her more than ever before on that night.

The next day I sent her massages regarding friendship but she did not reply any of them. It hurt me a lot.

"Kamal, it is usually said that love has many colours, but I don't believe in it. Love has only one colour and when it gets on someone all other colours fade. You are not able to feel any attraction in any other effect. This colour is so strong, it leaves behind all differences of race, faith and borders. It magnetises you to your beloved like steel objects to magnets."

"This was the case with me. My eyes remained in search for her all the time. I talked to her in isolation and thought of her always. I was always anxious to see just one glimpse of her." Ajay continued in his story,

"Once, she was serving customers when I came to start my

work. I went to see her as usual. When she saw me she became very excited. I greeted her and asked her, 'Can I go now'. She said, 'No, stay there with me'.. She said this in such a loving way as she had some special right over me. I told her about a girl who was after me in the store. She said, 'She is *fida*—dying for, you'. I said, 'No way, I have no interest in her'. But I could not tell her that I was *fida* for her not for any other girl. I invited her to go out for a dinner, she promised to spare some time for me. I told her that it was not my habit to ask people again and again. She said that she would let me know when she was ready to go out with me but she never replied me back".

It was her habit that she was very friendly at work but she never responded out of work. She came for the short time to work at Christmas time and went back to her university leaving me in turmoil again," he told him long story while looking into the space.

"Did she come back then?" Kamal asked him.

"Yes, she came in her summer holidays but I did not work during summer. I was on a long holiday in India," he said.

"When did you see her again?" he further asked him.

"After one year again on Christmas time," he replied.

"Did she keep touch with you during that time?"

"No, I sent her mobile messages but she did not bother to reply me. Even when I sent her birthday wishes she did not respond to me, except for sending me a short message of thanks," he said.

"Did her attitude make you angry?" Kamal asked him.

"No, I thought she would be busy in her studies. You know Kamal, I always keep my relations with my dearest people unconditional," he said innocently.

"Ajay *bhai*, you are such a wonderful person," he praised him.

"You know I would make screen savers on computer of her name every day and fill it with different colours", Ajay said.

"What was her name?" Kamal asked.

"Her name was Preya", Ajay said.

"Nice name!" Kamal praised.

"I have fallen in her love with all my feelings. I wanted her to feel my love before I expressed it to her in my words. But she was not going to feel it yet or avoiding it purposely. I decided when I would see her next time I take her hand, kiss it and tell her, 'I love you Preya'. I was waiting restlessly to see her again", Ajay said in romantic tone.

"What was the scene when you expressed your love to her? What was her first reaction?" Kamal asked him two questions in one breath.

"I will tell you next time. It's better if we go now to see my friend, for your job otherwise we'll miss him today," he said and started walking quietly towards the bus stop.

****

Nabeela was calm since her father announced the engagement date. She was not talking to anyone in the house. Her mother had tried to talk to her many times but she was not ready to talk about the issue. She was coming home late from work, which was unusual. When her father asked the reason, she said that she had some extra office work those days and was also seeing her friend Pooja.

Nabeela's family knew that she was a good friend of Pooja, an Indian girl, working in the IT department in the same bank.

At the weekend, when her father asked her to go for shopping for her engagement party she excused that she was not feeling well. She spent the whole weekend in her room not talking to anyone.

Her mother was worried about her. She could not see her in this condition. She went to her room to talk to her, when Raheem was not at home.

"My baby, I can not see you in this poor condition. You're not talking to anyone. You're not even eating properly. You know it hurts me," she sat with her on the bed and kissed her forehead.

"I am OK mum," she said softly.

"No, you are not OK, I can see it," she tapped her hands lovingly.

"My darling, don't worry about me, if your father divorces me I can live on social benefits, you refuse this engagement and go to the police station or any human rights organization to complain against this forced marriage," she said.

"This is not the solution mum," she said with seethe.

"My love, don't go ahead for this wedding if you don't like him. One wrong decision can destroy your whole life," she said.

"I never liked that idiot, you know me mum," she was apoplectic.

"I know sweetheart but your father is not going to understand."

"If my life was limited to this house I would never have minded this marriage, but I have a social life outside. I have friends, colleagues, and my bank customers with whom I have to mingle with. I want a life partner who can go with me to social events, who can talk to my friends, who has ability to socialise with them. I need a husband who I can introduce to my colleagues with admiration and reverence. I want a soul mate who I can feel proud of. Kamal is not my ideal by any definition," she burst out.

"I am feeling the suffocation of this house. Our father has always exercised our rights. He wants to use our rights of wedding too."

What a justification! He is worried about his old age but he is not worried about my life," she said with angst.

"I don't want you put in trouble because of me. I don't want to marry him. I don't know what to do?" she stroked her head with her hands.

"I told you not to worry about me. I have led my life. Don't ruin your life because of me," her mother said mournfully.

"What the world would think about me, Nabeela Chaudhry got her father arrested, got her mother divorced just because of her own wishes?" she said with great fretfulness.

"There is a law against forced marriages in this country. You are a British citizen. This law is to help girls like you. Don't afraid of the world, just use your rights," she encouraged her.

"There are thousands of Asian girls who are forced to marry their cousins or close relatives but how many have used this law, just a few of them. And you know why? Because they are put in the same situation or even worse than where my father has put me. I have to trade off my life or my mother's life? What a decision to take!" she said nervously.

"I cannot afford to loose you mum," she put her head in her lap and started wailing.

She ran fingers in her hair tenderly, a stream of tears also shedding from her eyes. They both kept weeping hopelessly for long time.

"Mum, why are women so weak before men? Why do men want to take hold of them all the time? Why do they exploit a woman in the form of a father, husband or brother? Why do they not want to know our feelings? Are all the male relations the same?" she said, sobbing.

"Woman has come to this world for sacrifice. First she sacrificed for her parents, brothers, then for her husband and finally for her children."

"My father did not send me to a college because he wanted to send my elder brother to university. He could not afford both of us at the same time. He preferred my brother over me, although I was better than him in studies. I had to sacrifice for my brother. He asked me to marry your father. I could not refuse because of our poverty. I did not want to be burden on my parents for long time. I sacrificed for them. Your father brought me here after wedding. He only took me back to Pakistan twice, in our thirty years of married life. He never took me to holidays. He kept me in this house like a prisoner. I was satisfied that I had my daughters with me. I kept quiet before him for you. I did not want to disturb your life at any cost. I sacrificed for my daughters".

"That is a woman life, honey," she said with different pauses, while fingering her hair.

"Will my life be same, mum?" she said softly.

"It is up to you darling. You will have to decide yourself. I had no option when my wedding was decided, but you have so many options in your hands. No one was there in my support, but you have support of your mum, this society, this country and the law. I was dependent and poor. You are independent and financially strong," she encouraged her to make a bold decision.

"OK, mum, I will decide it by myself," she showed her determination.

Sadiqa wanted her to register a complaint against this forced marriage but Nabeela was reluctant because she had a fear that if she did this her father could divorce her mother.

"I'll be there for you, to go to the police station, the court and the media to support you," the mother showed her support.

Nabeela kept quiet for long time in deep thoughts and finally said, "I will decide it myself". She repeated this sentence many times in a meaningful way.

****

Chapter 7

Kamal never thought that he would be labouring with masons in London, or even in Pakistan, but he was doing this because he had no other option. He badly needed money, for his engagement expenses. He did not want to disappoint his mother, who had planned a large gathering at home. He also wished to buy an expensive ring and good dresses for his proposed fiancée and for her family, according to his traditions.

While he was carrying bricks and heavy containers of mud, he was counting his total wage for working three weeks and estimated the expenses for his engagement celebrations.

"I'd send one week wage to my mother and spend remaining on shopping here," he was talking to himself.

He was working an eight hour shift but after four hours he was feeling severe pain throughout his body, because he was not used to this kind of work. The thought of his mother and the long list of shopping kept him working.

The first day was really hard for him. The spots of mud and brick-dust were very clear on his jeans and shirt. Three of his right hand fingers were badly wounded.

Today, it was his turn to clean the house. He already told his house mates that he could not cook, thus they had spared him from cooking until he learnt it. When he got home, he cleaned the whole house, including toilets and bathroom, although his body was aching.

Asif and Arsalan were busy in the kitchen. They knew he had gone to the building work that day. They were feeling very sorry for him.

"Chaudhry *Sahib*, did you enjoy the London life today?" Arsalan teased him.

"It is very hard to do something you've never done before," he said calmly.

"When we were in our homeland we didn't understand these things. We were flying high, thinking about life in the UK," Arsalan said.

"Our agents told us the false stories about life in the UK. If someone already living here had told us the truth, we were not ready to believe him," Asif said.

"What can we do? We are helpless there. This is our government's fault, they do not offer good job opportunities for educated people," Arsalan said.

"No, this is our mistake. We select incapable and crooked people again and again through elections. How can we expect social change, unless we vote for good people?" Asif said.

"Arsalan *bhai* did you drop my CV at your work-place?" Kamal, who was not very much interested in politics, asked him.

"Yes I did, but they told me that they would take people in at Easter time," he told him.

"I suggest you to do a security course. I can help you in finding a job with my company," Asif told him.

"How much it will cost me?" Kamal asked him.

"It will cost you one hundred fifty pounds, but once you get the certificate you can apply for a badge, which will cost you two hundreds and forty five pounds," he explained him.

"That means I need four hundreds pounds to get a security badge," Kamal said.

"Yes, you are right," Asif said.

Kamal had his dinner with them and went straight to his room to sleep, as he was feeling very tired.

****

Kamal and Ajay went to the Southall, a large sub-urban district of West London famous for hub of South Asian community and also known as 'Little India', for engagement shopping. Kamal has never been to this area before. As he arrived at the Southall he saw the station name was also written in Hindi along with English. They came out of the station and walked down to the South Road. Kamal was reading the sign boards along the both sides of the road with interest, Shahi Nan Kabab, Des Pardes Weelky, Himalaya Place, Punjabi Restaurant, Sambal Express, Roshni Sweets, Sira Cash and Carry and some other stores and restaurants carrying the pure Indian names. There was a beautiful and vast Gurdawara Sri Guru Sing Sabha on the right hand near to the station. He saw all kind of typical Asian foods, vegetables and sweets. They kept walking towards the high street. Kamal felt like he was wandering Satara Market in Rawalpindi in Pakistan not the high street of Southall in London. They visited Universal Shopping Centre, Bara Market, Sher-e-Punjab, Madha's Shopping Centre, Punjabi Bazar and Himalaya Shopping Centre for their shopping. Kamal also bought some bangles for Tanzeela along with other things suggested by his mother. He was very fascinated being in this part of London, where he could see his own people, culture and typical smell and market activity. They kept wandering in different part of this area for long time.

"Bhai, I'm feeling hungry. Let's find a good restaurant to eat", Kamal said.

"Don't worry, Southall is also a home of Indian resturants", Ajay said and led him to find a good one.

They reached to a restaurant to kill their hunger. Ajay saw a temple near the restaurant and asked Kamal to wait for him as he wanted to go there for some prayers. Kamal also wished to go to a Mosque as he rarely offered his prayers because of his busy life in London. The waiter of the hotel directed him towards the Mosque in the area. They handed over their shopping to the manager and went for their prayers. When they returned, they ordered some food.

"What did you ask to your god?" Kamal said.

"I asked for Preya", Ajay said.

"What did you ask for", Ajay asked the same question.

"I prayed for many things and for Tanzeela too", Kamal said.

"How selfish we are? We only go the worships when we are in need. Aren't we? Ajay said.

"This is human instinct, when he is in trouble he remembers his God", Kamal said.

"Once I called Preya to know whether she was interested in some over time at work but she did not answer my call. The next day she told me that she was busy in her prayers", Ajay recalled his past and started telling him some more things about Preya while they were having their dinner.

This was Ajay habit, wherever he went, whatever he did, he related it to his memories with Preya. He looked every thing with her eyes, thought everything with her mind and all of his talks ended at Preya.

"You know Ajay tomorrow Pakistan and India are playing a cricket match?" Kamal asked him.

"Yes I know that but I am telling you India will win this match easily", Ajay said.

"Pakistanis blowers are in good form they will not let Indian batsmen play so easily", Kamal said.

"Tendulkar will make century tomorrow, I bet you", Ajay said with confidence.

"Where are you going to watch the match?" Kamal said.

"I'd go to a pub near my house. It has a big screen. I always go there to watch football and cricket matches", Ajay replied.

"Come to my house, we have Sky Sports. We will enjoy match together", Kamal invited him.

"Good idea! I'll come", Ajay confirmed him.

"If Tendulkar makes a century you will give us a treat and if Pakistan wins we give you a treat", Kamal said.

"OK, I agree with you", Ajay accepted it.

"You know Ajay, Tendulkar and Raul Dravid are my favourite batsmen", Kamal said.

"I am also a big fan of Shoib Akhtar and Shahid Afridi. They are very thrilling players", Ajay said.

"Whoever plays good deserves appreciations", Kamal said.

"Yes of course, we should enjoy cricket as a game. I don't like those people who spread hatred and malice when Pakistan and India are playing", Ajay said.

"You are right Ajay, we should spread the message of love and peace through these matches", Kamal said.

****

Today was Kamal's engagement day with Nabeela. Raheem was very busy in decorating the house. His wife and daughters were not very enthusiastic to help him. He had invited some of his close friends. He denounced his wife and two younger daughters for not helping him. Nabeela had gone to the beauty parlour, with one of her friends.

He knew that no one was happy in the house on this engagement. He thought that once it done every thing would be all right.

He called his wife to help him dragging the big sofa into the centre of the room, for Kamal and Nabeela to sit on.

"Stop shouting, I am busy," she answered from her room.

"What are you doing there?" he shouted back.

"Sewing my coffin," she said angrily.

He walked to the room and found his wife cleaning the floor.

"Just come for one minute, I need your help," he looked upset.

"Can't you see I am busy?" she said rudely.

"I know why your mood is off madam. Today is our daughter's engagement so it is better for you to behave in a good way," he warned her.

"What am I saying to you?" she threw the mop onto the floor and walked to the drawing room with tears in her eyes.

"Don't show me your anger, I am talking to you," he said, following her.

"I am not saying anything to you," she said crossly.

"Help me to move this sofa to other side," he said imperatively.

"What is wrong with it if it remains here?" she said, putting her hands on her waist.

"To make some extra room for chairs, some of Kamal friends are also coming," he informed her.

She pulled her face in dislike and helped him half-heartedly.

"You see how Nabeela is happy today. She went to the beauty parlour to get ready," he told her, as she had bowed her head before him in his obedience.

"She is not really happy but just pretending to be happy," she said.

"Actually, you are not happy; so you think no one is happy in the house. She is my daughter and she knows well what I am going to do is for her long- life happiness," he said.

"OK, OK, I don't want to waste my time arguing with you. I am her mother and a mother knows her daughters better than anyone else," she said, in distress and left.

Tanzeela and Shakeela were also getting ready, but under the pressure of their father. Actually, they were not happy either.

Tanzeela was wondering about how easily Nabeela had agreed to the marriage. She could not believe that it was going to happen, without any big problem. She was feeling sorry for her; but the same time she was surprised about the engagement.

****

There was a huge gathering at Kamal's house, in his village. He had been known as *Kamal Chaudhry England wala*---- Kamal Chaudhry of England. The big yard of the house was full of women and children. They were all sitting on *charpies,* especially arranged to accommodate the guests.

The same arrangements were made for the men, outside the house.

Mubarkhan, Lakh lakh Mubarkhan---- congratulations, millions of congratulation, the atmosphere was echoing with this sentence. Whoever came said the same sentence, to Kamal's parents.

Khair Mubarak, Khair Mubarak----- blessed good, they were replying to every one with extreme happiness.

This was a first function of its kind in the village, for when the engaged couple were not physically present. Kamal's mother was running one *charpie* to another to greet the women; his father was doing the same to the men outside.

The *kammies*---servants, were doing their best to look after the guests. They were showing more happiness, than the households, to get maximum rewards from the Chaudhry family. They were carrying coloured liquid in pots mostly red, green and blue and sprinkling it on the guests with their fingers.

There is a custom in the village, at engagement events coloured water is sprinkled on the guests' clothes, to celebrate happiness. This is also a type of announcement, or advertisement. When they go somewhere, with those coloured water stains people ask them who has become engaged and they spread the information.

The engagement norm is, first of all groom's family go to the bride's house, with hundreds of invitees. They take dresses, shoes, jewellery and cosmetics for the bride and clothe for her other family members. They also take sweets and fruits. All the gifts are put on tables, or on *charpies,* in the middle of the gathering so that everyone can see them.

Usually, the guests are served the things brought by the groom's family. Then, both families are bound to tell the numbers of people, who they are bringing with them to each other houses, so that they can do proper arrangements to accommodate all the guests.

The bride's family treat the groom's guests with drinks, fruit and sweets, brought by the groom's family.

The sprinkling of coloured water is performed at the bride's house, during the engagement function. The girl, who is going to become engaged, sits on a *chapie* in a separate room amongst her friends. She covers her face with *dupata*----shawl, hanging to her lap.

This is mostly a female gathering, only few men close to groom's family attend this function.

The women, from groom's side, beat the drums, sing songs and dance at the bride house. Usually, they have a *Sheikh*----village drum beater, with them. They give him money called *vails.* Whenever he gets a *vail* he pronounces the name of the person and expresses good wishes for the engaged couple. Sometimes, the people get in competition for giving *vails* and give away lots of money. They regularly put the money on each other heads and wait for the drummers to come over to collect it.

In the same way, the women put money on the bride's head and there is *Sheikhnee,* a female *Sheikh*, who collects that money.

At the end of this ceremony, everyone comes to the bride, places their hand on her head tenderly and with affection. They communicate their best wishes for her and give her some money. There is a woman sitting beside the bride, with a note book, who registers this money for the record.

The next day, the bride's family goes to the groom's house and repeat the same things.

They send a plate of sweets to each house, in the village after the event. The people, who are not invited, or not able to attend the function, come to the engaged couple's houses to convey their congratulations on the days after and they are served with sweets.

Kamal's family was very happy, especially his mother who was flying high. They were all telling their guests how Kamal was doing so well in the UK in his studies and work. She told the village women that he had sent money to her, for his engagement function. Indirectly, she wanted to tell them that he was earning good money there and they had become rich. The village people were really envious of Kamal and his family.

Kamal's sisters were singing songs, along with their friends, by beating a small drum called a *dholki*. His brother was running in and out of the house, managing other things. The *Sheikh* was beating drums outside. The close relatives were giving him *vails* in the name of Kamal. They came to his father and circulated money on his head and gave them to *Sheikh* who pronounced their names and praised the Chaudhry family.

Inside the house, a woman was doing the same thing, collecting money in the name of Kamal and his fiancée. The women, especially, the close relatives were dancing around her and putting money on his mother's head in escalation.

At one stage, his mother and sisters started performing a traditional village dance called *Luddi* in an organized circle. *Luddi* is a form of dance where people move in a circle, bending their bodies onto the earth. When they bend they twist their bodies and strike their thumbs with the middle finger, rise up briskly and clap in a rhythm to make one sound and keep moving in the circle, repeating it over and over.

Kamal's brother was performing *Luddi* among the men, along with his friends and other relatives. Rehmat Chaudhry was throwing money on them. The *Sheikh* was flattering him, to make him throw more money. He was beating the drums obsessively, in his specific style.

The function continued till late at night with the same zeal.

****

Kamal was getting ready to go to his uncle's house, with his friends. All of his house mates took the day off to attend his engagement ceremony.

The previous night, he had been thinking about the letter once Tanzeela wrote to him asking him to leave the house. He did not want to go back to her house, but he was helpless before his family. So many times, he thought to inform his parents about that incident but he stopped because he did not want to create discord between the brothers. He knew that his uncle had always been in his favour. He respected him like his father.

He wondered how his uncle had made Nabeela agree to this engagement so easily. It was happening even earlier than he had expected.

He had heard Nabeela's words that he was not her suitor and she was not happy to marry him. He heard his aunty calling him an idiot, who did not know the dining manners. He knew, when he was leaving the house, how none of his cousins or aunty had asked him the reason for his sudden departure.

He remembered how Tanzeela had told him that she was not a friend of his sisters or his mother who had sent her *Salam*. He knew that they never had taken any notice of him in the house. He knew the reason why his uncle was bringing his dinner to his room, because his daughters did not like to dine with him. He used to make breakfast for him, just because his aunty did not bother about him.

He wondered how his uncle had so easily accepted his excuse

of abrupt leave from the house and why he did not ever force him to come back. He did not even ask him about his work-place and never came to see him. He just phoned him sometimes, to ask about his well being.

He was surprised about this decision for a quick engagement. He thought that perhaps his uncle wanted to punish his family, as he knew that they did not like him. The uncle knew this was the real reason why he had left the house and that was the reason he never forced him to come back.

Raheem wanted to show them his importance through this engagement. He thought so many things, but one question struck his mind again and again, how had Nabeela agreed to marry him?

He wanted to get a good job, pay off his debts and save some money to do his degree. He was very confused about this sudden change.

He thought out what would be the response of his aunty and his cousins, when they see him sitting with Nabeela wearing an engagement ring. Would they ignore everything and receive him warmly? What would they say to him?

He was really very nervous, and was not feeling easy going there. He pondered over his future life with Nabeela. Would she accept him happily and support him getting a good education? Would he be a family servant or a real husband to her?

He was just predicting things, but he was very uncertain. He was not ready to accept, easily, that Nabeela was going to marry him gladly or his aunty and cousins had changed their minds about him.

He believed it was a forced marriage, imposed by his uncle.

Two of his housemates had cars. They were ready to go with him.

Ajay had reached his house. He was making every one to laugh, telling jokes related to marriages. Kamal was trying to control his nervousness before his friends and pretended to be very happy.

****

115

"Nabeela, I don't think you are doing the right thing," Shahida, her friend, told her as they were sitting in the beauty parlour.

"I have been forced by my father to take this step. He knows well that I do not want to marry Kamal even then he is going to impose this arranged marriage on me. I still love Ibrahim and he loves me too," she said.

"You remember how your father became infuriated, when he came to know that you had a black friend at university," she reminded her.

"Yes I know. I stopped seeing him because I was dependent on my father then but today, I am independent," she said while looking at a fashion magazine.

"Friendship is something different, marriage is a big decision," Shahida said.

"I have no other option in this situation. I'm old enough to take my decision. I started seeing him again after my father declared his final decision of marrying me with Kamal. Ibrahim is happy on my decision of marrying him", she said with satisfaction.

"And what about you?" Shahida asked him.

"Of course, he was my first love in life. I left him just because of my father, he never left me," she said.

"You should think about your family before you make such a big decision," Shahida advised her.

"If my father is not going to understand my feelings, then why should I think about him? He threatened my mother to divorce her, if we reported this forced marriage to police. I love my mum so much; I don't want to create any problem for her. This is my personal decision. I did not even tell my mother about it. Once we settle down, I hope she will forgive me because she wants to see me happy in life," she said.

"Would your father not think your mother responsible for this?" Shahida showed her concern.

"I'd tell him that it was my personal decision," she said.

"I don't think it is fair to the parents, to run away with someone else on your engagement day," Shahida said deeply.

"Is it fair to force daughters to marry someone they don't really like?" she said angrily.

"You should have convinced them that you did not like him," Shahida said.

"I told my father that he was not my suitor and I did not like him but he insisted I marry him," she said.

"Don't you think this decision will affect your younger sisters?" she said.

"It will help them, and my father will never force them to marry someone they don't like. I want to save my younger sisters' lives too. If today I retreat, tomorrow they will do the same thing. This is the time for me to make a bold decision, for the sake of my sisters," she argued.

"Do you think Ibrahim will keep you happy?" she asked him.

"We both love each other, we will have a happy life *Inshallah*," she said with a flashing smile on her face.

"Will his family accept you?" she asked her.

"His whole family lives in Nigeria. He lives here on his own," she said.

"What is he doing these days?" she asked

"He is working in a private firm, as a finance control officer," she said.

"If you are going with him today, then what's the point of coming to the beauty parlour to have your face made-up?" Shahida asked her.

"We are going to marry tonight. He has arranged every thing for me. He will come here, in a short while, to take me to his house where he has arranged every thing for *Nikah*, and then we have a party," she told her the details.

Nikah is the formal, official and legal marriage. It is performed by the Imam, the official religious authority or any recognised person. It requires the presence of at least two witnesses, the *Mahr* (marriage gift from the groom to bride) and the *Khutba*--- a religious sermon, to join the couple together in the name of God.

Muhammad Ibrahim entered the parlour. He was their classmate at university and a mutual friend to them. He greeted Shahida with *Salam*.

She did not see any big change in his personality, gleaming black colour, large forehead, shaven head, big eyes and long big lips. He had put some weight on him but his tall height covered it and he was not looking like a fat man.

He was wearing a black wedding suit and looking a perfect man. He looked very happy that day. He chatted with Shahida for sometime. They talked about life after university, mostly regarding their jobs.

Nabeela left with him, to make a happy life but put her family into trouble.

****

Kamal had reached his uncle's house with his friends. He sat on the specified sofa in the centre of the room, along the wall leaving room for Nabeela to sit with him later; a table, made of glass, was put before the sofa with a small bouquet of fresh roses on it.

His friends sat on dining chairs, on his left side. On his right hand side, there was a long empty sofa for Nabeela's friends, who had not turned up yet and never did because they were not invited. There were also eight folding chairs arranged along the front wall, where some close friends of Raheem were sitting and gossiping. There were three long wooden tables, in the middle of the spacious sitting room.

Raheem was coming in and out of the room restlessly. He was trying to show his guests that he was busy doing other things.

His smile faded away. He was sitting speechless in his room, on a chair. His wife was lying on the bed, unconscious. Her daughters were trying to bring her to senses. Tanzeela was rubbing her hands while Shakeela was sprinkling water on her face, at regular intervals. They both were sobbing deeply, trying to control their bawling so it would not reach the sitting room.

"Sorry dad, mum, Tanzee and Shakee, I got married to Muhammad Ibrahim. You all know him very well; he was my friend at university. I believe this is shocking news for all of you and I feel it is bit unfair to you. I am sorry for that. It was my personal decision. I honestly apologise to all of you. I love you all. Nabeela"

That was the message she had sent to her family members, a short while ago, and had made everyone paralysed.

"What will I tell my guests---my daughter ran away?" he murmured. A stream of tears was soaking into his short black and white beard. He was twisting his hands in and out madly. Several times, he stood up and then sat down, went to the drawing room and came back from the door. He was feeling dizzy and trembling with shock. He did not know what to do. He kept walking through the house aimlessly.

There were some critical moments in life, when even the brave feel helpless. That moment had come to him. He was feeling powerless. He had spent his whole life, making a good family name and honourable position amongst his friends in the UK, his daughter had buried it into a grave today. You need years to build your nobility, but it takes one minute to finish it. He was now facing that one minute in life.

"Chaudhry *Sahib*; where have you been lost?" one of his friends called him from the room.

He gathered his powers, stood up, washed his face to look fresh and went to the room. "Sorry, my wife is not feeling well," he said.

"No problem, you take your time. I know mothers' hearts are very soft, it happens on such events," he comforted him.

He asked Kamal to come with him. He took him to a separate room.

"My son, my honour is in your hands today. Please help me out," he asked with an expression of grief.

"What has happened uncle?" he asked anxiously.

He took the mobile phone from his pocket and showed him the message sent by Nabeela. Kamal also went in shock.

"Oh my God, it is really bad," he said, while putting his hand over his head.

He collected himself and said, "We should postpone it and tell our guests that aunty is not feeling well and will organise it some other time," he suggested.

"This is not the solution. They will think negatively about us," he said.

"They will think badly anyway, when they come to know about Nabeela," Kamal said.

"I don't want to let them know that my daughter has run away with someone else on her engagement day," he said in nervousness.

"OK, you sit here I will do something," Raheem said and left the room.

He went to his room, where his daughters are attending upon their mother. He called Tanzeela and took her to a separate room.

"My dear daughter, my honour is in your hands today. I request you to help me out," he asked her with a weeping face.

"What do I have to do?" she asked, surprisingly.

"I don't want to be humiliated before the people today. I don't want them to know that my daughter has run away from the house on her engagement day" he said in anxiety.

She was looking at him in amazement. She still could not understand what he wanted to ask her.

"I ask you, please, save my honour today, daughters are honour for family and especially for their parents" he said helplessly.

"What should I do?" she asked bewilderingly.

He took a long pause to say, "Please, get engaged to Kamal."

When she heard this she felt like the roof had fallen onto her. She became paralysed. She saw a deep darkness before her eyes. She remained in this condition for some time, looking at her father with still eyes.

"Please Tanzee, help me out. I just verbally invited my friends, they don't know which of my daughters are going to get engaged today," he asked her feebly.

"No," she said and fell on the bed. She sank her face into the pillow and started crying.

She felt her father's hands on her feet who sat on the ground along the bed. She suddenly stood up and held his hands.

"No, please, don't make me be sinful," she put her face onto his hands.

"I can't do it," she repeated it madly, wetting his palms with her tears.

"For the sake of my honour," he said over and over.

"No, I can't do it, please," she kept saying.

He helped her to sit on the bed. He again sat on the floor and put his cap onto her feet.

"Here is my honour, please save it today", he kept repeating.

She took the cap and put it on his head again. She is screaming, "No, please no, I can't do it".

"I will kill myself, right now, if you refuse, I finish my life here", he said hysterically.

She looked at his face, all the fatherly loves he had provided her, in childhood, coming before her eyes, like a film on the screen. She had never seen him crying or so helpless. Daughters' hearts are always very tender towards their fathers. When a daughter sees tears in her father eyes she melts down. This is a natural instinct, which God has put in females. A young daughter can not see the tears of her old father.

Fatherly love had overcome Tanzeela. She hugged him intensely and said, "I am there for you dad. I love you."

"I will never forget this favour of you for my whole life," he said, thankfully.

She went to her mother, who had come to her senses and was sitting on the bed with the support of a pillow but was still and emotionless. Shakeela was sitting beside her.

"Mum, I have decided to become engaged to Kamal right now. I don't want you to feel shame before the guests. Nabeela has hurt you enough already. I am there for you. What I am going to do has not been forced by my father. I myself asked father to do it," she said hiding all her feelings from her mother.

Her mother was totally quiet, with still, stoned eyes. She did not show any reaction to the news. She was just expressionless.

Tanzeela was so deep in her father's love that she did not react before her mother. Raheem was hearing this, standing in the doorway.

"OK, everybody gets ready, give me the engagement dress Kamal has brought," she asked Shakeela.

"Dad, will you please go to the guests, we are coming in a while," she said with her full strength.

He passed them the two big bags, brought by Kamal. He went to Kamal and told him that Tanzeela was going to get engaged to him. He did not say anything but was just as surprised.

"Sorry, we kept you waiting," he said to the guests, as he entered the room after recovering himself.

Tanzeela realised that her mother was not well enough to go to the guests. She gave her some medicine and let her rest.

When she got ready, Shakeela called for her father. She told her about her mum's condition.

"We should tell the guests that Nabeela is attending upon her sick mother," Tanzeela asked.

122

Raheem took all the dresses, sweets and fruits into the sitting room and spread them on the table. He had also bought a golden ring, two dresses, and a pair of shoes for Kamal. He asked him to wear one dress. It was a light brown suit with a white shirt and a bright golden tie. Kamal took Ajay with him, into a separate room to ask for his help in knotting the tie properly.

"Ajay, Nabeela refused to get engaged to me. She protested a lot before her parents and made the mother sick. Now Tanzeela is going to get engaged to me," he had just lied to him, for his family's honour.

"This is amazing; forget about Nabeela, God is helping you. True couples are decided in the heavens. I strongly believe in it," he said, blissfully.

Tanzeela came to the room, a long dark blue embroidered shawl, with bright white stars and crescents, hanging over her face. She was wearing the same coloured dress. The trousers and *Kameez* had beautiful white embroidery at the end corners. Kamal bought this dress on Ajay's advice from Southall.

She sat with Kamal on the sofa, bowing her head to her lap. He tried to overcome his nervousness by finding himself so close to her.

"He is Kamal Chaudhry, the son of my elder brother Rehmat Chaudhry. He is doing an MBA degree here. Both families unanimously decided that Kamal will marry my daughter Tanzeela. We have sought their consent and they both are very happy with our decision. Kamal is a suitor for my daughter in age and education. She is also doing a masters degree from a good university. As soon as they finish their studies, they will marry," Raheem took attention of the guests.

"Mashallah, Mashallah," the atmosphere echoed praising God.

"This is compulsory, the girl and the boy must be equal in age and education," one man said.

"You are very lucky Raheem, you have found such a nice suitor within your family," another man praised him.

"I suggest that you find a suitable suitor for your other daughters and marry them together," one man said.

"This is good idea, one of my relatives did the same thing for his two daughters. It saved time and money too," another man said.

"OK, children stand up and give each other your rings," Rehmat said.

Shakeela helped her to stand up, and she gave her ring, to put on Kamal's finger. Ajay passed him the ring for Tanzeela.

They both put the rings in each other hands. Tanzeela did not look at him. He just raised his hand to her and she put on it. He took her hand in his to put on the ring. Ajay took some pictures of them.

An emotional defeat is the worst defeat in the world where one loses desire to react. Tanzeela had been defeated in an emotional battle against her father. Her body was with her but not the mind or feelings. She looked like a statue, wearing a bridal dress.

Kamal was more surprised than happy. He knew that it was an artificial engagement that looked real.

The guests extended their best wishes to the couple and gave them some money, as it usually happened at this event. At the end they were served food.

All the guests had left, except Kamal and his friends. His uncle was talking to him privately.

"Please don't tell your family about Nabeela," he pleaded with him.

"Don't worry I will not tell them," he assured him.

"She has died for me today," he said desperately.

"Sorry uncle, it all has happened because of me," he said sadly.

"No, this is not your fault. I never thought my daughter could do this to me," he said with a deep sigh.

"We should go to her and stop her from doing so," Kamal said. "No use, she has already got married and the law of this country gives her protection," he said.

"We can ask her to come back home, and we will do the honourable *Rukhusti*--- departure, for her," he said.

"No, I don't want to see her again in this life. She has put *kalak*---bad name, on my face," he said angrily.

Kamal kept quiet and did not say anything, as he knew that his uncle was already very disturbed.

"Kamal, you come back to our house please. I want to look after you," he asked him.

He was not mentally ready to move back to his uncle house.

"I will let you know uncle," he replied shortly.

He also left with his friends. He was rather quiet on his way back home. They were teasing him by talking about his fiancée. He put a fake smile on his face and gave them short answers.

He was very much worried about Nabeela and his mind was fixed on her. He was blaming himself for her escape. He was repenting why he had come to the UK. No doubt, he loved Tanzeela and wanted to marry her, but he did not want Nabeela to bring a bad name to the family just because of him. The way he was engaged to Tanzeela did not give him much happiness.

Tanzeela went back to her room. She looked at herself in the mirror and could not help crying. She changed the clothes, washed her face. She wanted to flush the ring into the gutter but the thought of the father stopped her and she wore it again.

She did not want to expose her anger and sadness before her parents, as she knew they were already in shock.

"Nabeela, you did not do well to me. You proved to be a weak person, who could not face challenges in life. It was better you fought against them remaining in the house. You did not realise how much emotional damage you were going to give us. Life is just not to satisfy ones own wishes but sometimes you have to

125

be considerate of other people as well. Family is not just a one person but a unit of people. You punished your mother and sisters just because of the father." she thought about Nabeela's rebellion.

She was just feeling remorse for her fortune. She never thought, even in her dreams, that one day she would wear Kamal's engagement ring. This was an accidental engagement.

If you paint green on withered leaves, you can not make them grow, if you water plastic flowers they will not give you scent.

Human feelings sometimes become like withered leaves or plastic flowers, you can decorate them with colourful objects but you can't give them life.

She fixed her eyes at the ring, which was not giving her any feelings for her proposed soul mate.

"You will never be able to get my love Mr. Kamal Chaudhry," she said finally.

****

Chapter 8

Decisions are never personal; they always affect the people related to us. We lead our own lives but we are not individuals at any stage. We are surrounded by people, all the time. We have only one reason to live in this world and that is we must have humans like us to deal with. If we think that no one has a right over us or we don't have any right over others and we are individuals then life becomes meaningless. We lose or win just because someone is competing with us. We don't want to play if there is no competitor.

Nabeela claimed that she made a personal decision but it affected the people related to her life.

The first question, Kamal's mother asked her husband was, "Why did Nabeela refuse to get engaged to Kamal? What was wrong with our son?"

Rehmat was also upset about this sudden move but he was taking side of his brother. He did not want to let him down before his wife.

"I told my brother that you wanted Tanzeela to marry Kamal. He did this according to your wishes," he pretended.

"Was it not a matter of shame the younger sister getting married first?" she said shockingly.

"They live in London. This is not a matter of shame over there", he said.

"She was older than Kamal anyway. I really wanted Tanzeela to become our daughter," she said happily.

"That's what my brother did for us," he said.

"But we have already told everyone in the village about Nabeela. What will we say to them?" she said worriedly.

"Who will remember the name, you mad woman, don't worry about it," he said.

"The people of the village will not remember the name but what we say to our relatives?" she asked her again.

"We will explain to them later on. You don't need to mention it to others at this stage", he said.

"By the way, what did Kamal tell you about why Nabeela refused to marry him?" she asked.

"He did not tell me anything," he said.

"I heard she was working in a bank," she said.

"Yes she was," he said.

"She was doing a better job and had a rather haughty manner," she made a right guess.

"God knows better" he replied.

Kamal did not tell his father the actual reason. He just told him that she refused to marry him because she was highly educated and older in age.

"Is our Kamal not doing a good job there?" she was curious to know why it happened.

"He is still studying, he does only part time work," he said.

"We should ask him to work in a bank, after all he is well educated too," she said innocently.

"He can do part time job only," he said

"Why? Ask him to go full time, anyway we will need lot of money for his wedding," she insisted.

"He will do full time but after he completes his degree," he told her.

"He is already highly educated; he doesn't need to study any further. He should do a good job, unless Tanzeela refuses to marry him.

"Once he gets a degree from there, he will be able to get a job in a bank," he explained to her.

"I am wondering he sent us a lot of money through doing a part time job. If he works full time he can send us more. I told you my son was very clever and hardworking," she praised him.

"I know him he is a very responsible person," he said.

"Is he working in an office?" she asked him.

"Yes, he told me that he was working in an office," he said.

"Only the office job suits him. My son is very neat and clean. You remember when we were building the new kitchen, he did not come home for three days because he did not like the smell of mud and bricks," she eulogised him.

"I never asked him to go to the fields with me because I knew he could not do hard things," he sympathised too.

"I am thinking about how my poor boy will have arranged his engagement ceremony without us," she said with all her motherly loves.

"He told me that some of his friends were with him," he said.

"That is good. I hope his uncle invited a lot of people because he is a very rich person," she guessed.

"Yes, he invited many people and gave lot of things to Kamal," he knew the exact numbers of the guests and the details of gifts because Kamal had told him already, but he did not tell his wife for the sake of his brother's honour. He knew his brother was a petty-minded.

"We should ask Kamal to live somewhere else. It does not look good to stay in fiancée's house," she said

"He has started living outside already," he told her.

He knew that Kamal had left his uncle house weeks ago, but he did not tell his wife and neither had Kamal told her. He just told his father the same thing he told his uncle, when he left the house.

His father did not tell his mother because she got worried about him for pretty things.

"Rehmat, I am worried. If today Nabeela refused to marry Kamal then tomorrow Tanzeela can do the same thing," she said.

"She got engaged to Kamal by her own free will; she will not do it," he said.

"But they are just engaged and this relationship is very weak that can be broken at any time," she said.

"It won't happen, Tanzeela is our daughter, she would not do that," he said.

"She could follow her elder sister, I have a fear," she said.

"Don't think stupid things, it won't happen," he pressed.

"I was thinking, if you ask your brother to perform the *Nikah*, and we do the *Rukhsti*, after Kamal finishes his studies," she suggested to him.

Rukhsati is a term used in Indo-Pak. It takes place within few hours after the *Nikah*, where the bride leaves her parents house to go with the groom. But sometimes families postpone the consummation of the marriage, or *Rukhsati*, for a later time, for some reason, by mutual understanding. There are many reasons for this postponement and it could be for few weeks, months or years. Most of time, people do that for immigration reasons. They can apply for a spouse's visas after *Nikah*, as they have all legal documents and do *Rukhsati* once the visas are approved. In the same way, if the couple are studying and the parents want them to complete their studies first, they postponed it. Once the *Nikah* is performed the couple is tied in legal marriage and they have to follow the legal procedure of divorce, if they decide to separate before *Rukhsati* even without touching each other.

Kamal's mother wanted to tie Tanzeela in *Nikah* to assure this marriage. She was pressing her husband to talk to his brother on this issue.

Eventually she made him agree to ask his brother for their Nikah as early as possible.

****

Kamal had started a new struggle to hunt for a job. He left early in the morning, with bundle of CVs and did not return home until he finished delivering all of them. The thought of his loan, his burning desire to do an MBA, and future dreams kept him walking for miles on foot, in the severe cold weather, without having lunch.

Finally, he found a job as the kitchen assistant in an Indian restaurant, at the weekend during the evenings, at three pounds per hour. His job was cleaning the dishes and keeping the kitchen tidy. There was another cleaner with him, who was also a student. He found that most of the waiters were students too. They all told him that they had no other option than doing this job. They all complained about the cold weather and tough life in the UK. He knew that back in his country, only the uneducated people did this kind of work.

An educated person had to kill his ego to do such dirty works. Whoever comes to the UK, on student visa, without bringing enough money has to do these things.

He thought about the revolt of Nabeela, his accidental engagement to Tanzeela, and future events while washing the dishes.

"I should not go back to my uncle's house. My aunty and cousins will have been holding me responsible for Nabeela. It would be a big problem if I lived among them in the current circumstances. Before, I was living as a guest but now I am the fiancé of Tanzeela, it does not look good to live in fiancée house. I will refuse my uncle by saying something reasonable."

"Nabeela was not willing to marry me just because I was not

131

her ideal man. She was a highly educated professional woman but I was nothing. Had my uncle not forced her to marry me, she would not have been left the house in such shameful way."

"It is not fair to ask a bank officer to marry a dish washer, but it is also not fair for a girl to run away from her home and cause humiliation for parents. It would have been better if she had gone to the police station to register a complaint against the forced marriage and the police had issued a warning to her father. She should not have done this."

He did not know that his uncle had threatened her that if she went to the police he would divorce her mother. She wanted to save her mother's life.

"How did uncle make Tanzeela agree to this engagement? Did she take pity on me or on her family? Whatever, it was a forced or courtesy engagement. She was not happy at all," he wondered.

"I would have to prove her that I am her suitor. I can only do this with a good education and an honourable job. There is no other option. This is a practical life; love and romance work only in Indian movies, where a high profile girl marries her servant. It won't happen in real life. This is a materialistic world, here you are judged by your social status not by the intensity of your love for someone."

"If I remained a dish washer, Tanzeela would do the same thing that her sister did," he thought as he poured washing liquid on the serving dishes.

"I must see Ajay, to ask him to help me in finding another job. I'll also ask him to find a good institution for me for my MBA degree," he thought about Ajay.

He could not see him, after his engagement party. He phoned him a couple of times and he told him that he was busy in his work.

****

Asif and Zaman, his housemates, were at home when Kamal got back after work. They were having coffee in the sitting room, after their dinner. Kamal was busy in the kitchen, heating his meal to eat. They were discussing the new points based system for student visas, introduced by the UK government.

Immigration matters are common issues of discussion amongst the international students in the UK. They remain informed about the new rules and regulations because they are directly connected to them. They chalk out their plans to prolong their stay in the UK in the light of the new policies.

"The new points based system is good for students. You can get points for your offer letter and for your bank statement. It is very easy to get admission to any institution that falls under tier 4. There are educational agents who help you in maintaining your bank statement. They put the required money into your account, for 28 days, and charge a heavy fee on it. So, the bank statement is not a problem. It is an easy way to come to the UK on student visa," Zaman said.

"What is the use of studying at a low profile institutions? The job opportunities have already been squeezed. It is easy to come but hard to survive. The agents are making a lot of money. They charge their commission from the colleges and also get consultancy fee from the students. They also charge big amount for bank statement, from the visa candidates. It is a very profitable business these days," Asif said.

"We should start this business then," Zaman said laughingly.

"No, this is deception, the agents mislead the students for their own benefit," he said.

"There agents deceive back home, here colleges deceive in the UK, where should the poor students go?" Asif said.

"If you really want to get good education, then you should go to one of the good universities, this is the solution," Zaman said.

"But you know their fees are very high, only a handful of students can afford them," Asif said.

"It is better to remain in your country then, instead of destroying your life here," Asif said.

"Most of the students, who come here for on less than a degree course, their aim is to earn money not to study," Asif said.

"This is the case with all the poor countries. There is corruption, cronyism, nepotism and high unemployment. The people come here to end their poverty," Zaman said.

"I think the government benefits from the inflow of students. They provide cheap and qualified labour. That is why the UK is the best in services. You go to a burger shop, any supermarket or even hire a cab and it is the masters' degree holder students who will be serving you. Look at yourself, you have done a masters degree in HR but working in McDonald's; look at me I done MBA and am doing a security job. What does this country want from us? We are working hard, paying taxes, without claiming any social benefits. We are not burden on the government."

"The government is worried about the international students. Every second day it introduces a new policy for them. They should look at how many taxes students are paying annually. They are providing the best services in the supermarkets and all over the UK. They want to finish the right of work of students and stop the right of work of their dependents. But if the dependents have got the skills they need in this country, they should be allowed to work rather than importing alternatively. I know one of my friends, who brought his wife here. She was a qualified teacher. She worked here and helped her husband complete his studies," Asif gave a lengthy speech.

"I've come to conclusion that if you can do something, in your country it is better to stay there and make your life unless you can afford to go to good universities. We have spent four years here. We have damaged our careers already. We are not able to go back and start from the beginning. We will continue to do minor jobs because we have no other option but we advise new comers, if you can afford a university education you must come here, complete your degree and go back to your country to make your life. If you stay here you will be doing same things that we are doing," Zaman said.

"Who will take our advice? I am convincing my cousins, who want to come to the UK on student visas but they do not understand. They think that I am just jealous of them," Asif said sadly.

Kamal was attentive to them, while he was having his dinner. His housemates' discussions made him stressed. He found lot of contradictions in their talks. Sometimes they carp governments' policies back in their country and here in the UK, they hold them responsible for the poverty of students', criticise agents, find fault in colleges, and complain about their jobs but they are still living in this country and no one talks about going back. They want to prolong their stay in the UK by fair or foul means.

He did not take an interest in joining them. He finished his meal and went to his room. He started writing in his diary, as was his routine before he went to sleep.

****

Today, Kamal was going to see Ajay to discuss lot of things. He went to the same place to see him. Whenever he thought about Ajay, the thought of London Eye came to his mind, which was always their meeting point.

It was still a mystery to him, why he spent most of his time sitting on the bank gazing at the waves of River Thames. He wanted to ask him, many times, but he always avoided telling him the whole story.

He was taking an interest in his love story and was always anxious to know what happened next.

He found him, sitting on the same familiar stone bench, in his usual pose putting one leg across the other, folding his arms under his chest, staring at the water and in deep contemplation.

"Ajay, you should write a will so that your ashes will be thrown into the River Thames, instead of The Ganges after your death," he said, as he approached him and they both started laughing.

"I feel cold with the thought of this place but you sit here for hours. Don't you feel cold?" he asked him funnily.

"When love is burning inside ---you don't feel the cold outside," Ajay said philosophically.

"Anyway leave it, tell me how is Tanzeela?" he asked him

"I don't know," he replied shortly.

"Kamal, the atmosphere was very tense over there, on your engagement day. I felt there something was going wrong inside the house."

"I told you that Nabeela refused to marry me. She created a big problem at home that made her mother sick."

"I wondered how Tanzeela so easily got ready to get engaged to you. It looked like an Indian movie, where a father puts gun on his head and makes his daughter marry someone." Ajay continued.

"I don't know any thing happened over there like that but if she got engaged to you, for the sake of her family honour, then she is a great girl." Ajay appreciated Tanzeela.

"Yes, she is very great. She did not want to let her father down before the guests after Nabeela's denial" Kamal agreed.

"Anyway, you must be thankful to Nabeela; she helped you to find your love. You are very lucky. Some people are very fortunate; they get the things without any struggle and some are so ill-fated they cannot claim the things they found in life." Ajay told him

"I don't know if I am lucky or unlucky because it was an accidental engagement" Kamal responded.

"You know, when your uncle was introducing you that you

were doing an MBA, I could hardly stop myself from laughing." Ajay recalled.

"Ajay, I have come to seek your advice, regarding this matter. My uncle thinks that I am doing a degree but you know the real situation. Nabeela refused to marry me because I had no qualifications, no career prospects. I fear if I remain in this position Tanzeela will do the same thing to me." Kamal revealed his fears.

"This is genuine concern, to be honest. If you don't improve your education your uncle will not be in position to support you against his family." Ajay concurred.

"Yes I know it but what I should do?" Kamal asked.

"It is best for you, to get your degree as early as possible. You seem to be a lucky person. It is possible you can get a good job." Ajay advised.

"How much will it cost me?" Kamal asked.

"I know one good institution, they charge seven thousands pounds for a postgraduate diploma and plus top up to an MBA" Ajay told him.

"How long it will take me to complete it?" Kamal asked.

"One and half year maximum." Ajay confirmed.

"Seven thousand pounds mean ten lakhs rupees in my currency." Kamal said.

"If you want to marry Tanzcela, you will have to spend this money. At least you will become equal to her in education." Ajay said.

"I not only want to marry her, but also to look forward to a better life." Kamal said.

"By the way, where you will get this huge amount?" Ajay asked.

"I'd ask my father to sell land in the village. Once I get my degree I can earn good money and we can buy it again," Kamal said.

"You are a son of a landlord!" Ajay said surprisingly.

"No *bhai,* we are not big landlords. We inherited some land from our forefathers. We are just living on them, nothing more than that." Kamal told him.

"This is good; you get money from your father for your tuition fees and do some part time work to earn your living expenses." Ajay said.

"That was the reason I wanted to see you. Please help me finding a job." Kamal asked his friend.

"I suggest you to get a security licence. It is easy to get a job in the security sector and money is also good." Ajay advised.

"OK, I have some money, which people gave me on my engagement. I can manage it." Kamal said confidently.

"Good, I'll send you tomorrow to a centre, to do the security course for three days. Once you get your certificate we can apply for badge." Ajay said.

"How long it will take me to get it?" Kamal asked him.

"It will take at least two months to get it. You should continue to do your current job until you get the badge. In the mean time I will try to get you another job." Ajay said.

"Thank you Ajay *bhai*" Kamal said.

"No worries, you are just like my brother," Ajay gave him a brotherly look.

"Ajay, you will organise my wedding ceremony, I am asking you today." Kamal asked.

"I will, don't worry. We will have a splendid ceremony" Ajay assured him.

"You know Kamal; once Preya told me that she was going to attend one of her cousins' wedding ceremony, I asked her not try to look very pretty because someone can lose life there and she said, '*Na*---no, there is nothing like that! I am not so much pretty."

He was lost in the memories of Preya.

"She was pure, innocent and pretty," he said, with his deep feelings for her.

"Ajay, what was her response when you expressed your love to her?" Kamal asked.

He closed his eyes, cupped face into his hands and said, "I was very happy that day because I was going to tell her that I was in love with her. I found her working on shop floor. I went to her and gave her a long deep hug. I wanted to take her aside to tell her how much love I had for her but it was Christmas time and store was very busy. I was looking for a chance to take her to a lonely place to tell her that I was *fida* for her.

We chatted and laughed on routine things. She was also very happy that day. I asked her that I wanted to take her to India but she said that she wanted to go to Australia. I asked her why Australia and she told me that she had found someone living in Australia. She wanted to marry him and settle down there with him. She further told me that the guy was their family friend and she was in love with him.

When she told me this I felt a cold wave running through my body. I was feeling a pain inside me which I never felt before in life. My very first love in life was telling me that she had found someone else before I expressed my love to her.

She was very happy. I had never seen her so happy before. Love is not self-interested, selfish or greedy; love is just love nothing else than. It wants to see your beloved happy all the time. I wanted to see her happy because I loved her. I extended my best wishes for her and buried my feelings inside me", Ajay told him.

"Did she keep contact with you after that? I meant did she ever talk to you on phone?" Kamal asked him.

"Just one time."

"Just one time!" Kamal said surprisingly.

"Yes, just one time" he confirmed.

"What did she say to you?" Kamal asked.

"She was looking for someone to cover her shift."

"Did you ever phone her?" Kamal kept questioning.

"Four times in total but she never answered it, every time she made an excuse that she was busy somewhere." he said

"What an amazing love story!" Kamal said astonishingly.

"Did you ever tell her about your love later on?" Kamal asked.

"No, you don't need to express your love, it speaks itself," Ajay said.

"But she did not listen to the voice of your heart," Kamal said.

"If someone does not listen to voice of your heart then there is no use to tell in words. If the people around you are not able to discover you then there is no use to explain to them by your words," Ajay said, looking up the withered leaves of a tree in front of him.

"Kamal l used to think about her:

'*Mujay yaqeen hai*

Keh zindgi mein woh lamha aiye ga

Jab mein tum say kahun ga jana!

Keh meri ankhuon kay ainnoun mein

Jo jam chukka hai woh aks tera hai, sirf tera

Woh aik khusboo

Jo meri sansoun mein ghul gei hai

Teri mohabat nahi tu kia hai?

Woh arzoo ke dhanak , saji hai

Jo mery ahsas kay ooffiq per

Teri wafa hai

Mujay yaqeen hai

Keh zindgi mein woh lamha aiye ga

Jab mein tum say kahun ga Jana!

Keh mery jazboun ke sari sachyian bhe teri

Heri rutoun mein jo dil ko seemab ker key rekh dein

Woh zard tanhayein bhe teri

140

Jo meri tanhanyuon ke pat jhard mein sabaz mousam ka
khawab thehrien
Woh bazam ariyan bhe teri
Mujay yaqeen hai
Keh teri khatar
Mein jitna sochoun ga, jitna lekhou ga, jitna boolou ga
Teen lafzoon mein karz sara utar dey ga
Ye keh kay muj sey tu
'SAME TO YOU'
Mujay yaqeen hai'.
I believe in
A moment will come in life,
When I'd say to you, my darling,
In the iris of my eyes,
That frozen is your reflection, only yours.
The scent,
That mixed with my breaths,
Is what if not your love?
The rainbow of yearn decorated
On the horizon of my senses,
Is my faithfulness for you.
I believe in,
A moment will come in life,
When I'd say to you, my darling!
All the truths of my emotions are yours.
That makes my heart mercurial in springs,
Those red isolations are also yours.
That becomes dreams of greenery in the autumn of my
loneliness,
Those companies are also yours.
I believe in,
For you
Whatever I think, whatever I write, whatever I speak,

141

You will pay me back all in three words,
By saying
'SAME TO YOU'
I believe in'.

"Still, I believe one day she would come to me and say 'Same to you'. My love is true for her and true love has a power", Ajay said with strong faith.

"What was her attitude towards you after that?" Kamal asked.

We kept greeting each other, in the same way but I never saw any real light in her eyes for me after that. She was happy, very happy and, at one stage, I became happy as well because I wanted to see her happy in life."

"Would things remain same in life, but it does not happen. The wheel of time keeps moving, crushing us under it."

"Preya went back to her university. She was busy in her studies. She came back after she finished her exams. I was waiting for her, as usual, with same zeal. I wanted to listen to her, talk to her, and laugh with her. I wanted to know about the boy she had found.

This time she had totally changed. She was cool, reserved and calm. She looked like an entirely a different person."

"What happened to her?" Kamal asked hastily.

"I'd tell you later," he said.

They both walked along the bank for some time in silence. Ajay stopped and started looking into the deep waters before he moved to the bus stop to leave from there.

****

The atmosphere had completely changed in Raheem's house, after Nabeela's rebellion.

His wife was in the hospital, he spent most of time in his room quietly, and Tanzeela was continuously attending on her mother, while Shakeela was looking after the house. No one talked to

142

each other. They were all quiet. They did not have a family dinner together after that day.

The first child is always very dear to their parents. Raheem was very happy on her birth. He remembered how she used to play in his lap. How he would get up early in the morning, to drop her at school and pick her up on time, ignoring all his business matters. How he used to buy dolls for her and gave her gifts for her birthdays. How she would play in the house.

He remembered, once she was sick, he could not sleep the whole night and sat beside her on the bed. He remained strict with her, when she grew up, just to play a positive role in being a father, to keep her away from unpleasant things.

"She forgot all my loves, sacrifices, cares and affections I gave her for twenty six years," he wondered.

He wanted to play his fatherly role, to arrange a suitor for her. He did his best for her, according to his own thinking, but she could not understand it. The punishment she inflicted on him was much more severe than his plans of marrying her to his nephew.

"You did not do well to me, Nabeela," he mumbled madly.

He questioned himself if parents' love was so weak when the children grew young they forgot every thing so easily.

"You did not think, even for one moment, about how much I loved you," he said helplessly.

He thought about how he had worked hard though out his life, to give a better future to his children. He sacrificed his own comforts and wishes. He bought property for his daughters. His wealth was pinching him that day. He had accumulated assets, became a rich person but could not make his daughter obey him.

He was not able to understand the feelings of his daughter. He thought, as he forced them to lead their lives according to his wishes, he would succeed in making decisions for their marriages but he was wrong.

Marriage is a very sensitive matter for any girl in this world.

You can not make her marry someone she does not like, just by giving her all the riches of the world. She always wants to marry a person who wins her heart. No power can compel a woman to love someone against her will.

Raheem just imagined Nabeela as his daughter but he could not see her as a woman. He was right in his claims of being a father but he was wrong in understanding a woman.

Had he realized the woman's feeling in Nabeela, he would never have been in such trouble he was going through.

He made the same mistake again, when he compelled Tanzeela to get engaged to Kamal, just to save his own honour.

****

Kamal had come to know about the illness of his aunty. He thought to go to see her in the hospital, but he was rather reluctant because she held him responsible for all the problems in her home.

He knew his aunty was against him and his visit could give her more tension. He wondered, if he did not go there, his uncle and cousins, especially Tanzeela, would think negative about him. He thought he should go to the hospital, not their house and it was a chance for him to prove to them that he was not a bad person. It was his moral obligation to attend upon his aunty, he thought.

After lot of pondering, finally, he decided to go there. He went to the hospital. He found his uncle in the lounge. He was looking pale and weak. The smile on his face had gone. It looked like he had not slept since Nabeela had left the house. Kamal could see the mourning on his face. He was a typical father, who was brought up in a respectable family in the village. He came to the UK when he was very young, but could not forget his culture and traditions. Kamal could understand what the feelings of a father were like, after his daughter had run away. If he were in the village, a number of people could have been killed in the name of honour. He got confused, in two different cultures. That was not only his case, but it was the same for the thousands of people who migrated to the UK, in the early 70s. They were facing the same dilemma, especially when they had grown up children. No doubt, they made good money but they could not get hold on their next generation. Although there were few exemptions, but most of them were having the same cultural clashes between themselves and their children.

"How aunty is feeling now?" he asked him, respectfully.

"She is not feeling very well," he said.

Kamal knew the reason, even so, he asked, "What happened to her?"

"She had been quiet since the bitch run away," he was cursing Nabeela.

"What do the doctors say?" he further asked.

"They say she is in total shock and it will take some time for her to recover," he said.

"I am so sorry to hear that," Kamal said.

"This is all because of that bitch. I did not know I was breeding a bitch at home," he kept calling Nabeela a bitch.

Kamal kept quiet on his remarks about Nabeela.

"How is your study going?" he asked him.

"It is going well," he replied, lying ashamedly.

"And what about your part time job?" he said

"My job is also going well. It is really helping me. I am getting some practical experience of the market," he lied boldly.

"That's sound good, keeping going, my son," Raheem appreciated him.

"I asked you to move back into my house. It would help you in your studies," he again demanded of Kamal.

"Actually, I talked to my employer he said he wanted a local person, who could be easily available at night time. And you know my college is walking distance from my work place. I could save four hours of travelling daily for my studies if I stayed there," Kamal told another lie skilfully.

"That's all right, if you feel convenient staying over there," he said contentedly.

"Your father was asking me to perform *Nikah*. The *Rukhsati* would be after you both complete your studies. What do you think?" the uncle asked his opinion.

"I don't think we should perform *Nikah* until we complete our studies," he said immediately.

"I told your father the same thing but he was insisting on it," Raheem told him.

"Don't worry uncle, I will speak to him. I hope he will understand," he assured him.

"OK, I need to collect some reports from the laboratory. You can go upstairs, to see your aunty," he told him the room number and walked outside the hospital.

Kamal went to the room and knocked at the door slightly. His heart was beating hard. He was feeling very nervous.

Tanzeela opened the door. When she saw him before her, she also got nervous. He greeted her quietly but she did not give any expression in return and left the door wide open, to let him in. His aunty was laying on the bed, in deep sleep, fully covered with a hospital blanket.

"How is she feeling now?" he asked softly.

Tanzeela who was looking at her feet, replied, "She is not feeling very well."

Kamal saw his engagement ring on the right hand of her ring-finger. He meandered off his ring in puzzlement.

"I am sorry to hear this," he said in lower tone.

There was another knock at the door. A nurse entered the room; she took some notes from the file and asked them before she left, "Your patient needs complete rest, it is better if you leave her alone."

They followed the nurse and came out of the room. Tanzeela

walked to the canteen silently, Kamal also walked after her. She sat on a chair in one corner. He also dragged a chair near to her and sat in front of her. She was totally inattentive to him. He remained quiet for some time.

"I am sorry Tanzee, it has all happened because of me," he said apologetically.

She did not say anything in response. She was gazing outside the window turning her face aside of him.

"Actually I did not want...," he wanted to say something but she burst out before he spoke further.

"What you did not want? You did not want to come to the UK to marry one of us, you did not want to stay at our house, you did not want to marry Nabeela, you did not want her to run away, you did not want to get engaged to me, you did not want to destroy our peace or you did not want my mother in the hospital."

Thick tears were floating at the corners of her eyes.

"You did not want anything; we wanted all of this," she wiped falling tears with her fingers.

"I wanted to come to the UK for my studies, I wanted to marry you but I did not want anything else," he said in puzzlement.

"Do you think marriage is a commodity that you can buy from anywhere in the market," she said agitatedly.

"I wanted to work hard, I wanted to become equal to you in education and status, getting married was my last preference. I did not want it so early. But unfortunately we have become victims of our family circumstances," he said in a bit of a high tone.

"When you knew none of us wanted to marry you, could you not refuse it? Could you not ask your family to stop this engagement? Could you not refuse before our father? Couldn't you?" she protested to him.

"You know we don't turn down our elders' decisions but if I knew that things would go so wrong, I would have never let it happened," he said ruefully.

"But if you want, I could refuse it now," he said lightly.

"I lost my sister, my mother is going to die, now you want me to lose my father too," she said mournfully.

"What should I do then?" he said anxiously.

"There is nothing left to do," she said regretfully.

"This is not my fault, Tanzeela," he said.

"You'd refuse now; do you think my father has no respect in the society, he has no feelings, no emotions, do you think he is made of stone? The people will say one daughter ran away and the other broke the engagement," she said deeply.

He was ashamed of his remarks. He did not say anything. There was silence for a long time. He was just looking at the table, bowing his head before her.

"OK, thank you very much for your visit. I will let my mum know about it," she left, leaving him ashamed and regretful.

"I am sorry Tanzee," he said as she was leaving.

"Its OK," she said, gently this time.

He sat there in the same position for long time after she left.

****

Chapter 9

Kamal asked his father to give him 10 lakhs rupees for his education. He explained to him all about the situation, apart from Nabeela's escape. His father got worried about him. He did not want to let his son down, before his brother's family. He also wanted him to get good education. He wanted him to marry Tanzeela, because it was a matter of honour for him too. He was very sensitive about his self-esteem. He had never asked his brother for financial help in his life, nor did he want to ask this time.

He had already 5 lakhs loan on him, which he had to pay back very soon. He knew that Kamal would not be able to help him. He thought, if Tanzeela also broke engagement with his son, at any stage, it would be great disgrace for him. The people of the village would laugh at him. He decided to sell some of his land, to meet Kamal's educational expenses in the UK.

"It is a matter of shame, to sell land of our forefathers. What will people think about us?" his wife said.

"I know, but I want to give happiness to my son in his life," he said.

"Happiness is reached by marrying a person of your choice not with his educational transcripts," she said.

"If husband and wife have good education, they can have better life," he said.

"We both are uneducated but we are having a better life, aren't we?" she said.

"Times have changed now. It is need of this age. When we were married the needs were different," he said.

"Tanzeela is his first cousin; age, education and wealth don't count in blood relations," she said.

"She was born in England, the things are different there", he said.

"Why do people change when they go to the other countries?" she argued.

"This is not their fault; the system makes them to change" her husband answered.

"Rehmat, will our Kamal change too?" his wife asked.

"What can I say?" he did not have an answer.

"Will Kamal's children be like Nabeela and Tanzeela?" she fretted.

"If they were brought up there, they would be like them" he assumed.

"Will they not marry their cousins?" she kept asking startlingly.

"They could be like them," he said strongly.

"Will Kamal not help his sisters and brother?" she further asked.

"He could be like his uncle" he responded honestly.

"This is not good. We should ask Kamal to live with us in Pakistan after his marriage. I don't want to lose my son" she said.

"We can't force them to live with us" her husband reminded her.

"I will ask him. I am sure my son will take my advice," she said affirmatively.

"Tanzeela would not agree to live here," he said.

"She will be his wife and a wife has to live where her husband wants" she told him.

"I told you that things have changed. It is the opposite now, husbands live where their wives want them to live" he said.

"Our Kamal is not among those men who follow their wives," she said proudly.

"No man wants to be changed; these are circumstances that compel him to change."

"Did you talk to your brother about the *Nikah*?"

"I did, he agreed but Kamal was not ready though. He said that the *Nikah* would be after he finished his studies."

"I am afraid that Tanzeela would refuse to marry him in future. She could follow her sister," she supposed.

"It won't happen," he said and went out to see Gama *mochi* who was waiting for him outside.

"*Salam* Chaudhry *Sahib*, I told Chaudhry Noor that you would buy his land soon. Everyone in the village is praising Kamal's splendid engagement ceremony. Some people are feeling jealousy, especially Chaudhry Noor," he flattered him as he met him.

"I told everyone in the village that Kamal *Sahib* was making good money in *Walliat*," he further said.

"Kamal wants to go to a big university, he needs more money, I want to sell some of my land, find a buyer for me," he ordered him.

"Land is for children, this is good decision. When Kamal *Sahib* returns he will become a big officer," Gama veered off and suddenly changed the topic, like a good servant who always speaks his master's mind.

"He wants to go to the same university where the prime minister's children are studying. This university is very expensive, which is why I am going to sell my land," he told him so that he could tell this to the people of the village.

Someone knew that the prime minister's children were studying at the University of Oxford in the UK. The rumour spread in the village that Kamal was going to study at Oxford and his father wanted to sell his land to afford it. The people, who could not pronounce or remember the name of Oxford, said 'the university where prime minister's children are studying'. This story gave Kamal more respect and greater reputation in the village. The people started gratifying his family more, as they thought Kamal was going to be a big man in future.

The most difficult thing for a villager to do is sell his forefathers agricultural lands. It is considered disgraceful, in a rural culture. This is not only the source of income but the pride for the family. Your social status is measured by the number of acres of land you have. Most of the disputes and murder cases are due to lands. Sometimes a number of people have been killed just for a small piece of it.

Rehmat Chaudhry sold a part of his land, to pay off the previous loan he got for his son's education and to pay his further fees in the UK.

****

Kamal was admitted to a new college for a one year post graduate diploma. He was told that he had to submit just a dissertation to earn his MBA degree, after the successful completion of his current course. He started working hard wholeheartedly.

Arsalan, his housemate, who was a lawyer in Pakistan and did a LLM degree in the UK and now working in a supermarket as a sale assistant, helped him in getting a job in his company.

He went to the college regularly, but did not find any local students there. All of his classmates were international students. The administration and teachers were all Asian. Most of the teachers were ex-students of the college, or inexperienced like those who were teaching on 15 to 20 pounds per hour.

The college was situated in the upper part of a plaza and had five small teaching rooms, with basic facilities. The library consisted of a shelf only and long corridor was being used as a computer lab, with eight desktops connected to internet.

He found most of his classmates were more interested in finding a job, rather than studying. Their discussions were about immigration matters and employment, instead of academic talks. They did not look very serious in their studies. They were just coming to the college for a piece of paper, which could prolong their stay in the UK. It was compulsory for students to attend the college at least twice a week.

He wondered why the local students did not come to these types of colleges. Why were they only for international students? He reached the conclusion that such colleges provided an easy route to enter into the UK on student visas. Most of them were just the homes of fake students. That was the reason such educational institutions in the UK had no attraction for local students.

Whatever the environment was, he was trying to do his best in his studies. He knew his father had sold land for his degree. He knew what it meant for his family to sell the land.

He understood well that his uncle was waiting for him to complete his degree, to marry him to his daughter. He did not want to give an opportunity for his aunty or cousins to accuse him of not being well educated. These things were forcing him to work hard.

The letter from Tanzeela, the hatred of his aunty, the fleeing of Nabeela, his accidental engagement, the expectations of his uncle, his last meeting with Tanzeela, the thought of his sold land and his future dreams, were all the motives behind his hard-work.

Although he was not satisfied with his college but it was a mean for him to reach his targets. He was behaving in a totally different way, from the other students. He came to the college four days a week, with full preparations like a school child. He attended all the lectures, took notes and met with the teachers after the classes to ask them more questions; to clarify the things, which confused him in his studies. After he finished his college he went to the local library and spent several hours there, to concentrate on his homework.

He worked three days a week in a supermarket, in the produce department. This new job was very thrilling. He learnt the names of all the vegetables and fruits in English. He was happy with this job because he had a chance to work with his White colleagues. He was improving his language skills day by day. He found his colleagues very helpful. They encouraged him to speak English if he spoke wrongly, they did not mind it and guided him to speak correctly. If he had to face a customer enquiry, a colleague came to help him. He was feeling very confident.

He was learning practical language skills, which he could not learn at any institution. He realised that the best way to improve English was to work with native speakers. He thought that the supermarkets were the best source of learning, for the newcomers to the UK.

Sometimes, he had to face very awkward situation at work. One day, he was sitting in the canteen, among some of his female colleagues. One of them asked him, "Do you have a girlfriend?"

"No," he said. He had come to know what the word 'girlfriend' meant here.

"Do you have a boyfriend then?" she asked him again.

He did not know yet about this term. He thought she was asking about his male friends.

"Yes, I have many boy friends," he said confidently.

"What?" they were all surprised at his reply.

"Are you a gay?" the other one asked him.

He was completely unaware of the meaning of 'gay'. He had never heard this word before in his life. He realised that he had spoken something wrong, from their expressions.

"Sorry, I could not understand you?" he said in puzzlement.

"I mean, do you sleep with boys?" she explained him.

"No, I have my own separate room in the house," he said hastily.

They all laughed madly and left him in total confusion. When he came back home, he told this story to his housemates and they laughed a lot. They explained to him what the girls actually had asked him and he was very ashamed. The next day at work he went to them, one by one, and cleared the position of his sexuality. The girls laughed again at his innocence.

Once, he was working early in the morning. A customer asked him where she could find the meringue shells. He could not understand what she had asked for. He said, "I'll find for you." There were none of his colleagues around to help him. He was going one aisle to other, blindly. She was looking on astonishingly at him, when he went to shampoo aisle, to find the meringue shells. He wanted her to move away and to ask someone else but she was still standing there. He supposed she might have asked Michele, one of his colleagues as he could only pick the last sound 'shells'. After wandering through the aisles he came back. He gave her a big smile, as he was trained to when serving the customers and said with confidence, "Sorry, she is not working today." She raised her eyebrows and said surprisingly, "Who is not working today?" He realised that was not the answer to her question but he had no other option than to say, "Michele is not working today."

"Who is Michele? I did not ask about her," she said surprised.

He got nervous and he could not understand what she was muttering, when she walked towards the customer service desk to seek help.

This was not the only incident he faced. He was facing this kind of situation while working on the shop floor, everyday.

Most of time, when he could not pick up the accent, he went to another colleague to ask them to help the customer. He learnt new things each day.

It was not an easy job. He had to pull heavy pallets of vegetables and fruits, from the warehouse to shop floor and fill the empty shelves under a time pressure. He had never helped his father in the fields, but here he was doing heavy work. He thought about those poor shopkeepers in his village, when they went to the city at dawn to bring vegetables and sell them in their shops. He realised the hard work of those cart men, who load and unload heavy sacks of potatoes. He thought to himself that he was like a cart man, who was using pallets and pumps not the donkeys to carry vegetables, not for a street shop but for a supermarket. He was a modern labourer, wearing a neat and clean coloured uniform with his name badge 'Kamal', but he was not sensing any difference between a cart man and himself. The only difference was the place and the tools, but the work was the same. When he trailed huge cages, with his full force he felt like a donkey on the front of a cart.

This is human nature, when you have aims, goals or a lack of things in life you really work hard to reach them.

"The people who live a dream life are not productive. This world is for practical people, not for the idle," he thought, while pulling a heavy pallet of potatoes.

Kamal was showing his dedication and persistence to reach his goals in the UK.

****

His housemates were really impressed by him. They did not think he could be so sedulous. Arsalan told the stories of his hard work to his housemates because they both worked in the same company.

"If we work so diligently in our country, we can have a better life there," Zaman said.

"We run after dreams and come to the UK. Kamal's dream is to get a degree and marry his cousin; you want to apply for

HSMP visa and I want to become a barrister. We are all killing ourselves for our dreams, but dreams seldom come true," Arsalan said intensely.

"I went to the solicitor to consult him about my HSMP. He told me that I had to show more than thirty five thousands pounds in my account, for one year, according to the new rules. I hardly earn one thousand pounds per month, how could I arrange such a huge amount?" Zaman was depressed.

"Don't worry there is a solution for every thing. The three of us will put one thousand into your account every month. You just need to show the transactions not the savings. I know one accountant who will help by showing you a self-employed. This is not a big deal, everyone doing the same thing. Only those who earn more than forty thousand pounds, annually, have the executive jobs in this country, not people like us. It will cost you around three thousands pounds to get a HSMP visa," Arsalan gave him a solution.

"What would you do after your post study work visa finished?" Zaman asked him.

"I am planning to get married to any European girl. I have already talked to someone about it. I am arranging to save five thousands pounds for this purpose," Arsalan said.

"Will it be a real marriage?" Zaman asked.

"No, just a paper marriage," he said.

"But five thousands pounds is lot of money!" Zaman said.

"If you get a five year spouse visa, for that money, then it is not a bad deal," he said.

"Why don't you think to apply for a HSMP?" Zaman insisted.

"It is even expensive and risky too. You spend about three thousand pounds in accountant and solicitor fees and get just a two year visa and then you will have to spend the same amount to get an extension. There are lot of headaches and paper work, which I can't take," he said.

"There is the same risk in the paper marriage, isn't it?" Zaman said.

"No risk man, the European girls who are involved in this business have poor back grounds. They need money and five thousands pounds is a big amount to them. They don't give you any trouble, after you get visa, usually they go back to their countries," he said.

"Why you don't think about a genuine marriage instead?" Zaman asked him.

"Who will marry us here? It is very hard these days. The English or British born Asian girls don't trust us. They think we want to marry them for the British passport," he said.

"You can prove to someone your sincerity and love," Zaman said.

"They don't even give us chance to prove it. They avoid us like a prohibited object," he said.

"You should be able to get any Pakistani girl," Zaman said.

"I tell you my personal experience the British born Pakistani girls seldom go out with students like us," he said.

"I don't believe it. It could be your personal experience but it does not happen all the time. I know one of my friends has good friendships with such girls," Zaman argued.

"I bet you, he would be a professional or a very rich person," he said.

"Yes, he is doing a good job," Zaman said.

"I told you that they would not date labourers like us who are doing menial works and have no good career prospects," he said.

Asif entered the house. He seemed to be very upset and down that day. He did not want to talk to anyone and was engaged in heating his meal. He listened to his friends' discussion, about the curtailing of working hours for students and subsequent problems".

"You look very sad today. What is wrong with you," Zaman asked him.

"Today, I saw a student begging on the high street. He told me that he came here one year ago but could not find a job. He borrowed some money from a man back home, on 20% interest rate to afford to live in the UK. The man was demanding his money back, with interest, and threatening his parents. He had no other option than to beg," Asif told them.

"That is a real tragedy," Arsalan said with grief.

"The point based system is an easy route to enter into the UK on student visa. The agents help them maintain their bank statement and give them a false picture of the job market. The desperate poor people come here, by borrowing huge amount, with hope they will earn lot of money in England but the reality is totally different," Zaman said.

"If the situation remains the same, I tell you today, those students who come to the UK with purpose of earning money will be soon begging, committing suicide in depression or involving in criminal activities to cover their losses" Asif said.

"You are right, I totally agree with you," Arsalan said.

"The government should introduce an effective policy, to stop the misuse of student visa entry into the UK. The NGOs and educational bodies should also spread awareness in other countries to discourage fake students and their agents", Asif said.

"To be honest, we can not blame the government, we are all cheating the system one way or another for our own benefit," Arsalan said finally.

"What can we do? We are forced by our needs to cheat the system. We are not doing this happily," Zaman said.

"As long as the world remains divided, between the very rich and the very poor, this problem will always be there. If the rich countries want a permanent solution, to their immigration problems, they should help the poor countries to become developed. If you have bread to eat at home, you never have to go out to kill your hunger," Asif said indisputably.

****

Ajay was missing Kamal. He wanted to see him, to know how he was doing. He asked him to come to the London Eye, many times, but he could not make it because of his busy life.

Today, he has promised to meet him after his college. He wanted to tell him that he got the security licence. He was also very interested in listening to his love story. He really enjoyed his poem from their last meeting. He felt the poem fitted him, more than Ajay. He wanted Tanzeela to say to him one day 'Same to you'. He knew well that his engagement with her was an accidental one, but she did not want to break it for sake of her father's honour. He regretted that he had asked her in the hospital to break it.

He knew she did not like him, but she was his fiancée anyway and he wanted to win her heart. He was doing what he could, to improve himself and to become acceptable to her. He had great respect for his uncle, who paid a heavy price, in form of Nabeela's fleeing, to marry him to his daughter. He was determined to meet his uncle's expectations. He wanted to go before him, with a degree and a good job. He wanted to prove to his aunty that she was wrong about him. He intended to show Tanzeela that he had not come to the UK mere to marry her but to make his life, a respectable life where he could give her all the matrimonial happiness. He wished to see his younger sisters and brother well educated. He yearned to give a wealthy life to his parents. Most of all, he had a strong desire to find Tanzeela. He wanted, again, to listen to that poem, from Ajay.

This is a human instinct, when you love someone you want a response. You remain restless until you get it. The happiest day of your life is when your beloved says to you, 'I love you too'. You forget all the troubles and pains you carried after your darling.

The both friends are still waiting for this day to come to their lives.

He went to London Eye to see Ajay according to the set plans. After the formal conversation, about his studies and work, he asked him to narrate that poem for him once again.

"Ajay, love is very painful without expression," he said after listening to it.

"You are right Kamal," he said with a deep sigh.

"OK, tell me why Preya was so changed when she came back to work?" Kamal continued his questions.

"I asked her about the guy once she mentioned to me and she told me that was over then. I asked her the reason and she said that her parents had not agreed with her."

"She left him in obedience of her parents?!" Kamal asked surprisingly.

"I told you, she was purely a domestic girl; fully submissive to her parents."

Kamal's mind was spinning around Nabeela, who did not care about her parents and left the house to marry a person of her own choice.

"You know Kamal, she told me about it in such an innocent way. I wanted to go to her house to sit at her parents' feet, to beg them to give her what she wanted but we are all bounded to some limitations in life."

"I think that was the reason she went quiet and calm," Kamal said.

"Yes, a person breaks when expectations are shattered."

"Her obedience to her parents only increased my love and respect for her. I loved her more than ever before."

"One day, she was serving me and I was trying to make her laugh. I said, 'OK, let me find which card I have some money on, to pay. I don't want to be ashamed before you if my card is declined. You might think me a rich person'. She smiled and said, 'I don't care who is rich and who is poor. I look into the person not in his pockets'. Her words still echo in my ears."

"When she told me about the boy she wished to marry, I asked her if he was handsome and she said, 'I don't look at faces, I look into hearts'. See how positive she was! Any sensible boy in this world would love to marry her."

Ajay continued.

"She looked normal, but her real smile had finished and it hurt me. I tried to make her happy by my jokes and funny remarks about work, colleagues and customers. I told her the stories about the girls who were interested in me".

"One day, I asked her that I wanted to go back to my village and marry a simple village girl. She suddenly said, 'will she keep you happy?' for the first time she made me realise that she took care of me and was worried about me. All the time I shared my personal and even pretty things with her, like a child. Once, I told her about a girl at work who was after me like anything, but I did not take any interest in her, and told her that Preya was my only friend in the store. Actually, I told her that I loved Preya and she became jealous of her, but I could never tell Preya that I loved her."

One day she asked me if I had found a girl for me. I said no. I asked her the same question and she said that she was not thinking about any boy that time. I wanted to tell her that I was in deep love with her but I was not brave enough to tell her. I told her that there were some girls who touched my heart but I could not go ahead with them because of some reasons. I said to her that you touched my heart too and I liked you very much. I realized that her face went pale on my claim. I further said that if I went to your parents to ask your hand they would not be agree with me even if I sat at their feet and begged them for you. She smiled and said, 'you make good jokes'. I said that there were so many things related to me regarding you if I told you would get hurt. She just said in response, "Oh is it".

I said, 'Tu Janay Na'----you don't know.

'Tu Janay Na'--- was a line of famous Indian song. 'Kaisay batayian kyu tuj ko chayein—Yara bata na payian---Tu Janay Na', 'how I do I tell you—why I am loving you—but my friend I can't tell you---and you don't know this.

This time she looked very serious and bit nervous. She realized me as if she was taking my words as a joke because she always asked me that I made good jokes.

"I remained sad and worried because Preya was sad. I wanted to hold her hand for ever but every time I tried to express my love to her some unknown fear stopped me. Indirectly, I told her all my feelings about her.

Then things changed, suddenly and unexpectedly. I never thought in my life that it could happen to me. But this is life, it never remains the same. I had some good opportunities for another job but I did not leave because of Preya. I loved her, wanted to see her and talk to her. I did not avail myself of any opportunity, for a better job, just because of her."

"Kamal, humans change in no time. Before I take her hand, kiss it and tell her about my love, one day, I resigned from my job because of Preya", Ajay said with tears in his eyes.

"How did it happen?" Kamal asked, shocked?

"This is the end part of my story. I'll tell you next time," Ajay said and turned his face aside to hide his tears falling like a stream.

He looked at a bird that just flew off the tree and away to an unknown destination. Ajay's eyes followed it until it disappeared.

"Life is like a bird in flight, you don't know in which direction it will move to, in the next moment," he said and kept quiet for long time, staring into space and trying stop tears by pressing his lips in.

****

Tanzeela's mother had come to home from the hospital. She was feeling better but still she was not talking to anyone. The doctors advised that she should have maximum rest and comfort. Both of her daughters were attending upon her constantly. She shed tears in silence, whenever she looked at Tanzeela's ring finger.

"I am happy mum, I am really happy. No one has forced me to wear this ring. I love you, I love my father. I'd do whatever he asked me to do. I'd never leave you," Tanzeela hugged her when she saw tears in her eyes and tried to comfort her.

But Sadiqa knew the feelings of a woman, when she wore an engagement ring against her will just to keep her parents happy. She did not say anything and just shed tears quietly. This ring tortured her more than Tanzeela getting hurt by wearing it. It reminded her of Nabeela. She supported her, but she never thought she would take such a horrendous decision of leaving the house and marrying a black man. She just wanted her to report against this forced marriage to a concerned authority.

Raheem went out only for necessary things. He had restricted himself to his room. It looked like this family had never laughed in life. They only talked to each other when needed. A constant hush had prevailed in the house.

Time never stops. It keeps moving the humans with it. No one is able to bring back past moments. Time always pushes us into the future. This is a natural cycle and we all bound to the nature of time.

Raheem's family was going though this natural process and becoming normal, as the wheel of time kept going. His wife held him responsible for Nabeela's revolt. She was in favour of bringing her home or making good family relations with her. She was a mother and a mother's heart is always soft for her children. Although she was very angry with her, at the same time she had tender feelings for her. She remained worried about her and sometimes phoned her secretly.

Tanzeela hated her more than her father did. She blamed her for her engagement to Kamal. She thought that she was being punished in life because of her. Nabeela tried to talk to her on the phone many times, but she never responded to her.

Raheem did not want to see her in his life. He always said that she had died for him. No one talked about her to his face in the house. She was a banned topic to discuss in front of him, even his wife did not dare to talk to him on this issue.

On the other hand, Nabeela was living a happy life with her husband. She was not ashamed of her decision. Some of her friends, who encouraged her marrying Ibrahim, were appreciating her. They were satisfied with her that, with the passage of time, every thing would be all right.

A husband's love is everything for a girl, after marriage. She forgets about all other things in life. However, Nabeela remained worried about her mother and phoned her occasionally to ask about her well being. She did not want Tanzeela to marry Kamal but she was helpless, as Tanzeela was not ready to listen to her. She was expecting a baby soon and was very happy.

****

It was Eid-ul- Adha—a festival of sacrifice or Greater Eid, the second most important festival in Islamic calendar, when Muslims commemorate the willingness of the Prophet Abraham to sacrifice his son Isma'il, as an act to obedience to God.

The devil tempted Abraham, to disobey God, in the love of his son but he remained committed. As he was about to slaughter his son, God stopped him and gave him a lamb to sacrifice instead. This story is also found in Jewish Torah and the Christian's Old Testament.

Muslims all over the world, who can afford it, sacrifice lamb, sheep, goat, cow or camel as a reminder of Abraham's obedience to Allah. They share out the meat among family, friends and the poor, who each get a third.

There is a tradition, in the rural society, for the groom's family to send meat, money and gifts to the fiancée, as they consider her a family member. The same thing happens at Eid-ul-Fitr, which is celebrated at the end of Ramadan, where sweets are sent instead of meat.

Kamal's mother asked him to give gifts and some money, from their side of the family, to Tanzeela. He bought a golden wrist watch, a dress and put one hundred pounds in a coloured envelope to give to her, from his parents.

His uncle had already asked him to celebrate this festival with them, but he made an excuse to be busy with his friends, during the day time, and promised to come in the evening for a dinner. Actually, he was working, even on Eid day, to reach his goals.

He got up early in the morning, to go to the mosque to offer Eid prayers. He found his house mates, Manzoor and Asif, were going to work while Zaman and Arsalan had not come back yet, from their night shifts. He remembered how he would prepare for Eid with his family in the village. His mother would be busy in cooking; the sisters would be making clothes ready for their father and the brothers. The smell of nice foods would be airing through the house. Everybody used to be in hurry; in taking bath, wearing new clothes and going to the mosque, to find an easy place for prayers.

But here, things were totally different for him. He went to the local mosque. It was full of people. He offered his prayers, but none of them embraced him. He was standing at the mosque door; hundreds of people were coming out. They were hugging and exchanging greetings with known people, but he was like a stranger amongst the crowd. He was looking for any familiar face, to hug and greet, but he could not find a single person to satisfy his hugging and greetings desires.

He recalled the Eid day in his village, when he had to hug hundreds of people after prayers. He was badly missing his family, friends and the people of the village that day. He was remembering; family dinner, sacrificing the cow, distributing the meat and the warm company of his friends, when he was on the bus on his way to work.

He worked during the day and went to his uncle house in the evening. He was feeling guilty, for asking Tanzeela to turn down the engagement. He guessed that he would take the dinner with his uncle, in the same small room where he used to live. He also supposed that Tanzeela, Shakeela and his aunty would not come to see him.

He was surprised, when all of them greeted him in the normal way and they all gathered at the dining table. His aunty and Tanzeela were quiet as usual. They were not wearing special dresses, as women usually do on such festivals. It looked like they had no interest in the celebration.

He found that Tanzeela did not look at him, at all, during the dinner. As the dinner finished they all went to their rooms, apart from his uncle.

It looked to him, as they joined him under the pressure from his uncle and he was very right in his thinking. They greeted and dined with him, to Raheem's satisfaction.

The uncle took him to the sitting room, where they had tea together and talked about routine things.

"You know your aunty spoiled Nabeela. She always supported her against me. Basically, she was a daughter of a *chowkidar.* She has got a poor mentality. This is my personal experience in life, it is always better to get married to a good family."

"Kamal you are a son of Chaudhry and a Chaudhry should get married to a Chaudhry. Tanzeela and you will have a good life because you both belong to a Chaudhry family." Raheem continued,

"I feel proud, when I tell my friends that my son in law is my nephew and doing a master degree in business administration," he kept repeating the same things over and over and Kamal listened to them patiently.

He had to go to college early the next day, so he left after taking tea, without seeing anyone else at home.

Tanzeela threw the watch and dress pack, Kamal brought for her, on the bed, in hatred, with her full force. She opened the envelope and found two fifty pound notes. She immediately decided to give this money to a charity.

"These things have no meaning for me. He cannot win my heart by giving me gifts. I'm wearing his ring to please my father. I'm praying for the day he realises that he is going to tie me in an unnatural relationship and the chapter of Kamal Chaudhry will be closed in my life," her mind was always buzzing with this kind of thinking.

****

Chapter 10

Tanzeela was coming out from her university library, when she saw Nabeela standing at the door, with one of her classmates. She walked towards her warmly but Tanzeela started running in the opposite direction. She ran after her and approached her on the lawn.

"Please Tanzeela, listen to me," she said in uneven breaths.

"I don't want to listen to you; go away," she said, sighing heavily.

Nabeela spread her arms around her and started to cry, emotionally. A sisterly love took over Tanzeela, she also wrapped her arms around her, unintentionally, and wept bitterly, uttering in broken voice, repeatedly, "Please go from here."

"I love you honey," Nabeela said in a quivering tone.

Tanzeela pressed her hard and kept saying, "Please go from here."

"I called you many times but you always rejected my call. I sent you dozens of messages but you never replied to me," she said sadly.

"I don't want to talk to you, please go away; please leave me alone," she said, sobbing.

They both sat on the bench. Nabeela was still holding her hands and patting them gently.

Tanzeela held her ring finger and started looking other side.

Nabeela took it, looked at the ring, pressed her palm and said, "I am sorry Tanzeela, I never thought it would happen to you."

"You should have refused it," she said immediately.

"It wasn't in my control to deny it." Tanzeela revealed.

"Did dad force you?" Nabeela asked.

"He threatened me to kill himself if I refused." she told her.

"Oh my God, it is an emotional black mailing." Nabeela said.

"You left the house on the day of your engagement. The guests were sitting at home. Mum and dad looked like they were dead. I had no other option," she explained the situation to Nabeela.

"But everything has gone back to normal by now, you can refuse it," Nabeela suggested to her.

"Dad is already very disturbed, Mum has just recovered from her illness. I don't want to give them any further tension. This was my fate. I would have to go along with it."

"You are not so misfortunate, darling. I advise you to refuse, unless it is too late for you," she provoked her.

"No, I will never do it. I don't want my parents humiliated again because of me," she showed her respect for the parents.

"I am really ashamed of you. It all happened because of me," Nabeela expressed her sorrows.

"One of us has to sacrifice, anyway, if not Nabeela then Tanzeela, if not Tanzeela then Shakeela. So, I'm going to do this," she said deeply.

"But how will you be happy with him?" Nabeela asked.

"This is not about my happiness, it is about my father's," she said miserably.

"Why do parents sacrifice their daughters for the sake of their own honour?" Nabeela said angrily.

"This happens in Asian families. They want to live here, in pursuit of a wealthy life but they don't let their children adopt modern culture. This is called a cultural clash and we are victims of it," Tanzeela said.

"If I knew it would happen to you, I would never have left the house," she said and repented.

"There is no use to ask forgiveness now. Live your life happily and let me live my life as it is," Tanzeela said.

"I've talked to my boss, about a job for you. I know you are going to finish university soon," she said.

"No, thanks, I don't need your help. I'd find job for myself." Tanzeela said.

"Are you still angry with me?" she asked.

"I am not angry with you. I am angry with my destiny," she looked at her wrist watch and said, "Sorry Nabeela, I have to attend my next lecture, I must go now."

Nabeela wanted to talk to her but she was not interested. She was feeling suffocation in her presence.

She walked to the lecture room bowing her head in deep thought leaving Nabeela ashamed and repented. Nabeela kept looking at her until she disappeared from the scene.

****

Rehmat Chaudhry remained worried about his son, after Nabeela refused to marry Kamal and he asked him for more money for his education. He had a fear that Tanzeela would also do the same thing and all of his investments would go to waste. He wanted his son to settle down, in the UK and become a rich person like his younger brother, Raheem. He knew that marriage could secure his son's immigration status over there. He visualised that if Tanzeela and Kamal both earn good money, he could buy a large piece of land in the village and become a big Chaudhry. He also had a strong desire to contest the next local election.

Someone told him that his brother had number of properties in London. He imagined that all of his brother's property would equally be distributed amongst his daughters and Tanzeela would get a big share too. He would make Tanzeela and Kamal agree to sell some property, in London, and buy huge piece of land in the village.

He pictured himself, a big landlord of the area, in the future in light of that marriage. That was another reason he sold his property, for Kamal's education to make his wedding possible.

On the other hand, his brother, Raheem, had the same kind of thinking. He did not want to transfer his property out of family. He had persuaded him to send Kamal to the UK, so that he could marry one of his daughter's. He was also thinking of marrying Shakeela to Kamal's younger brother, but first he wanted Tanzeela's wedding to Kamal to be successful, so that he could easily clothe his plans.

Both brothers had a hidden agenda, in their minds, and they were using their children as a tool to reach their goals.

In the village, the popularity of this family had increased after the engagement ceremony and the selling of land. The people thought that Kamal studying at Oxford and his father was investing lot of money on him.

Rehmat and his family had become very snobbish in the village. They told false stories about Kamal's life in the UK. He told the people that he was paying fifty thousands rupees per month, for his accommodation only. He spent one hundred thousand rupees on his clothes this month and so on.

They also told false stories about his friendships, with English people and high profile students at university, to impress the poor people in the village. His mother, always, makes mountains out of a molehill. She would tell the women that there was a competition, among his cousins, to marry him and he selected Tanzeela. She sketched her out to be like a princess and praised her son like a prince.

Each mother, in the village, wished her children to be like Kamal and Tanzeela. Every young person dreamt a life like

Kamal's. The fathers were ready to sell, even their kidneys, to send their adults to the UK. Every young person, who had some education, was now crazy to go to England. They were zealously working on how to get student visas, to reach the dream land. They were gathering resources, by selling their ornaments, cattle and land to meet the heavy expenses for their visa mission.

****

Kamal's health had deteriorated, by working beyond his limits. He was looking very skinny. He had no proper routine of eating and sleeping. His life was limited to the college, library and the supermarket, where he was working. His housemates only saw him at home when it was his turn to cook and clean.

He was filling his daily dairy with his feelings, regarding life in the UK and his future dreams. He did not go out for recreation and he was not having any hobby. He was just killing himself in order to get his MBA degree, to show to his uncle's family and prove to them that he was a successful person.

Ajay, his only close friend in London, was worried about him. He forced him to spare some time for an outing. One day, he went to his college and took him to central London, for some fun. They wandered for hours, through the busy and colourful streets of London.

Finally, he took him to his most favourite place, the London Eye. Ajay was always lost somewhere, whenever he saw the running waves of the River Thames. Kamal wanted to know the end of his love story.

"What did Preya do to you that made you to leave your job?" Kamal asked him, while walking along the bank.

He looked towards the dark black clouds, arising from the eastern horizon, and said, "Preya would come for a short period and then go. She disappeared and did not keep any touch with me. I always waited for her, fanatically. I had a hope to find her, after she told me that she had broken-up with the guy she was in love with. This time I have decided to express my feelings to her openly. I've been in love with her for the last four years. Her love was making me crazy. I was waiting for her impatiently.

One early morning, the weather was chilly, the sky was covered with black clouds, and it was drizzling, she came to work. I was standing on her way in the store, she came close to me, putting her hands in her fleece pockets, but unexpectedly, she did not hug me or take my hand, as she used to do. I gave her my hand; she shook it half-heartedly, without giving any warm expression."

He stopped walking, held his back against the river wall, closed his arms around his chest in his unique style and said, "Kamal, I had heard about breaking of hearts, but I had experienced it for the first time in my life. It was really very painful. I felt like there was nothing around me. It looked like all the colours had faded away and the people walking around me were robots not human beings. I was not able to hear anything, it was like someone had put copper into my ears. The love, feelings and emotions that I had bred for her, in four years, were badly wounded, I felt like the earth had stopped moving and I was not a man, but a statue."

"But you know this love is cruel. I finished work, did some unwanted shopping and went to her to be serviced. She served me in a formal way, taking her eyes off me. The next day, when she saw me, she said that she was not expecting me to be there. Then she started ignoring me. I was forced, by my heart, to go close to her but she showed me a cold attitude. Every time, she was uncaring toward me, it hurt me more than before."

"She made me realise that she felt uneasy and disturbed in my presence. If I passed by her she got busy in other things, just to avoid making eye contact with me."

"I faced this situation for one month, but there was no change in her behaviour. Each time, she looked distant and was more reserved towards me. She had no idea how much I loved her and to what extent I was being hurt. I was getting mad under this situation. I lost my interest in work and even in my life. I tolerated every hardship in this country, bravely, but I proved to be very weak before her and could not face her stony attitude with me. Whenever I had a chance to go near her I told her about my intention of leaving job for some other reasons but I could not tell her that her icy impressions for me were tormenting me. Eventually, I left my job."

"Did you ask her the reason for her unkind attitude?" Kamal asked him.

"She brought me down so quickly, I could never ask her this question," he said.

"What do you think what was the reason?" Kamal asked.

"I think she had come to know that I was in love with her and she was doing this to discourage me, or simply to get rid of me," he said.

"You told me that she was purely a domestic girl, fully obedient to her parents, she might be doing this intentionally, to give you a message that what were you thinking would not ever happen," Kamal made a guess.

"She was very sensitive, she fell in love with someone and her parents did not allow her to marry him. She could not rebel against them and left it over to them, being a dignified daughter. It is very hard for sensitive people to love again in life. I think she lost her interest in boys," Ajay said.

"If she wanted to marry according to her parents' wishes then she was right not to be frank with boys," Kamal said.

"But she could remain my good friend. I wasn't creating any problem for her. She punished me for unknown things," he said.

"You loved her but she did not ever love you. She might think of you as just a friend but you fell in love with her. It was your fault not hers," Kamal argued.

"I fell in love with her at the very first sight. It was beyond my control what I could do?" he replied.

"She knew her parents would never accept you. I think she did right thing to you. She wanted you to forget about her and make your own life with someone else," Kamal said.

"Whatever was the reason I did not deserve such hurting treatment," he insisted. I simply loved her and still loving her and will love her through out my life. She is my real and natural love. My love is true for her and one day I will find my love. That is my belief, a firm belief. One day she will come to me and say, 'SAME TO YOU', Ajay had become rather emotional.

The clouds had covered the sky completely. A cold wind was blowing. It was becoming hard for them to stay there. They were tired, as they roamed around the town for hours.

Kamal was feeling sorry, for the tragic end of his friend's love story and surprised on his self-belief of finding her. Ajay yet believed that one day he would find Preya.

Still, one question was unanswered, what was the link of the River Thames with this story? Why would he come to this place so frequently? Why did he recall his past memories only when he was here? Why did he become so sad, while looking into the deep waters?

He wanted to know about it in his next meeting with Ajay.

****

Kamal was facing new challenges every day. The UK boarder agency had visited his college and there was a gossip that the college had been degraded because the agency had found some scams there. The students were agitated, but the administration convinced them there was nothing wrong. They were constantly keeping an eye on their college name, among the Tier 4 institutions, which had approved by the boarder agency.

One morning when Kamal reached there, he found students standing in groups in the corridor and some others bending over computers to make sure the news was true. The college's name had been removed from the list of sponsored institutions, by the boarder agency. The key administration had disappeared, and students were angry, arguing with the other staff. They were telling the students that the principal was in a meeting with the concerned authorities, to clarify things. The office staffs were trying to control the situation but the anarchy was getting worse.

They were telling their friends, on the phones, about the college's degradation. They were all rushing to talk to them about this news. Kamal saw a large number of people, who he had never seen before in the college. They were all the students who rarely came to attend the classes. There was total mayhem. No one knew what was actually going on. Some were demanding their fees back and others were just protesting noisily.

By the afternoon, the whole building was crowded with students. They were waiting for the principal to arrive with some good news, but he did not turn up till the evening.

Kamal was equally worried, about this situation, because he had deposited his course fee in full in advance. Seven thousands pounds was not a small amount for him. His father had sold his land, to pay his fees. He had already lost three thousands pounds to his previous college. He could not afford to lose more money.

He came back home, with a hope that the next day everything would be all right. He could not sleep well the whole night. Some terrifying thoughts were coming across his mind but he was forcing himself not to think about them. He was satisfying himself, on the bed, that everything would be fine.

The next day, he was not supposed to go to college but his anxiety to know the situation dragged him there. He saw a horde of students, leaping each other's shoulders to read something on the main door of the college. His heart was beating hard. He was not going to believe what he heard from the other students; he wanted to confirm it by himself. Each word on the notice sheet was hitting his heart, and mind, like an arrow.

"This college has been found to have many irregularities, contrary to the immigration polices of the UK border agency. An inquiry has been launched to investigate the things. Thus the college is closed till further notice."

The notice was stamped and signed by the UK border agency.

He was feeling like a stamp had been put on his dreams, ambitions and targets and even on his luck. He was aghast and stood there, speechless, for long time, looking at the people around him in astonishment.

He was walking along the road, without knowing where he was going, like a traveller who forgot his route in the desert or like a child who had gotten lost on his way back home.

The largest loss in this world is the loss of hope. He was facing this loss. It was not only the loss of ten thousands pounds, that he had drowned in bogus colleges so far, but the loss of his aspirations, objectives and goals. The loss of his family's dreams, his uncle's expectations, and, above all, the fear of losing Tanzeela was making him mad.

He was feeling tired and defeated. He was confused about what to think, what not to think. He kept walking for hours and hours in frustration.

He knew he could not get any more money from his family. He had no energy to repeat the same tiring exercise of studying and working-hard. Dozens of questions were coming across his head and he had no answer, for any of them.

He supposed to work in the evening, but he had no interest in working. He phoned his manager to make an excuse of sickness.

One question was striking his mind, over and over, whether he would be able to get his fee back from the college, or transfer his course to another institution. This was the only hope left for him.

He arrived home and asked his housemates about it. They told him that it had happened to some of their friends already, they did not get their fees back. The Home Office wrote them a letter to get admission to another recognised college otherwise their visas would be cancelled. He got more stressed after hearing that.

He wanted to go to the Home Office the next day to get the exact information about it. He did not sleep the whole night. He wondered what his fault was. He was a genuine student, who was studying hard and going to the college regularly. When he took admission to the college, it was among the approved Tier 4 institutions. It was not his fault, so why was he being punished for others' frauds? Why was there no policy to protect the authentic students, studying in such colleges? Why did the border agency not distinguish between the real and the fake students, whilst they decided to close this college? Why did they not think about those students who had paid thousands of pounds in fees to the institution? Why were these colleges not bound by the law to refund the fees?

One of his housemates told him that this was a very beneficial business those days in the UK. The parties open a college, get it approved by the border agency, recruit hundreds of international students, and collect fees in the millions, by the end of year they get them closed intentionally, because they know that there is no law, which would force them to refund the fees paid by students. The next day, they open another college, with a different name, repeat the same thing and make millions every year.

He thought out, what he would say to his family, uncle and cousins, especially Tanzeela. How could he make his dreams come true? He was going crazy, thinking about all of those things.

He went to the Home Office for his satisfaction. He argued, about the same stuff, at the reception but nothing happened. They took a statement from him, regarding this matter.

He thought about Ajay, he wanted to discuss his new problem

with him. Ajay was very informative, about immigration things and colleges in London. He once again had to go to the London Eye, to see him.

"Forget about Preya, the River Thames and its running waves; just tell me what I should do now. My mind is going to burst," he said, in absolute anxiety.

"This is a big problem. Who asked you to deposit seven thousand pounds in advance? You stupid guy!" Ajay denounced him.

"You sent me this college. I wanted to pay my fees in advance, to get some discount. I never thought it would be closed," he said, desperately.

"I asked you stay with the previous college. You just have to pay two thousand pounds extra to get an extension for the next fifteen months. You wanted to do an MBA as early as possible, to prove to your cousins that you were a successful person. You wanted to become equal to Tanzeela, in education. You did not realise that there was a big difference between them and us. They are home students, they go to good universities and colleges, the government helps them, their parents help them, they don't need to pay rent, and they don't need to do rubbish jobs like we do. They get better jobs because they were born here. They can speak the native language; they know the system, the culture, better than we do."

"You wanted to compete with them, by studying in bogus and low profile institutions. You are an idiot, an absolute idiot," he said angrily, but with sympathy.

"Ajay *bhai*, I got tired. I am just sick of all these things," Kamal said forlornly.

"You just need a piece of paper, not a degree, to satisfy your uncle's family, forget about competing with them. I'll arrange it for you, just show it to them and get married and make your life," he said intensely.

"I did not want that. I wanted to study, working-hard to prove to them that I'd be a successful person in life," he said, innocently. "You have seen the results of studying in sub standard colleges. What did you get?" Ajay was upset, too, at his loss.

"I did not know about these things, when I was in Pakistan. I had dreams and ambitions. I did not even imagine in my dreams what had happened to me so far."

"We all have the same kind of thinking, when we apply for visas, anyway forget about it tell me how much money do you have on you?"

"I have got nothing. I just have a credit card, of twenty five hundred pounds, which my bank gave me recently," Kamal told him.

"OK its fine. I have an overdraft of one thousand pounds. We can manage it. I know a person who will buy us a post graduate diploma for two thousands pounds, from a college. We will pay just fifteen hundred more, to the same college, and only submit a dissertation to get an MBA degree from its affiliated university. You need not to worry about the dissertation, I know someone who will do it for us for three hundred pounds. You've almost completed one year, in the UK. You will get your degree in three months. You can proudly invite your uncle's family to your graduation ceremony," Ajay explained to him the best possible option.

"I did not want to get my degree this way but I can't help it now," Kamal said.

"If the system cheats you, then you have the right to cheat the system," Ajay said.

"The system does not cheat; there are some people who cheat us." Kamal responded.

"You know Kamal, I would just spend two hundred pounds to get a diploma, for a new extension in visa, before the introduction of the Tier 4 system. Now that things have changed, you have to pay out three to four thousand pounds, every year, to maintain your student status in this country. The government is trying to stop fake colleges and fake students. They want to control the net immigration. The economy is not able to accommodate more people. The government wants only those immigrants who can bring financial benefits, not those who take the jobs of the native people." Ajay answered.

"But how can the government get benefit-addicted people to work, replacing the hard working work force in form of students?" Kamal kept asking questions.

"It will take years to change the state of mind of benefit-addicted people. The government has no solid policy, or magic stick, to bring people back to work, in days or months. But on the other hand, it is acting briskly to cut the number of immigrants. This will be a big disaster for economy, in the future." Ajay had the answer.

"You can do full time work now. My security company is recruiting new staff these days. You already have a security badge; apply for this job, I hope you will get it. But continue with your supermarket job, do twenty hours there and for the rest of the days do the security job."

"You are right Ajay; I have to cover my losses by doing the maximum work I can."

"You can easily earn more than thousand pounds each month," he told him.

"You mean, I can earn back my money just in one year." Kamal asked.

"You could earn more than you lost." Ajay told him.

"Thank you Ajay *bhai*, you have always been very helpful to me. Sometimes, I think that if I hadn't have met you, what would have been happened to me by now. You are a super star," he thanked him.

Circumstances change humans. Kamal was standing among

those who wanted to reach their goals hook or by crook. He was doing two jobs and making good money. His only aim was to make money. He forgot about colleges and studies. He started sending money, to his family, on monthly basis. They were becoming richer day by day. They were showing off the money and their riches to the poor villagers, to become prominent.

He followed Ajay's advice and got his MBA degree. His family was over the moon with this news. His uncle was telling his wife and daughters, every second hour, about his degree. His cousins wondered, how had he got his degree in just fifteen months when he had told them that it would take him two and half years?

The uncle invited him many times to dinner but Kamal was very busy, working his two jobs.

He invited his uncle's family to his graduation ceremony but, as usual, no one turned up except Raheem. He sent pictures of his graduation ceremony to his family, who were showing them to every one in the village. The story of Kamal's MBA degree made him a hero in the village. His father told everyone that he was doing a managerial job, for a big firm in London. The intensity of the young people to go to the UK, had increased and was now higher than it had ever been before.

Both families were planning an excellent wedding ceremony for Kamal and Tanzeela. His mother was insisting that they have a wedding ceremony in the village, while his uncle wanted it in London.

Tanzeela had started a job in a bank. She had no interest in Kamal or his success. She was quiet, just because of her father. Her mother was not interfering in anything. She had a bad experience, with Nabeela, so she was just a silent spectator in the house. Shakeela does not take interest in family affairs. She always remains busy on computer and most of her time spent on the 'Facebook' making new friends.

Just as one success can give you all in life, in the same way, one incident can take every thing from you. One occurrence alters humans, their ideas and their views. Your life is always at one happening; just one incident can change the whole course of your life.

Something same happened with Kamal and just one confrontation with Tanzeela changed his life completely and everything turned the other way round.

****

Chapter 11

Rehmat, his wife and children were gathered for dinner. They were chalking out a plan for Kamal's wedding.

"We will hold the *'Drum sitting'* ceremony for ten days," Kamal's sisters said.

Drum sitting is purely a woman's ceremony. Both the groom's and bride's families celebrate it, at night time, for at least one week prior to the main wedding event. A female, from the drum beating family in the village, sings bridal songs to the beat of drum whilst sitting among the women and receives lot of money in form of *vails*. The surrounding women clap and sing, rhythmically, with her. The young girls prepare special wedding songs, for this occasion, and compete with one another.

On the very first day, the groom's family gives molasses, sugar or sweets to the participants, in a measured quantity. If someone is not able to come on the first day, then their share is reserved for the next day and it has to be made sure that everyone one gets it.

"We will give out sweets, not treacle or sugar," Rehmat's wife said.

"Mother is right; treacle and sugar are given by poor people. Our brother is in the UK, we will distribute *Laddoun*--- a special yellow coloured costly sweet in a round shape," the elder daughter said.

"Nazim, is the closest friend of Kamal's; he already asked me if he would be his *Sambhala*," their son said.

Sambhala is usually a close friend of the groom, who accompanies him during the whole event. His role is very important. The groom remains quiet all the time, *Sambhala* speaks on his behalf, especially at bride's house. The bride's cousins and friends tease and make fun of the groom by performing different customs and it is the *Sambhala* who defends him. If the bride has a younger sister, she offers a glass of milk, wrapped in a colourful paper, to the groom and negotiates a large amount for it. The *Sambhala's* job is to get good bargain and make her agree to less money. In the same way, there are number of customs like this, where he has to protect the groom.

"Nazim is a clever guy and also a bosom friend of Kamal's. He will be right for this job," Rehmat approved of him.

"I'm anxiously waiting for the day when I'll carry my son's *Ghrowly*," his wife said.

Ghrowly is a very special custom at weddings. A pitcher, full of water, is wrapped with colourful papers, usually used to make kites. All the women, in the village, are invited to celebrate this custom. They all gather, at groom's house, wearing bright dresses. The drum beaters are called to beat the drums. The women of the groom's family carry this pitcher, one by one. At the end, the mother of the groom carries it and leads all the women to the Miran Shah Shrine. The close female relatives of the groom perform the *Luddi* at the Shrine. They pour the pitcher's water on to the Shrine, when they finish this ceremony.

"You should make your brother to bring Tanzeela here. I want to celebrate my son's wedding in the village," his wife insisted.

"Don't worry, I'll make him agree," Rehmat satisfied her.

"I'll demand one lakh rupees from Kamal, on his *Sehra Bandi*," his younger daughter said.

Sehra Bandi is the main custom at weddings, when a garland is worn, on the forehead, by the groom. Usually, a younger sister of the groom fixes the garlands, made of different golden coloured stuffs and fresh flowers, around his head and demands money for it. There is no bargain on this occasion and the sisters are paid whatever they ask for. The sisters ask him to salute them after *Sehra Bandi*, once he salutes, all the money is given back to him and if there is a married elder sister, she gives him some extra in return.

This is very heart touching custom. This is the moment that the sisters wait for a long time to see, garlands on their brothers' foreheads. They can't keep control of their feelings and shed tears in happiness. If their parents, both or one of them, are not in this world they are specially remembered on this occasion. The groom's family shed tears by recalling them. They all hug the groom emotionally, kiss his garlands and howl. This is solely a family ceremony, within the house. If the groom is an orphan, then the sensitive and weak- hearted relatives avoid attending this function.

After *Sehra Bandi*, the groom comes out the house and sits in open place, where his friends and other invited people, called *Barati*, put garlands on him, which are threaded with money and flowers and also give him some cash called *Naindra* or *Bhaji*. A person is sitting with the groom, to write the amount down against each name. When the groom's family go to their wedding ceremonies, they pay them back and add some extra.

After *Sehra Bandi*, the *Barat*---wedding procession, leaves for bride's house, with drums beating. The *Barati* performs *bhanghra*—a typical Punjabi dance, in front of bride house. In the past, the groom would go to take his bride by riding a horse but these days a decorated car is used, instead of a carthorse.

Rehmat's family keeps discussing Kamal's marriage for a long time and finalise all the arrangements verbally.

****

Although Kamal got his MBA degree, he was guilty cautious because of the way he earned it. His uncle always asked him about his job hunting activities, he told him a different story every time, about his efforts in searching a good job. Sometimes, he lied about going for interviews at various banks and firms. His uncle wanted him to get a good job, as early as possible so that he could marry him to his daughter. Unlike Nabeela, he was not forcing Tanzeela to get married Kamal before he settled down in life, instead he was asking Kamal to find a good job.

Two of his housemates had gotten good masters degrees from recognised universities but could not find a suitable job. They told him about their long tiring efforts to secure a job, in their relevant fields but all in vain and now they were working as security guards or sales assistant in supermarkets.

He used to think that he would not be so unlucky in finding a job, like his housemates. He believed in his hard-work and fortune but after he received his degree, by unfair means, he lost interest in searching for a respectable job. He had accepted the reality and worked as a security guard and also as a sales assistant on a part time basis.

He had not seen Ajay for long time. He wanted to see him to find out the answer of his long- running question, what was the link between his love story and the River Thames. He fixed a meeting with him and went to the London Eye.

"Ajay, please tell me today what is so special about here?" he asked him after formal conversation.

Ajay stood along the river wall, looking down into the deep waters, as he spent most of his time in this position whenever he came over here. He kept quiet for short time and then said, "The very first day I saw Preya, at work, and she touched my heart at first glance. For the first time in my life, I felt love for some girl.

188

Every young man has a picture, in his mind, of his ideal girl. The features I had in my mind, I saw in her. She was my ideal girl, by all definitions. I started loving her, at first sight and it was a natural love. I came home and wrote each word she said to me. Later on, it became my routine, I used to write down all her conversations with me words by words and all the texts she sent me, our telephonic talks that just happened once, our chatting on the internet, which happened only five times in four years and the e-mails she sent me, merely two times. I recorded each and every moment with her, even how many times I saw her with loose or tied hair, with uniform or causal dress and how much time I spent with her. I even kept a record of, which part of the day or night I met her at work, and how many times I saw her in life. You know even I counted all the alphabets, smiley, punctuations she used in her texts, emails and internet chatting. How many times she hugged me, shook my hand or walked with me on the shop floor. At the end, how many times she ignored me. Each time I saw her I wrote my feelings about her. I did this till my last day at work." Ajay continued.

"After I left my job, I invited her to a dinner to give her this diary because it was full of her memories. It gave me pain, all the time whenever I had a look at it. I wanted to get rid of it by giving it back to her but she did not come to my invitation." he said.

"Did you ever tell her about this diary?" Kamal asked him.

"No, I had never mentioned it before," he replied

"Did you tell her, when you invited her?" Kamal further asked.

"No, I wanted to give it to her, as a surprised gift," he answered.

"You told me that she started ignoring you, then how could you expect her to come at your invitation." Kamal asked.

"I thought, once we had a good time and she knew that I was leaving so she might turn up."

"Did you tell her about it later on?" Kamal asked him.

"Yes, I messaged her that I only wanted her to come, just to give her this diary." Ajay answered.

"What was her reaction?" Kamal again asked.

"She replied to me, 'Wooow!!! That's very surprising! Why would you do that, *pagil* (mad)? No one has ever studied me like that before; no one has ever observed me like that!!" Ajay revealed.

"What did you say to her?" Kamal asked.

"I replied, that I was impressed by her, at my very first sight of her, and it was very natural and beyond my control. I could not help after that." he replied.

"What was her response then?" Kamal continued with his questions.

"Aww bless you Ajay! Hug!" that was her last message to me, the final message of this story, he said miserably.

"What happened after that?" Kamal asked again.

"Nothing, the story finished with her last text." Ajay told him.

"But what is the link between this story and the River Thames?" Kamal wanted to know.

"I waited for few weeks but she never asked me for the diary. I realized that it had no importance for her. Every night I read a part of it before I went to the bed and lost in Preya's memories. I could not sleep for hours and eventually I fell in insomnia. I did not go to the doctor because I knew the reason for this disease. This diary made me sick. At one stage I felt that I would die if I remain in this condition for long time. There was only one solution to come out of this disturbance and that was to get rid of the diary. I wanted to burn it but every time I tried, some unexplained feeling stopped me. One day I wrapped it in a red velvet cloth and threw it into this river." Ajay exposed.

"I thought I could forget Preya by doing that but it was not like that. Her memories still chase me, wherever I go. As much as I try to forget her, she comes to my mind more powerfully. I threw the diary into the river but I could never throw her out of my mind and heart", he continued.

"I've handed over my memories of her, to the waves of this river. I come here to share with them my past. They know what was in it. My reminiscences are buried under the water. I come here, as a pilgrimage, to visit the River Thames and its running waves" he said sacredly.

Kamal saw a wave of thick water floating on the corner of his eyes. He was madly repeating, "My reminiscences are buried under this water. I come here as a pilgrimage. I love Preya, I can't forget her...I can't forget her."

"She will come one day and say to me, 'Same to You'. I'll take her hand, kiss it and tell her, 'I love you Preya'. This river is witness of my love", he was saying uncontrolled with tearful eyes. But when Kamal put his right hand on his shoulder he started crying bitterly. Ajay put his head on Kamal's shoulder and wailed for long time. Kamal comforted him but could not control himself and also stared crying. They hardly stopped howling. They were not talking to each other. They were just sitting there sad and quiet.

Ajay was gazing at a boat, tied with a rope along the other side of the bank and thinking that one day Preya would come. He would take her to the love island, competing through the lashing waves of this river and never come back to this selfish world again.

****

At night, Kamal read every thing he had written about Tanzeela, so far, and wondered, what was the reason Preya had never responded Ajay's love? Tanzeela had also never responded to him. He did not have the courage, yet, to even ask for her mobile number. He had only two chances to talk to her directly since then, once on the lawn, during his early days in the UK, the second was in the hospital. She had written him one letter, when she asked him to leave her house. But he had written dozens of pages in her appreciation. What was this? A stupidity or was it really a true love? "Could we continuously love someone, without getting any response?" he mediated.

Why did Preya never respond to Ajay? Did she not want to marry a person with no immigration status, no good education and no career prospects or was she just simply obeying her parents? She never told him that her parents had found a boy for her better than she found by her own. Maybe her parents could not agree about the boy she found. If she was purely a domestic girl, depending upon her parents for selecting her soul mate, then why had she chosen a boy by herself? This showed that her parents had given her the right to find someone but acceptable to them. She could have introduced Ajay to them, or tell him what the preferences of her parents were, but she completely ignored him, at one stage, when she realized that he was in her love. What kind of girl was she? Once she was praying to see him but some other time, not even bothering to look at him. When he told her about the diary and the reasons for why he had written it, it was a clear expression of his deep love for her and she was surprised but she never wished to see that diary nor responded to his love, after knowing every thing.

Why could Ajay never be able to win her love? Can you compel someone to love you? Is it possible to mould someone, by showing them the intensity of your love? Do Asian families marry their daughters based on the sincerity and loyalty of the boys? Or, do they look at other elements, like his immigration status, family background, education, nature of job and career prospects. If they consider only the deep love of a boy for their daughters, then Preya could have introduced Ajay to her parents. The case was totally opposite, though. Ajay had only profound love for her but not the other characteristics to meet their standards. Although, she had told him that she did not care about beauty or riches but rather the person, however, her parents might have had other preferences. It could be the reason she avoided him.

He was wondering over the different aspects of Ajay's story and feeling very sorry for him.

Actually, he was applying his story to Ajay's and thinking, would he ever be able to earn Tanzeela's love. Engaged couples normally plan for their future, develop an understanding, go out to dinner, and talk for hours on phone, at night time. Kamal did not have even the phone number of his fiancée. It was very clear that she was not taking any interest in him. He could have her body but not the feelings. Marriage was not only the joining of two bodies but it was about feelings, emotions and the meeting of two souls. He could be her bed partner but not her soul mate.

He was satisfied that Preya had never been Ajay's fiancée, while Tanzeela was his and he was engaged to her. Once they got married, he would prove his love to her. Eventually, a wife fell in love with her husband. He was just thinking these things.

Then, he wondered whether all women were the same when it came to feelings. If Ajay could not earn Preya's love how he could get Tanzeela's love. How long you could love someone one-sidedly.

Basically, he got confused whether the one-sided love is a stupidity or a true love because he was also one-sided lover like his friend Ajay.

Actually, Ajay's story affected him badly and it made him more depressed than ever before. He was comparing Preya to Tanzeela. They were both women and they could not be impressed just by the intensity of a man's love for them. They were looking at the other social and economic factors too.

"Ajay did not try to become equal to Preya in education and social status while I was trying to become a proper suitor for Tanzeela but I earned my MBA degree by foul means and doing a security job. If I had earned it by fair means even then I would have been doing the same job. I also could not come equal to Tanzeela in social status", he accepted the truth.

He thought out-loud, 'One day, I might have to throw my diary into the River Thames'.

****

Nabeela had a baby girl, but her husband had left her and had gone back to Nigeria. He wanted to take her with him but she insisted on staying in the UK. He had his own family problems and wanted to live in his country. He did not want to leave her alone and tried to force her to go with him but she refused. This was the reason of their separation.

She was on maternity leave and living in one bedroom flat. Her family had come to know about her separation. She was feeling alone at home. She wanted to go back to parents' house but his father was still very strict about her. He did not want to hear her name spoken in front of him. Her sisters and her mother had a soft spot for her and wanted her to bring home but the father was not going to agree with them, at any cost.

She was depressed and became mentally ill, living all alone. She felt the importance of family and was feeling guilty about running away from the house. For the first time in her life, she was living such a boring life. She wanted to talk to someone and share in bringing up the baby.

Pooja her colleague and friend often came to see her. She had got a fair colour, beautiful black eyes, small rounded forehead, about five feet height, long black hair twisted at the end, and she was putting some weight on her. She was born and brought up in India. She was married to a British born Indian guy two and half years ago. This marriage was an arranged one through family friends but it did work hardly for two years.

Pooja did graduation in computer sciences and was also

working in a big IT firm in India before her wedding. Her husband was living with his English girlfriend and also had a baby girl but his family kept it secret from her before marriage. They wanted him to marry an Indian girl and led a proper family life but he was completely a spoiled boy and had no respect for his parents. They forced this marriage on him with a hope to get him on the right track. They thought when he would see how an Indian girl love, respect and serve her husband, he leave the White lady. Pooja came to know about his girlfriend and a baby in the very early days of her wedding but even then she struggled hard to make her marriage successful. Her husband was a daily drinker and beat her on pretty things. Pooja belonged to a poor family and did not want to be a burden on her parents after the wedding. She tolerated every brutality of him for two years to make him realize that she was the best wife in the world but all her efforts went fruitless. Eventually, she got separation. She found a job in IT department in the same bank where Nabeela was working. She was also living alone in a one bed room flat.

Loneliness is itself a disease. At one stage, it leaves humans mentally sick. It is a state of mind, when people take the wrong steps in using drugs, committing suicide and so on. No human is an individual in this world but connected with other people. Only death can end this connection.

Pooja became victim of isolation. She started smoking in the beginning and now she was on drugs.

Nabeela tried to go back to her parents but her father did not allow her. She was already having a depressed life but when Raheem closed his doors to her she fell in further stress. She started smoking and was soon on drugs too in Pooja's company. They smoked and used drugs together to get out of their depressions.

****

195

Security is the most boring job ever. A security guard has to do nothing, except stand or sit for long hours, silently. It is human instinct when you are awake, but silent, you keep thinking about different aspects of your life.

It was the same for Kamal. Most of time, when he was working as a security guard, his mind was always buzzing with new ideas about his future with Tanzeela.

One day, his company sent him to a bank to cover one of his colleagues, who was on holidays. He was standing inside the bank, at the main entrance, wearing his security uniform. A security licence, with a long blue strip, was hanging on his chest. There was some repair works going on, inside and outside the bank. His job was to keep an eye on the workers and open the door for the customers. The door had an electronic fault and the technicians were fixing it. Behind him there were cashiers' counters, fully covered with a mirrored wall. On his left hand side, there was a wooden cabin, which used as the manager's office. At the front, there were two round desks, made of wood, with a luxury office chair, one telephone line and one flat computer screen on top, specified for the customers' relations officers. Two small office chairs were in front of each desk, for the customers. He was standing opposite of these desks.

He was opening the door for customers. It was exactly 9:00 AM, when he saw Tanzeela walking towards the bank, from the opposite side of the road.

He started looking to other side, to avoid being seen by her, but he was shocked when in the next moment, she was pushing the door open, to enter the bank. He helped her open the door, lowering his eyes. He did not look at her face because he did not want to know her first reaction. She sat right in front of him, at one of the customers' relation officer's desk. She was working as customer relations officer at this bank.

Kamal was feeling like his body had lost all powers. He felt drops of sweat dripping down his forehead. His face went pale, his mind went blank. He forgot to open the door for the customers.

"Mr. Security Guard, could you please help that old lady to open the door," Tanzeela's voice was echoing in his ears but he was still motionless. The old lady was struggling to push the door in. The lady sitting next to Tanzeela rushed to door and helped her to come inside.

"Are you there Mr.?" she asked him, surprised.

"Oh, sorry," he came back to the world.

"Are you feeling alright?" she asked him.

"I'm alright," he replied, puzzled.

"Then do your job properly," she told him and went back to her desk.

There was just a few feet distance between him and Tanzeela but he was feeling far from her, like he was a many miles from her. She was busy in her work and not paying any heed to him, however, she was also not feeling easy, finding him standing before her. He was looking outside turning his back to her.

It was morning time, the bank was not very busy, there were only two persons standing at cashier counters. The manager was with some other staff, examining the repairing works upstairs. Tanzeela and her colleague, sitting next to her desk, were chatting with each other.

"Hey Tanzee, you haven't told me about your fiancé," she asked her.

Kamal heard this and paid attention to their conversation. Tanzeela was quiet.

"How does he look like? What does he do?" she further asked her.

"He has an MBA degree," she replied.

"Wow! Wonderful, he will definitely be doing a good job in the City then," she remarked.

Tanzeela remained silent.

197

"Have you tried him in bed?" she whispered.

Kamal did not know the reaction of Tanzeela on this question because she was sitting behind him.

He was puzzled, confounded, ashamed and also humiliated by standing as a *chowkidar* in front of his bank officer fiancée. He thought about the *chowkidar* of his school, *Baba* Bashir, a short old man with white beard and small round cap on his head. He would open and lock the main gate of the school, every day. On the annual results day he congratulated students and their parents, who gave him some money in return. He recalled his office *chowkidar* in Pakistan. A tall man with long thick moustaches heavily rounded at the both ends. He saluted all the staff in the morning, in a military style. They all gave him some money from their salaries. At the Eids, he went to each person especially to say Eid *Mubarak*---greetings, and received a lot of money. The case of the office peon was different; he needed everything all the time. He told different, painful, stories of his parents' illness and the miserable condition of his family to get sympathy and money from the staff.

He brought to mind poor Nosheen, the prettiest girl amongst the staff. She was criticised by all, just because she would give a smile to the security guard when she came to work in the morning. The staff did not consider it appropriate, to greet the doorman in such friendly manner.

He was at a complete loss, when a woman with a baby buggy was struggling with the door.

"What's wrong with this doorman?" the lady officer murmured.

"Hey! Mr. are you there?" she said loudly.

He was alerted by her shouting and helped the lady to enter by opening the door wide. An emotional war was going on inside him. He was feeling like, if he stood there till 5:00 pm, his mind would split open. He controlled himself for two hours but then the moment came when he decided to do a dramatic thing in his life.

He walked out the bank, quietly, without telling the staff.

Tanzeela told her mother and sisters about her confrontation with Kamal at the bank that day. She still believed that he was the main cause of all the suffering her family was going through.

"This is the revenge of nature, Raheem always taunted me being a daughter of a *chowkidar* but, today, he is going to marry his own daughter to a *chowkidar*," her mother thought.

Tanzeela was sitting in her room, holding her head and wondering about her future with Kamal.

"How can I tell my colleagues that the person standing at the door is my fiancé? If I told them, what they would think about me, my personality and my family? There was a story at the bank that I was going to marry the doorman. Where was my respect before my colleagues?"

"I know what the importance of family is and I don't want to hurt my father but how I can lead my life with him? What is the state of mind of a person, who has done an MBA degree and is working as a doorman?"

"When my colleague was speaking ill about him, I was embarrassed. I could not ask her, 'please stop it, he is my fiancé'. How would I introduce him to my friends?"

She thought out all the things Nabeela once thought. She did not know what to do? How to convince her father? Her mind was just confused. She was just wishing that her colleagues will never come to know that she was going to marry a *chowkidar*. She was praying to God to help her in this matter.

One question was coming across her mind, again and again, what was the reason why he ran away from there after just two hours and the company had to send another guard on emergency basis?

She knew that he was not feeling easy in her presence, but why had he left at once, without telling anyone? What made him to leave all of a sudden? She wondered and wanted to know the reason.

****

Shahida, Nabeela's friend, revealed to Tanzeela that her sister was on drugs. When Sadiqa came to know about it she got worried about her daughter.

"Look Mr.Raheem Chaudhry this is the result of your obstinacy which put Nabeela on drugs", she argued with her husband after a long time.

"Did I ask her to run away with a black man?" he argued back but he was also worried about her.

"She stopped seeing him on our demand but when you forced her to get married Kamal she went against you. Had you not forced her she would never have been done it", she said in frustrating.

"I was doing my job being a father", he said angrily.

"If we make our daughters to marry against their wishes they will do the same", she warned him.

"You meant Tanzeela is not happy marrying Kamal", he said.

"She is not happy at all", she said.

"She is happy. She is not like Nabeela", he satisfied himself.

"I can't see my baby in a miserable condition. She needs our attention and family support to get rid of a depressed life. I'm taking her home tomorrow", she said.

After all he was a father and could not see her daughter dying like that. Sadiqa brought her home the next day. Her condition was very poor and she was immediately admitted to a hospital. The whole family was looking after her. After few days she was admitted to a rehabilitation centre.

Kamal had come to know all about Nabeela. He was feeling so sorry for her. One day he went to see her in the rehabilitation centre.

"I'm sorry Nabeela it all happened because of me. I never thought the things would go so wrong", he said bowing his head down.

Nabeela was coming to the norms. She kept quiet and started staring into the space.

"Can you please forgive me?" he said apologetically.

"There is no your fault Kamal", she broke her silence eventually and went back to her room without saying anything.

****

Tanzeela did not have to wait long to find out her answer. Kamal had come to her house. The whole family was sitting in the TV lounge on Saturday evening. Nabeela was still under treatment. She spent weekends with her family at home according the doctors' advice. Raheem was very polite to her as she was going through the rehabilitation. Shakeela and Tanzeela were looking after her baby at home.

They were surprised at his sudden visit.

"Sorry uncle, I don't want to marry Tanzeela," he said with out any preamble.

They were all astounded at his unexpected remarks. Tanzeela, who was about to leave, remained seated.

"What do you mean?" Raheem asked him, surprised.

"I don't want to marry Tanzeela," he said again.

"You know what are you saying?" Raheem said.

"I meant what I said," he said with confidence.

They were all looking at him, startled. He was looking to his feet. Raheem had fixed his eyes on him and he was speechless, in shock. The mother and sisters were looking at each other and feeling bewildered. There was a silence for some time.

"What is the reason?" Raheem asked him, after a long pause.

"I am not her suitor," he said lowering his head further down.

"How can you make such a big decision on your own?" he said angrily.

"This is my life, I know it better than anyone else," he said.

"But this is the decision of two families, not of any individual," Raheem said.

"If families are doing wrong, then the children have a right to express their opinions," he said humbly.

"Do you think that you are wiser than your elders?" he said

"No, I am not, but I am more realistic than them," Kamal said.

For the first time his aunty and cousins were impressed by him, because what he was speaking suited to them.

"You need to talk to your parents first. I think you have gone mad." Raheem told him.

"I have told them about my decision already." Kamal answered.

"What did they say?" he questioned.

"They were not happy." Kamal humbly answered.

"How can you make this decision without them?" he insisted.

"They don't know what I'm doing here." Kamal revealed.

"I'm not going to accept your decision. You are letting me down. Ask your parents to talk to me," he said intensely.

"What can my parents do if I don't want it?" Kamal said.

"Do you know what the meaning of breaking an engagement is?" his uncle said angrily.

"Yes, I know it very well." he replied.

Tanzeela looked at his ring finger and found it empty. She was more surprised, than the others, about his sudden decision.

"This is an association between two families, not just a relationship between two individuals," Raheem said.

"I know, but if the individuals don't want this relationship, how can the families force them to establish it?" Kamal said.

"Did someone from my family say something to you?" he looked at his wife and daughters, one by one.

"No, they did not say anything to me. This is totally my personal decision."

"I do not agree with you. No one has ever broken engagement in our family before. You can't do that," he said firmly.

"No girl has ever run away from house on her engagement day before, in our family," Kamal said rudely.

Nabeela felt uneasy about his statement and squeezed herself into the sofa. She was feeling disgraced. The whole family was perturbed on his uncharitable comments.

"Are you taunting me about my daughter," Raheem said, wrathfully.

"No, I am not; she is my cousin and equally respectable to me. She is my family honour too. But I am just facing the realities and the reality is, if we force our girls to marry against their will, they can do anything beyond our imagination," he clarified, that he had not meant to put them down.

"You will marry Tanzeela, this is my final decision, don't try to become our father," he said, more powerfully.

"Do you want to marry your daughter with a chowkidar", Kamal repeated.

His wife looked at him with ironical eyes. Tanzeela was looking at her lap. Nabeela and Shakeela were also looking at their father's face. He was puzzled at this question. He was staring at Kamal in stillness.

"Do you want to marry your daughter a *chowkidar?*" Kamal repeated.

"What do you mean by this?" he asked, gruesomely.

"I am working as a *chowkidar,* in the same bank where Tanzeela is an officer," he said.

Raheem was totally shocked at hearing this. He was speechless. During the whole discussion, for the first time, he had lowered his head in deep thought.

He had always looked down on his wife, being a daughter of a *chowkidar.* He was not able to say something on this question before his family. For the first time he was defeated in an argument.

"Have you not done an MBA degree?" he said, in lingering tongue.

"I did not do it, I bought it and even if I had done it by myself, I would be in the same position. There is no difference whether I do it by studying hard or buy it with money. My housemates, who went to good universities, are doing the same jobs. This is our future in this country anyway," he said.

"But you told me that you were going to the college," he asked.

"I wanted to study properly. My first college was bogus one. After I got engaged to Tanzeela, I asked my father to give me more money, to go to a good one. He sold land in the village and gave me seven thousand pounds. I took admission into another college and studied hard but this was also closed down by the UK border agency, on suspicion of being a fraud. Then I bought this degree, for thirty eight hundred pounds."

"After spending fourteen thousand pounds on education, in this country, I became a security guard."

"I don't think myself suitable for Tanzeela. It is not fair for her to get married to the *chowkidar* of her work place." Kamal revealed the truth.

He was speaking non-stop, bowing his head to his lap. Everyone had fixed their eyes on him. His aunty and cousins were respecting him, for his realistic approach and truthfulness.

"She should get married to a bank officer or a person equal to her in status. Islam teaches us to ensure suitability and compatibility in marriages not only the blood relations. I struggled hard to become equal to her but I was an idiot in my thinking. Whatever I do here, I will not be anything more than a *chowkidar* or a sales assistant. If I go to low profile colleges or good universities the case will be the same for me in the current situation of the economy of this country.

Nabeela has already destroyed her life because of irrational family demands. I don't want to destroy Tanzeela's life under the family pressure."

Tanzeela gave him a quick glance. She thought him to be a

realistic person and felt sorry over his loss of money in the fake colleges.

"I've decided to go back to Pakistan, next week, for good. Life in the UK has taught me to work hard. I want to lead a respectable life in my country, where I do not to hide my job from my fiancée, where my wife and children can feel proud of my profession and they can introduce me with confidence to their friends."

He finished his long speech and then kept quiet. His cousins and aunty had pools of water in their eyes. They were looking at him as a person, with ego and self-esteem, not as a forced husband or unwanted guest.

"My son, I ask you to stay with us until you leave the UK," his aunty said lovingly. She wanted to compensate him, for her cold behaviour in the past. His cousins had the same kind of feelings. She looked at her husband to ask Kamal the same thing but he knew his rural cultural and family character. He was aware that Kamal would never come back to stay in this house, but even so he asked him.

"No, thank you, I am OK there," he said, as Raheem expected.

He took out the engagement ring from his pocket and put it on the table. Raheem was bowled over before his family. He could not say that he was happy to marry his daughter a *chowkidar*, just because Kamal was his nephew. He remained quiet.

"I do apologise for the disturbance I have caused you," he said.

When he was about to leave, his aunty asked him to have dinner with them. He refused and made an excuse of having already agreed to see one of his friends.

Raheem hugged him and sobbed bitterly. Family affection took over all of them. They all stood up and gathered around him. They saw him off with tears.

He came out of the house, found a dark lonely place and cried for long time.

At night he read his whole diary, word by word, about his life in the UK and his dreams with Tanzeela.

He received a text from Tanzeela, late at night. She wanted to see him and asked him to send her his door number and the post code.

He knew that she had gotten his number from her father; he wondered why she wanted to see him.

He guessed that she might want to give him back his engagement ring and all the gifts. He sent her his postal address.

****

Chapter 12

Ajay came to know about his decision, of going back to Pakistan, and his confrontation with Tanzeela, in the bank. He opposed this decision and was anxious to see him. He wanted to go to Kamal's house but Kamal was not ready to see him at his house. He asked him to come to the London Eye. Ajay was surprised why Kamal was asking him to come to London Eye this time. When he reached there he found Kamal sitting the same stoned bench where Ajay used to sit and remember Preya. He was holding his daily diary wrapped in red velvet cloth and gazing at the running waves of the River Thames in deep thoughts.

"I'm astonished you called me at this place today. You used to criticise me for being here," Ajay said as he approached.

"Today, I am going to do the same thing once you did," Kamal replied.

"What do you mean?" Ajay asked surprisingly.

"*Bhai*, we both are same kind of idiots, who were running after dreams," Kamal said.

"What is this in your hand?" Ajay looked at a book type thing, wrapped in red velvet cloth but he did not know it was a diary.

"Come with me," Kamal took him to the same place where Ajay would stand, looking down into the deep waters.

He threw the diary into the river and said, "Those were my dreams, I buried them today for ever, now I will lead a real life."

"What was that?" Ajay asked surprisingly.

"I used to write in this diary about my dreams of the UK life, about Tanzeela, and the same things you wrote for Preya one time".

"Are you crazy?" Ajay asked.

"Whoever faces the realities of life, people think him crazy." Kamal told him.

"Just one incident changed you completely, I can't believe it." Ajay said.

"How long we will live on dreams?" Kamal asked.

"But we can't forget our past." Ajay replied.

"Only the coward lives in dreams, the brave confront reality." Kamal told him.

"This is silliness, to leave the country, you have no courage to face the realities you want to run away from them," Ajay pressed him.

"You want me to come here, every day, and keep watching the deep waters, like a mad man?" Kamal said

"You think me a madman," Ajay asked.

"Yes, you are a madman; you are not ready to face reality. You wrote a diary for Preya for four years but could not find her love. You could not stand her avoiding you and left your job. You invited her but she did not bother to come. You told her about the diary but she did not take notice of it. Now you talk with the waves, like a mad man."

Kamal walked here and there as he was delivering a lecture.

"She was not troubling about you, whilst you were torturing yourself by remembering her sitting on this bank, in severe cold weather." Kamal continued.

"If you spent the time in some other productive activity, you wasted after Preya, life would have been so much better for you. You could neither win love nor her friendship. Have you ever thought about what the reason was?"

"She was studying at a good university and had a bright future before her. She wanted to marry a person with good career prospects. She observed you, for four years, you were still doing the same job. She could not see any progress or ambition in you."

"You buy diplomas, every year, from fake colleges and get an extension for your visa. This is your reality. You are just cheating yourself and she is moving towards a better life by getting good education. You are a security guard who is called a *Chowkidar* or a *Darban* in our language."

"I believe you, when she told you that she did not care about riches and appearance but she certainly looked at your immigration status and career aspirations."

"What is your immigration status in this country? If tomorrow your visa is refused, you are finished. What is your career here? You are a doorman and will remain a doorman through out your life in the UK. This is your reality."

"One day, Preya will come with her husband to visit the London Eye. She will find you sitting there and will change her path. She even will not bother to look at you."

"You are not only cheating yourself but also your family. They think that you are getting good education in the UK. Have you ever thought about them? Have you ever thought about your old mother in the village, who is waiting for you to come back? She illuminates a lamp for you at every *Diwali* and wishes that you were with her. Every day she will ask the postman for your letter."

"You are sitting here to recall; 'Preya said this, Preya said that, Preya did this, Preya did that'. One day, you will die here, by the bank of this river and there will be only two lines news in the media, 'Ajay Kumar Sharma, a young man of Indian origin was found dead on the bank of the River Thames. The police are investigating his death'. No one will trouble about you, not even Preya."

Kamal was speaking emotionally and Ajay was just looking at him phenomenally.

"Dreams, dreams and dreams. We all run after dreams in this country. You are dreaming that one day Preya will come to you. I used to dream that one day, I would be equal to Tanzeela but I've come to the reality. You have lived in your dreams for four years. You are a bigger idiot than I was."

Kamal sat with him on the bench. Ajay was still looking at him in deep solemnity. There was a long pause.

"*Bhai*, I have been defeated by my dreams," Kamal said tiresomely.

"I was working as a doorman, in front of my fiancée and she refused to acknowledge our relationship. She called me Mr. Security Guard," he said, crying.

"You wasted lot of money on your education, you broke your engagement and now you are determined to go back. It doesn't look sensible to me," Ajay spoke, after long time.

"I also lost my identity here. I never thought of my future as a security guard, dish washer or a sales assistant. I was working in a telecommunications company, in my country and I was looking forward to becoming a customer services manager. I was very ambitious and motivated. I was improving my skills and doing better every day, by competing with my colleagues. I had clear career objectives in my mind."

"The golden dreams and high expectations dragged me to this country, I was totally wrong. I couldn't get good education as I thought. I lost my striving for a good life and worked as a labourer to cover my losses."

"I want to lead a respectable life and give a reputable education to my children, so that they can grow in society with confidence. I don't mind if I earn less money but I want an identity and personality in life."

"I know this country can give me little bit extra money but no one can earn real respect with money in this world. You can only get appreciation through your identity in life. I don't mind if my children live in a small house, I want them to feel proud of me. I want to become a role model for them."

"Just think for a moment, if my wife working as a bank officer whilst I am working as a doorman, in the same bank or I am standing as a peon at my children's school gate, what they will think about me? Will they feel proud of me?"

"Have you taken your family into confidence, about your decision?" Ajay asked him.

"Yes, I have." he replied.

"What was their response?" Ajay asked.

"They were shocked and opposed me, but when I told them the truth about my life in the UK they agreed with me," he told him.

"What will you do there?" Ajay wanted to know.

"I'd start my old job again." he replied.

"Are you sure you will get the same job back?"

"I'd convince my employer that I went to the UK to improve my education, when they see my MBA degree they offer me better position in the company", Kamal reassured him.

"OK, you do whatever you want to do but I won't leave this country." Ajay said, determined.

"If you want to live in your dreams, you can, but I am fed up now." Kamal responded.

"Love happens only once in life. I love Preya with all my heart and soul. No matter if I can't have her yet. She lives in this city and I feel her smell in the air every time I take breath. I will stay here till my last breath, with the support of her memories. I believe, one day I will find her love," Ajay said romantically.

"That is not your fault, Ajay, we've been watching romantic Indian movies since our childhood and we live in dreamy world all the time. But my dear, a director can get favourable results in a movie but not in practical life. What we see in the movies rarely happens in real life." Kamal reminded him.

"I am not able to forget her. It is out of my control. I loved her in a real life, not in a movie," Ajay said.

"Anyway, Ajay, this is your life, you live it as you wish," Kamal finally said.

"You know Kamal, I love her too much," he said childishly.

"OK, come with me, we will go to her house and tell her parents that you love their daughter and want to marry her." Kamal said.

"How can we do that? I never have seen them in my life." Ajay replied, astonished.

"OK, we go to Preya, she knows you very well, I tell her about your love for her and ask her to introduce you to her parents." Kamal answered.

"I've not been in contact with her since I left my job. It does not look nice, to go to her like that." Ajay said, making excuses.

"Fine, give me her telephone number and I talk to her right now," Kamal insisted.

Ajay hesitated, to give him her mobile number, but Kamal took his phone out of his pocket by force and started scrolling it to find Preya's number.

"OK, here is Preya's number," Kamal found the number on the contact list and wanted to call her, but Ajay stopped him by saying that she would not answer it.

"No problem, I'll call her from my number," Kamal dialled her number into his phone and turned the speakers on. Ajay's face turned pale with unknown fear.

"Hello," Preya said.

"Oh, hello, sorry to disturb you, my name is Kamal and I'm a friend of Ajay--- Ajay Kumar Sharma, I hope you know him." Kamal greeted her.

"Yes I do," she said.

"You know he is dying for you. I have not seen any boy so deep in love with a girl. He loves you with his heart and soul," he said with confidence, without going into further details.

212

"What rubbish you are talking about? He was my colleague at work and I never thought him more than that. He is not my friend anymore", she said in annoyance.

"He wants to marry you, please don't reject him", he pleaded her. I'm working in a prestigious fashion and design company in London at a high position. I want to marry someone equal to me in education and social status. How can I marry him?" she said more angrily.

"Look Preya, after all love is something in this world and believe me he loves you so much", Kamal kept insisting her.

"Listen Mr. I need a house to live in, a regular income to maintain life, a well educated husband to introduce my family and friends----a life partner with a good job, having some sort of career prospects and full of ambitions. A soul mate with who I can feel proud to lead my life. You need other things in life apart from romance. Romance only works when you have a comfortable life", she explained her ideas about love and romance.

"He is sitting with me, would you like to talk to him?" he said.

"I don't wish to talk to him and don't phone me again," she said furiously.

"He loves you madly, please talk to him", Kamal insisted.

"I don't care, I never loved him and I don't need to talk to him", she said more harshly.

Before she cut the call she said loudly, "Idiots."

Ajay listened to their conversation and stilled his eyes like a stone. He looked like a statue, not a human.

Kamal started laughing madly and repeated his words, "She lives in this city and I feel her smell in the air every time I take breath. I will stay here till my last breath, with the support of her memories. I believe, one day I will find her love".

He kept laughing, until tears started pouring from his eyes. He sat beside him on the bench, cupped his face with hands and cried painfully.

"This is our reality, Ajay."

Ajay was still expressionless, in shock. He was just looking at him with hollow eyes. It looked like all of his senses have been snatched away.

"She thought you a colleague not a friend even," he said in the depressing tone.

"The girl, you worshiped like a goddess, does not want to speak to you. This is a modern age, an age of competition. You are weighted here according to your material introduction in society not by what is in your heart and mind. Your social position is your identity not the status of your mind, not the sincerity of your heart. You love Preya, dreaming to marry her, but what is your identity in this country-an international student of bogus colleges- what is your introduction here- a *chowkidar*", he shook his head and said heartbreakingly.

"She might be enjoying her life with a person equal to her in position and status and you are sitting here at the bank of the River Thames to die in her memories", Kamal took his face in hands, sat beside Ajay and wailed for long time.

He wanted to say many things but he lost his control and kept crying. Ajay was completely quiet but a stream of tears falling down to his cheeks. He had stilled his eyes at the running waves of the River Thames. They were running up and down as usual. Everything was same as before at the London Eye but not for him.

"I'm going back to Pakistan this Saturday. I'll text you my flight details and departure time. I hope you will come to see me, at the airport," Kamal left with tears in his eyes.

Ajay sat there for long time, deep in thought. His possibilities denied and hopes dashed. The waves of the River Thames were mourning his fate and he was looking at them with empty eyes.

****

There was big news in the village, Kamal had completed his education and was coming back to visit his parents. His family knew the actual situation but they were avoiding telling the truth. They pretended, before the people, that they were missing him and asked him to come for a short period. They also told the people that, if he found a good job over here, they would not let him go back. They said it was hard for them, to live away from him. His mother started telling the village women that she wanted to keep him near her after the marriage, and had asked his uncle to bring his daughter here and asked her to live in Pakistan, otherwise she would look for another girl for her son. The women appreciated her decision and flattered her that there were hundreds of girls, who wanted to marry Kamal. To some extent they were right, if not hundreds then dozens of parents in the area wanted their daughters to marry Kamal, because of his reputation being in the UK.

Actually, they were trying to hide their past boasts about their son's excellent life in London.

"Rehmat is it true Kamal is working as a *chowkidar* in London?" Kamal's mother, did not, easily, believe that *'her son... a chowkidar'*.

"Yes, it is true and he is working in the same bank where Tanzeela is an officer," he told her.

"Oh my goodness, now I understand why Nabeela refused to marry him." she said.

"Yes, she was right." he agreed.

"But I wonder, why did Tanzeela agree to marry him?" she asked.

Rehmat had come to know about Nabeela's running away, through Kamal, but he did not tell his wife, for the sake of his brother's honour.

"She said they were blood relatives, so there was no problem for her to marry Kamal," he said.

"Then why did Kamal break the engagement with her?" she asked.

"He thought that he was not her suitor and it was not fair to marry her." he told her.

"Was Kamal not able to find a good job, in the same bank where Tanzeela was working?" she asked.

"He tried but he could not find one," he answered.

"Why? He was well educated and also did degree in the UK," she kept questioning.

"He told me so many things," he shortly replied.

"And you know he had to work with masons," he told her.

"Oh my goodness, Kamal worked with masons!" she had one hand clamped over her mouth in total disbelief.

"Yes, this kind of life he was living in London," he said.

"Ask him to come back as early as possible. We don't need to become rich. I don't want money, which my son earned by working with masons and as a *chowkidar*. I don't want my son to kill himself to make us rich," she said genuinely.

"I have not slept, since Kamal told me all about his life in the UK. I also don't need to become a big landlord in the village. God has already given us every thing. The real wealth is the children not the land," he said fairly.

"Rehmat, I'm worried about those poor people, who are selling their assets to send their children abroad." she said worriedly.

"If I tell them the reality, they won't believe us and think we are jealous of them," he said thoughtfully.

"We had some land, to pay our loan back, what about the people who have nothing and are just borrowing to go to *Walliat*," she said sympathetically.

"This is a matter of honour for us we can not negate the things we told them already about Kamal," he said.

"Rehmat, do all the students do same kind of work in the UK?"

"Everyone who has not enough money to support the education

does same or even worse things." he told her.

"How our sons earn money though such difficulty in foreign lands, but we spend it here, lavishly, as if money grows on trees over there. If I had known Kamal had to work with builders to send me money for his engagement ceremony, I never would have held it," she said.

They both kept talking for long time but he did not tell her the painful things Kamal had told him because he knew that mothers' hearts are weak, regarding their sons.

They both are agreed on one point that they did not need wealth but an honourable life for their son.

****

All of the housemates were gathered at home after a long time. They were making dinner and chatting about immigration matters, as usual.

Kamal was listening to their discussion. He never participated in such talks at home but that day he was going to lose his self-control.

"Zaman, what were you doing in Pakistan?" Kamal knew it already, but asked him for a reason.

"I was a lecturer at a government college," he said.

"That meant you were a gazetted officer, weren't you?" he asked him.

"Yes, I was," he replied.

"What are you doing here?" he asked.

"I'm working in McDonald's, you know all of this," he said.

"A grade 17 officer in his country is working in McDonald's in London just to earn a little bit extra money," he said, ironically.

"What do you want to say?" he asked him.

"How much money do you save here, each month, after your expenses? Two hundred, three hundred or maximum five hundred pounds? You were doing a respectable job in Pakistan. You were called 'Sir' by your students, now your identity is a burger man. Would you not able to earn this amount in your country? You have become a burger man, from being a lecturer. What a sensible trade off it is!" Kamal ridiculed him.

"I came here for education. I did master degree in human resources management at a good university. I did not go to any bogus college, like yours," he criticised his college.

"Now you are teaching resources management to burgers not humans," Kamal kept criticising him.

"This is not my permanent job. I'm trying to find a job in my field," he said nervously.

"I've been looking you doing the same job for long time. I don't think so you can get a better job," Kamal said.

"You are a weak person, which is why you are going back. This country is not for lazy people like you but for determined ones like us," he said.

"I am weak because I don't want to be known in life as a burger man or a *chowkidar*. I am lazy in not cheating the immigration system for long time. I am determined to make a good life in my country, where I have some recognition and respect," he said.

"You are also letting me down by calling me a *chowkidar*," Asif said

"OK, what a security guard is called in Urdu? If you not happy being called a *chowkidar* I call you a *darban* then, now you are happy", Kamal said more ironically.

Asif kept quiet.

"You did an MBA degree in the UK. You were a bank officer in your county. What is the link between an MBA or bank officer and a security job?" he said.

"You think we are doing these jobs happily? We have our own compulsions," Asif said.

"Not compulsions but dreams. You are all running after dreams.

A dream of a rich life! This is lust for money! A greedy man can never be a wealthy man," Kamal said in hatred.

"You are crossing the limits Kamal," Asif said angrily.

"I am not crossing the limits; I am showing you the mirror so that you can see your real faces in it. You are living an artificial life. You have no daring to face the reality because you have lost your identities. Once identity is lost, everything lost. You always blame your country but you've never thought of a solution. You are part of problem not the part of solution. Who will change the system over there, if educated people like us do minor jobs in this country? What is your end goal here, a big house, a luxurious car or a huge bank balance? If you think that you cannot survive in your country, with a higher education, then what about the majority who are living there with no education at all."

"In the future, your children will write your history, they will write, 'my father did a masters degree at a good university in Pakistan. He went to England for a higher education and also did a masters degree there and became a burger man'. The other children will laugh at them and ask if someone needs two master degrees to become a burger man in the UK. This is the introduction, motivation and aspiration you want to transfer to the next generation. You can't change your identity by living in a big house, driving an expensive car or accumulating a large bank balance. You will be known as a burger man or a *chowkidar* throughout your life."

"But if you become a professor, a solicitor or a bank executive, your children will feel proud of you, regardless of if you have a big bank balance or not, if you live in a small house or in big one or if you travel by public transport or in your own car."

"We are living here by our own choice and we know better what is best for us. We are not idiots, like you, who are leaving this country. We have a long term planning. We will bring our families in the UK, in near future. Our children will get good quality education. They will enjoy better health facilities. They will grow under an exemplary social justice system and when we get old the government will look after them.

"There is nothing over there, not even security of life; you can be killed anytime, in a targeted killing or in a bomb blast. When you leave the house in the morning, you are not sure you will come back alive or not. If you buy a property, the land mafia usurp it. If you buy a good house or a new car, your children are kidnapped for ransom. You can't find a good job, until you pay huge amount in bribes or have some strong reference from a big politician. If you can't afford expensive private doctors, you are left to die in government hospitals."

"You have electricity for only twelve hours a day. You have access to gas for only a few hours in a day. There is shortage of flour and sugar. You will have to wait in a queue for several hours, just to get a bag of flour or one kilogram of sugar. There is no control of prices. The prices of basic necessities of life are reaching the sky. There is no social security at all."

"You are talking about social change. The 65% of our population lives in villages, under the immense influence of feudalism. Those feudal lords are kings of their areas. Agriculture is the main source of our GDP but they don't pay any tax on their crops. They are also part of government and so strong that the land reforms have been pending since the creation of our country. No one can compete with them in elections. How can we bring social change, until we win elections against them?"

"Actually, there is a kingship, in form of family politics and in the name of democracy. No one can be a leader of a party, apart from family members. Is this a democracy?"

"In this country anyone can contest elections but over there, you need to be a feudal lord or an industrialist."

"We will live in this country; at least there is security of life and peace. Here, people are not known by their professions but in our country, your profession is your caste and social identity. We treat people according to their social identity but here, everyone has equal respect and rights."

"This country is giving us everything we need in life. Why should we leave it?" Zaman gave a lengthy speech and they all listened to him patiently.

"This is our basic problem; we curse the system but don't want to play any role in fixing it. More than 65% population comprises on the youth in Pakistan. They can play an important role in social change. If, today, they stand against corruption and militancy, two of our main problems, then change will not be far away. The change starts from a family, a street, a village, a city and then spreads across country. This is not the solution, to run away from the crisis, the solution is to fight against them within your capacities. We must play our individual roles for the betterment of our country". Kamal said.

"Patriotism is a good thing but finance is more important. We feel that we have a better future here, so we live here regardless of whatever we do," Arsalan said.

"You know, my one friend, who was MBBS doctor in Pakistan, is doing a pizza delivery job here. If professional people, like him, can do minor jobs, why should we not do them?" Asif said.

"This is your family matter, so we don't have any right to speak about it, but if you will allow me, I want to say something," Zaman said.

"Go ahead," Kamal said.

"You have come to this country, to marry your cousin. We realised, on your engagement day that she did not like you. I reckon this engagement is not going through, you are desperate and that is why you are running away, from this country," Zaman said.

"I want to make clear to you that I did not come to this country just to marry my cousin. I came here to make my future better, by getting a good education. Unfortunately, I was cheated by fake colleges and could not complete my education, as I thought. When I saw your situation, I was discouraged to go to any recognised university. I realised that my future would be the same, wherever I studied in this country. I worked as a labourer with builders, as a dishwasher in a hotel, a salesman in a supermarket and finally as a security guard."

"My fiancée is a bank officer. I broke this engagement by my own choice. I did not want a bank officer marry a chowkidar, only on the name of kinship. It was not fair to her."

"I'm going back because I can't see a better future for me in this country. I don't mind less money but I want to work equal to my educational level. I want to give an honourable introduction, to my family. I can do it easily in my country. I can understand that there are lot of problems there, but I want to become a part of solution. I want to build up my career over there, which I can not do here," Kamal explained in detail.

Manzoor was busy in the kitchen, listening to their discussion. He came out and said, "I am totally in agreement with Kamal. My personal experience is that we can progress in life, in a better way in our country. I did an MSc in Physics but am doing a security job here. I came here with high dreams on HSMP visa, but could not find job in my field. My colleagues are doing far better than me in Pakistan. They are earning good money, having a good life and furthering their careers, day by day. I am just waiting to get British citizenship, and then I'd love to go back."

"Kamal, I suggest this, don't be silly leaving empty handed, get married to your cousin, once you get indefinite leave to remain, then you can go back," Manzoor advised him.

"I don't want to marry someone here, for immigration status only," he said.

"Don't be stupid Kamal, you will repent later on. There is a golden chance for you. You can't understand the benefits of the British citizenship," Manzoor insisted.

"Whatever they are, I don't want to do it," he said firmly.

"He is an idiot, I am telling you," Asif looked at his friends, to approve his judgement about Kamal.

"You are all idiots, who are running after dreams in this country," he said impatiently and went to his room.

Kamal received a mobile message from Tanzeela, *"I'm coming to see you this Saturday after noon"*.

****

Chapter 13

It was Friday, 12th November 2010, Kamal's second last day in the UK. He wanted to do some shopping, for family and friends. He knew that he was not good at shopping. Ajay always helped him, but that day he was not ready to go with him. He told him that he was also very busy somewhere, but he promised to see him at the airport the next day.

"I should not have phoned Preya; at least Ajay was happy in life. I made him angry," he cursed himself.

He spent the whole day, wandering around different shopping centres and buying gifts for his family and friends. He did not forget to buy a tea thermos for the wife of *Gamma mochi* and woollen jacket for *Bhagee machin*.

His brother and sisters demanded mobiles phones with cameras from him. He bought the phones for them. His parents did not ask for anything. They just asked for him to come back safely, even so, he bought a wrist watch for his father and some clothes for the mother. He also bought some perfume for his friends in the village.

The most demanded things are mobile phones and perfumes, in Asian families. If you check their luggage at the airport you will find these two things in large quantities.

There is a custom, in the village, if someone comes to see you after you have returned from abroad you will give him a gift. Perfume is the most common gift for this occasion, unless someone has demanded a particular thing already. The women are especially keen to know, about the stuff someone brought from foreign lands. The mothers show them the gifts their sons brought, from foreign countries, with as much pride as when they show off the dowry at their daughters' weddings.

When family members use these things, they don't forget to tell their friends that these items are from a foreign country. A person, who lives in Europe, or America, is considered rich and his gifts have special importance.

Kamal purchased a lot of gifts, keeping in mind his rural traditions. He also bought a gift of thanks for Ajay, for all his help and warm friendship.

He remembered his early days in the UK, when he used to roam about those centres in search of a job. His past memories were running, like a movie on the screen of his mind. He laughed at some incidents at college and at his work place. But his confrontations with Tanzeela, in the bank and her letter asking him to leave the house, always punched him. He would never be able to forget them. He became sad and disheartened, each time they came across his mind.

He remained busy, packing his bags for almost the whole night. While he was packing, he thought that it was as if he was packing all of his memories of life in the UK. Although he was leaving of his own accord, still he was feeling sorry.

****

It was Saturday, his last day in the UK. He got up very late because he went to bed late the night before. All of his housemates had gone to work, but they had promised him to come early, to see him off. He took shower and had a light breakfast, as he was not feeling well enough to have a heavy one.

It is very natural, when you are sad, you don't like to eat much. He was missing Ajay and his housemates. He had spent more than one and half years with them and it was hard for him to say goodbye to them. It was not his turn to clean the house, even then, he still cleaned the whole house and remembered some good memories, made in this house, which brought tears in his eyes.

It was mid-day. He was having a cup of tea, in the sitting room, when he heard the door- bell. His sixth sense told him that it was Tanzeela, he was expecting her to come after noon but she came earlier. He went to the main door, carrying the cup in his hands. He was right--- it was Tanzeela standing at the door.

He greeted her and, unexpectedly, she replied more warmly than ever before. He led her to the sitting room and offered her a cup of tea. She did not refuse. He went to the kitchen, to make a cup of tea for her. He wondered why she had come empty handed and had not returned his gifts, as he was expecting.

He pulled a small table before her and put the cup of tea onto it. They both looked nervous and did not look at each other while talking. She sipped tea and said, "Oh, you can make good tea."

"I learnt it here," he replied shyly.

"Then you have definitely learnt good cooking too," she said with a smile.

"Not as good as you are thinking, but I can cook few things very well," he said.

"For example...," she continued conversation.

"Like, chicken curry, rice and some vegetables," he said.

"Wow, that's wonderful," she said warmly.

The silence prevailed, for some time, in the room. She was sipping tea comfortably. Kamal was scratching his left thumb nail with right index finger.

"When are you leaving?" she broke the silence.

"Tonight."

"Pay my compliments, to your family, especially your mother and sisters." she asked him.

He suddenly remembered the day, when he conveyed their greetings and she said that she was not a friend of them. But he did not want to go into the past.

"Of course, I will." he assured her.

"I guess you have bought a lot of things for them," she wanted to engage him in conversation, to gain confidence for the further things she wanted to ask.

"Not really, just few things." he told her.

He replied shortly.

"How many people share this house?" she asked.

"Five."

"It looked like two bedrooms house," she said surprisingly.

"Yes, it is two bedrooms." Kamal confirmed.

She did not know that here, sometime the two bedroom house was even shared by eight students. She was surprised how the five of them shared it.

"You share your room with someone." she further asked.

"No, I have a separate box room." he told her.

"You mean each bedroom is shared by two people." she asked.

"Yes."

"But even then, it looks very neat and clean." she noticed.

"Yes I cleaned it today." he told her.

"You cleaned it!" she surprised.

"I'm leaving today, so I thought to clean it one last time because I have some good memories of this house." he told her.

"I know you are very sensitive person." she revealed.

Kamal remained quiet on her remarks but his mind was spinning around a lot of things, more sensitive than his association with this house.

"You are speaking good English, I am surprised", she said with a big smile.

"Thank you", he said.

"Kamal you must be thinking that I have come here, just, to return your ring and engagement gifts", she said.

He still remained silent.

"But it is not like that. I have kept every thing, including the engagement ring as a gift from my cousin." she told him.

"I'm sorry, I just thought of you as my fiancé, not as a blood relative. I was totally wrong. You made me realise that we had a kinship as well. A relation of blood is more powerful than any other relation in this world. I have come to see you today, as a first cousin." she revealed.

Kamal was listening to her, looking down into his hands, still scratching his nails.

"We cannot blame each other for what has happened between us, up till now. Actually, we are all suffering from a generation gap. Our parents have the same old ways of thinking but they don't know that we were brought up in a modern age, which has its own requirements. They want us to live in their past and this is an unreasonable demand of them. The problems occur when they want to impose things on us, against our will."

"I was brought up in a totally different culture than you. My schools, curriculum, college, university and social life were completely different. I even could not speak your language properly. I visited Pakistan, only few times in my childhood. I don't know much about it. I wished I could learn Urdu. I watched Indian movies with English subtitles. So many times, I wished to spend some time in my ancestral country when I reached to the maturity age but my dad never encouraged me to go over there. He never gave us a chance to develop understandings with our relatives back in Pakistan. He always told us negative things about the country and the people." she continued.

"When you came to us, we had all negative views about you. Our mother told us that dad wanted one of us to marry you. It was very natural that we disliked you and whatever happened after was an outcome of it. I knew that I shared some part of my childhood with you in Pakistan. But it was just childhood enjoyment nothing else than that".

She took a long pause to start again. Perhaps, she was feeling guilty on her behaviour towards him.

"Would you like to eat something?" Kamal asked her.

"No, thanks, I'm OK," she said.

"It does not look nice for me to treat guests to just a cup of tea. I must order pizza for you," he said.

"I'm not your guest. We are cousins. There is no formality among cousins," she said.

He was not in mood to eat, even then he pretended that he was feeling hungry and ordered pizza, garlic bread and some soft drinks just to serve her to his satisfaction.

He was a product of the rural culture, where it was a matter of shame to treat guests to only a cup of tea.

"I became engaged you after my dad threatened to kill himself, in case I refused. He was mentally disturbed after Nabeela's flee from the house." Tanzeela continued.

"Did he?" Kamal's hearing was alerted to that because he did not know about it.

"Yes, he did." she confirmed.

"I did what I was asked to do but to be honest, I was not happy at all." she told him.

"It wasn't fair to you," he said.

"Yes, it was a completely unreasonable demand, of my dad, when he knew that none of us wanted to marry you", she said.

"How is she feeling now?" he asked her.

"She is still going through rehabilitation. It will take her long to recover fully. We are all supporting her to come back to a normal life. She was at initial stage of drug addiction that is why she is making some good progress", she said.

"I noticed that the uncle was also very polite to her", he said.

"Yes, he is taking much care of her these days", she said.

"Do you think if he had not forced her marrying me she would not have gone in that condition?" he asked.

"I think she would not have been", she took a long sigh.

"I wish she recover soon and live a happy life", he prayed for her.

"I wish so but it looks very hard to me. She will have to compromise with her life as it is", she said sadly.

"The uncle wanted to join two banks of a river. It was very unnatural thing," Kamal said.

On mentioning the banks of a river he suddenly remembered the two diaries, he and Ajay had thrown into the river. His face went pale and he felt a wave of pain in his heart.

The door bell rang. It was the pizza delivery. He arranged everything on the dining table and asked her to come over there.

"Who usually cook at home?" she asked.

"We have fixed turns. Each of us cooks on his turn," he said.

"That is really interesting, my mum does all the cooking in our house," she said.

"I have four specialised cooks here," Kamal said and they both laughed.

"You are enjoying your life," she said.

"Not really, it is very boring," he said.

"When you are all at home, it will be a real fun," she said, cleaning her mouth with a kitchen roll.

"We rarely get together at home. We all work different day and night shifts. If sometimes, they are all together, they only talk about immigration matters and how to cheat the system, to prolong their stay in the UK," he said.

"Are they educated?" she asked.

"Not only educated but they are highly educated. Two of them have done masters degrees from good universities, in

London, but they are working as security officers or sales men in supermarkets," he said.

"This is sad. Why they don't move to somewhere else, to find jobs in their relevant fields?" she said.

"They are running after their dreams. They want British citizenship, to secure their future," he said.

"But it is waste of education, if you don't work in your field," she said.

"One of them has done a masters degree in law but he is working as a sales assistant," he said.

"That is not fair, with your education," she said.

"It is not even fair with life," he said, stressfully.

"I reckon that is the reason you want to go back to your country," she said.

"Yes, I want to build my career over there," he said.

"This is rational thinking," she said.

"They think me an idiot because of my decision," he said innocently.

"No, you are not, they are idiots for working differently than their skills and education" she said.

"When I saw that you were working as a doorman, I really felt bad for you," she further said.

"Being a fiancé or a cousin," he made her laugh.

"I think both," she replied, laughingly.

"You really impressed me, with your positive thinking, when you came to our house last time." she told him.

"To break the engagement," he smiled big.

She smiled too and said, "I felt proud of you, being a cousin."

"Not being a fiancé," he kept joking.

She gave a big laugh and said, "Both."

"I hope you marry someone who is your best suitor," he extended his wishes for her.

"Let see what is in my fate," she replied.

"You know Kamal, when you left we talked about you, the whole night. My mum and sisters were all very impressed with you," she said.

"I did not do anything, to impress them, but I did what I thought was the best for both of us," he said.

"I am blessed that I have such great relatives," she said.

"This is a gift from me, for my great cousin, Kamal Chaudhry;" she took out a cheque and gave it to him.

He did not take it and said, "No Tanzee, sorry I can't take it".

"I have kept all your gifts. Will you not accept my gift?" she forced him to accept it.

"No, Tanzee, I can't take it, I am sorry," he persisted.

"If you think me as a cousin, then take it for my pleasure, please," she again, forced him.

"You are my cousin but it is a matter of shame to take money from a female cousin," he said moderately.

"This is a gift. Don't people accept gifts from their female cousins?" she took his hand and put the cheque in his palm.

"Ten thousand pounds! No Tanzeela, this is a big amount, I will not take it," he threw it onto her bag.

"If you don't take it, I will not forgive myself all my life. You can buy your land back with this money. I can't marry you, but please don't make me feel that I am a mean person and have no blood relations with you," she took her face in hands and started to cry loudly.

"I lost fourteen thousand pounds in bogus colleges but I don't want you to compensate my loss. It was my mistake. I can't blame you," he said.

"I asked you to leave our house. You faced all those troubles because of me. I am feeling guilty. You deserve more than what I am giving to you. I am not taking pity on you but acknowledging your greatness, feeling proud of you and I want to become your good friend, in the future. Please accept it for my satisfaction, please make me feel like I am your cousin and a friend," she passed him the cheque with a stream of tears.

He took it, with a thought that when she got married he would return it to her as a gift.

"OK, please stop crying," he tapped her head gently.

He led her again, to the sitting room. She composed herself, wiping her face with tissues paper, which she had in her hand bag and tiding her hair with her fingers.

Again, a dead silence prevailed. He went to his room, to check how much cash he had in his wallet. He had two hundred and sixty pounds, which he had withdrawn last night to empty his account. He put two hundred pounds in an envelope and wrote on it, 'with millions of loves, to my dear younger sister Shakeela'.

"Please Tanzeela, give this to Shakeela from my side. She is the youngest of us and has rights over us," he passed the envelope to her, which she took happily.

"OK, I have to go now," she was ready to leave.

"OK, thank you very much for your visit, for your gifts and please also pay my greetings and thanks to your mum and sisters. I'll call uncle later on," he stood up with her.

She again extended her greetings to his family, her best wishes for him and asked him to keep in touch. They exchanged e-mail addresses and their IDs on facebook.

He went out with her, to the car and opened the door for her. They briefly farewell each other, before she leaves.

Tanzeela was satisfied, after giving him all of her life savings.

Kamal went back to his room and was lost in memories. He thought about his uncle's family, his own family matters, the generation gap, and the social and cultural differences between the two families.

****

Kamal was sitting in the airport lounge, waiting for Ajay. He came a bit earlier, to have a brief meeting with him. His eyes were fixed on the ramps where passengers were coming out of the departure lounge, to catch their flights.

He was restlessly waiting for him. He tried to call him but his phone was switched off. After a long time, he saw him dragging one big suitcase and a large bag hanging from his right shoulder. He thought he was serving some old passenger, according to his helping nature. But there was no one around him and he was walking all alone. He was looking here and there to find Kamal, struggling with his heavy luggage.

Kamal waved his hands, to draw his attention. He approached him, unloaded his bags and took a breath of relief.

"What is this, stupid?" Kamal asked him.

"I tell you but first buy a drink for me," he said, sighing heavily.

He went to the vending machine and came back with two cans of coke. He gave him one can and asked, "What is this?"

He took a long gulp of drink and said, "I'm going back to India, for good."

"What?" Kamal was not going to believe him, easily.

"How come you are going back?" he asked again, surprised.

"I was an idiot, running after dreams. Thank you Kamal, you brought me to reality," he said.

"What are you talking about? Are you joking with me?" he was still in doubt.

"I know it is hard for you to believe but it is true." Ajay confirmed.

"But you never told me before." Kamal said.

"I wanted to give you a surprise." Ajay explained.

"What is the reason of this sudden decision?" he asked.

"My father passed away when I was young. I only have one younger sister and my mother at home. They live a simple life in the village. I wanted to buy a house in the city. This dream hauled me to the UK, although I was doing a good job at a private company. I was not interested in my studies in this country. I struggled hard for five years to save some money but I was standing back where I started from. My average income was one thousand pound per month, whereas my expenses were a minimum of five hundred pounds. The maximum of my savings went to the bogus colleges and to visa extension fees. Since the rules changed, for international students, it became harder to save any money."

"My mother has always asked me to come back and live with her but I fell in love with Preya. I've loved her for the last four years. My love was true but I forgot that I was living in a materialistic and competitive world, where you are weighted by your education, nature of job, career prospects, social and immigration status. The feelings, emotions and sincerity of your heart are worthless commodities here. I wanted to come out of this dreamy world and live a real life. I'll serve my mother in her old age, as she brought me up after my father. I don't want a big house in the city, I'd prefer to live in my village and do a reasonable job to earn my livelihood. I'm just sick of this dream land." Ajay explained all.

"I really appreciate your decision," Kamal hugged him happily.

They both were laughing at their dreams of the UK life and on their romances. They also were sharing their future plans. They made light jokes at each other's expense.

"Kamal, you are right when you say, 'one-sided love is foolishness', just waste of time and mere a dream. The practical life is something different", Ajay said his final words about love.

"Yes bhai, it is good to have some dreams in life but they should be based on rationality not on stupidity", Kamal replied.

****

If it were an Indian's movie, the day Ajay told Preya that he recorded each and every word of her for four years, she would have rushed to him, embraced him emotionally and said with tearful eyes, 'I love you Ajay'. She would have taken him to her house and told the parents that she wanted to marry him. They opposed her decision and she would have tried to commit suicide. She would by lying on a hospital bed, calling Ajay's name in faint. Her parents would be standing by her side and shedding tears. They would have called Ajay to save their daughter's life. He would have sat beside her, took her hand, kissed it lovingly, and sung a sad romantic song. During the song she would try to open her eyes. When the song finished, Ajay would run his hand in her hair and say, 'Look Preya I have come'. She would open her eyes, hug him and say, 'I can not live without you Ajay'. The doctor and the nurses standing around them would be shedding tears and in the next scene they would be getting married. The viewers in the cinema hall clapped loudly on the happy ending of this love story.

Or, when Kamal went to his uncle's house to break his engagement, after his emotional and realistic speech, when he was about to leave the house, Tanzeela would have stood up and said, 'stop there Kamal'. She would run towards him, held him in her arms, wailed in pain and said, 'sorry I made mistake in judging you. I liked your truthfulness. It did not matter if you were a peon or a chowkidar, I'd marry you, and after all, you were my cousin." She would take the engagement ring and put it on his finger again and said with a romantic voice, 'I'd marry you Kamal' and the whole family would become happy. In the next scene, she would be sitting on the bed, wearing a bridal dress and Kamal would be entering the room as a groom. He sat beside her, took her hand, kissed it romantically and said, 'I love you Tanzee'. She lied down on the bed, closed her eyes and allowed him to touch her wherever he wished. He started loving her and there was a nice loving song played on in the background. The movie ended with a happy end and the viewers also become happy.

If Tanzeela embraces Kamal at the end of this story and Preya does the same thing to Ajay, the name of this novel would be 'Power of Love'. The readers become happy and satisfied with the end.

But practical life is not as easy as when we watch in the movies or read through the romantic novels.

Tanzeela only went to see him, for her kinship with him. She gave him money, to compensate his losses or for the natural attraction of blood relatives. Or it could be a reward for going out of her life. She might have thought that ten thousand pounds was not a big amount for her, but she knew it could help him a lot. It was also possible that she was feeling guilty about her attitude towards him and wanted to satisfy her culpable feelings of the past by giving him all of her savings just being a nice person.

Whatever her feelings were behind this kindness, one thing was clear, she did not come to put on engagement ring on again or request him to change his decision of going back to Pakistan.

Preya was never impressed by the romantic attitude of Ajay. He picked each word she spoke before him, in four years, like a flower and knitted it in a garland of her memories to wear all the time and was living on hope that he would win her love one day. But she just thought of him as a co-worker, to pass the time at work. She never met him outside the workplace or kept any contact with him after he left the job. She did not think him suitable, even for long-run friendship.

Preya was neither impressed by Ajay nor did Tanzeela agree to marry Kamal, because it was not a romantic Indian movie or a love novel but a matter of practical life.

Their departure time was almost the same. They were sitting in the lounge, planning for their future, by coming out of their dreams. They were not telling each other their loves stories, but thinking about the genuine and practical things in life.

Finally, the time had come when they had to say goodbye to each other, for good. The most difficult thing, in this world, is to say goodbye to your true friends when you know you will never see them again in life.

"Hey *bhai*, you go first," Ajay asked Kamal.

"No, you go first," Kamal said.

"Please *bhai*, you go first," Ajay insisted.

"No, please you go first," Kamal said.

They both started crying like children and kept saying each other to go first.

Two young men were passing by. They looked like Indians and were over the moon on their arrival in the UK. When they saw Ajay and Kamal, crying, they came to them and asked, "Hi brothers are you OK? Can we help?"

"Thanks, we are fine," Ajay said.

"Why are you crying then?" one of them asked.

"Have you just arrived in the UK?" Ajay asked him.

"Yes, we have come here on student visas," they replied happily.

"What is your college name?" Ajay asked them.

They told him the same name where Ajay had spent five years. He knew the reality of that college very well.

"You know, when I came to this country I was happy, like you, even more than you are right now. After few years, you will be sitting here, like us, crying painfully and some new comers would be asking you the same question you asked us. When you would tell them the truth about the low profile colleges or hardships of life in the UK, they would not believe you. So, I am not telling you the reason for our tears because you will not believe us this time. Welcome to the dream land," he said to them.

They thought that he was making fun of them. They murmured something under their breath and walked away.

"You know what they muttered?" Kamal said.

"Yes, I know," Ajay said.

"What?" Kamal asked.

"Idiots," Ajay said and they both had a big laugh.

"OK *bhai,* you are going to be late, go to get your boarding card please" Kamal said.

"No *bhai,* you go first," Ajay said.

"You know me, I won't go before you," Kamal said.

"The same problem is with me *bhai,*" Ajay said.

They started to cry, hiding their faces with their hands and forgot that they were sitting at the airport, among dozens of people.

Eventually, they stood up at the same time, walked towards their boarding counters, did not speak while walking, stopped at their separation point, and hugged each other for long time and again cried like children.

"Thank you Ajay, *bhai,* for all your help and support in the UK," Kamal said.

"Go away you idiot," Ajay said, lovingly tapping his back.

They both walked to opposite sides, with tears in their eyes. After a few steps, Kamal stopped and turned back to have a final look at his friend. He found Ajay standing facing towards him. He smiled, with a weeping face. Kamal waved to him, cleaning his tears with his hand, shook his head in pain and said fondly, "Go away, you idiot."

They both disappeared into the crowd.

****

Lightning Source UK Ltd.
Milton Keynes UK
UKOW021414201211

184131UK00001B/19/P